$16.99

Gr 1-3

Mr. PANtS

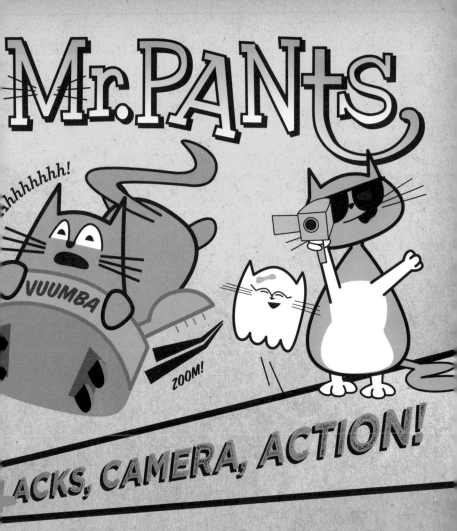

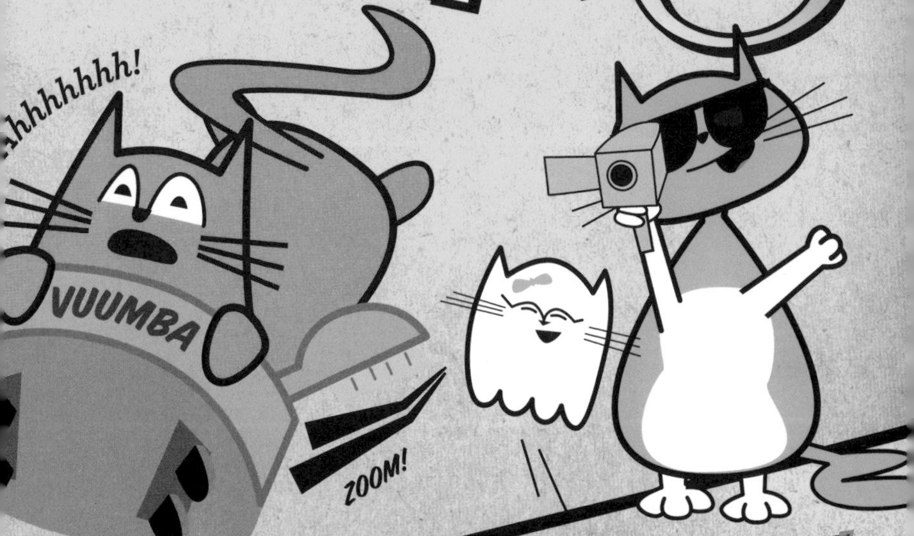
VUUMBA
ZOOM!

ACKS, CAMERA, ACTION!

WORDS BY
SCOTT MCCORMICK

PICTURES BY
R. H. LAZZELL

Dial Books for Young Readers
an imprint of Penguin Group (USA) LLC

FOR MY MOM, WHO WAS EVEN MORE EXCITED ABOUT THIS THAN I WAS.
". . . THE . . ." —S.M.

FOR MY FAMILY, FRIENDS, AND CHOCOLATE CHIP COOKIES EVERYWHERE. —R.H.L.

Dial Books for Young Readers
Published by the Penguin Group | Penguin Group (USA) LLC
375 Hudson Street | New York, New York 10014

USA / Canada / UK / Ireland / Australia / New Zealand / India / South Africa / China
PENGUIN.COM
A Penguin Random House Company

Text copyright © 2015 by Scott McCormick | Pictures copyright © 2015 by R. H. Lazzell

Library of Congress Cataloging-in-Publication Data   McCormick, Scott, date.
Mr. Pants : slacks, camera, action! / words by Scott McCormick ; pictures by R. H. Lazzell.   pages cm
Summary: Mr. Pants is determined to win a film contest, but his sisters and their friends are not eager to participate.
ISBN 978-0-8037-4009-9 (hardcover)
[1. Brothers and sisters—Fiction. 2. Cats—Fiction. 3. Video recordings—Production and direction—Fiction.
4. Behavior—Fiction.] I. Lazzell, R. H., illustrator. II. Title. III. Title: Slacks, camera, action!
PZ7.M47841437Mr 2015   [E]—dc23   2013038372

Manufactured in China on acid-free paper
3 5 7 9 10 8 6 4 2

Designed by Jennifer Kelly | Text set in Archer

CONTENTS

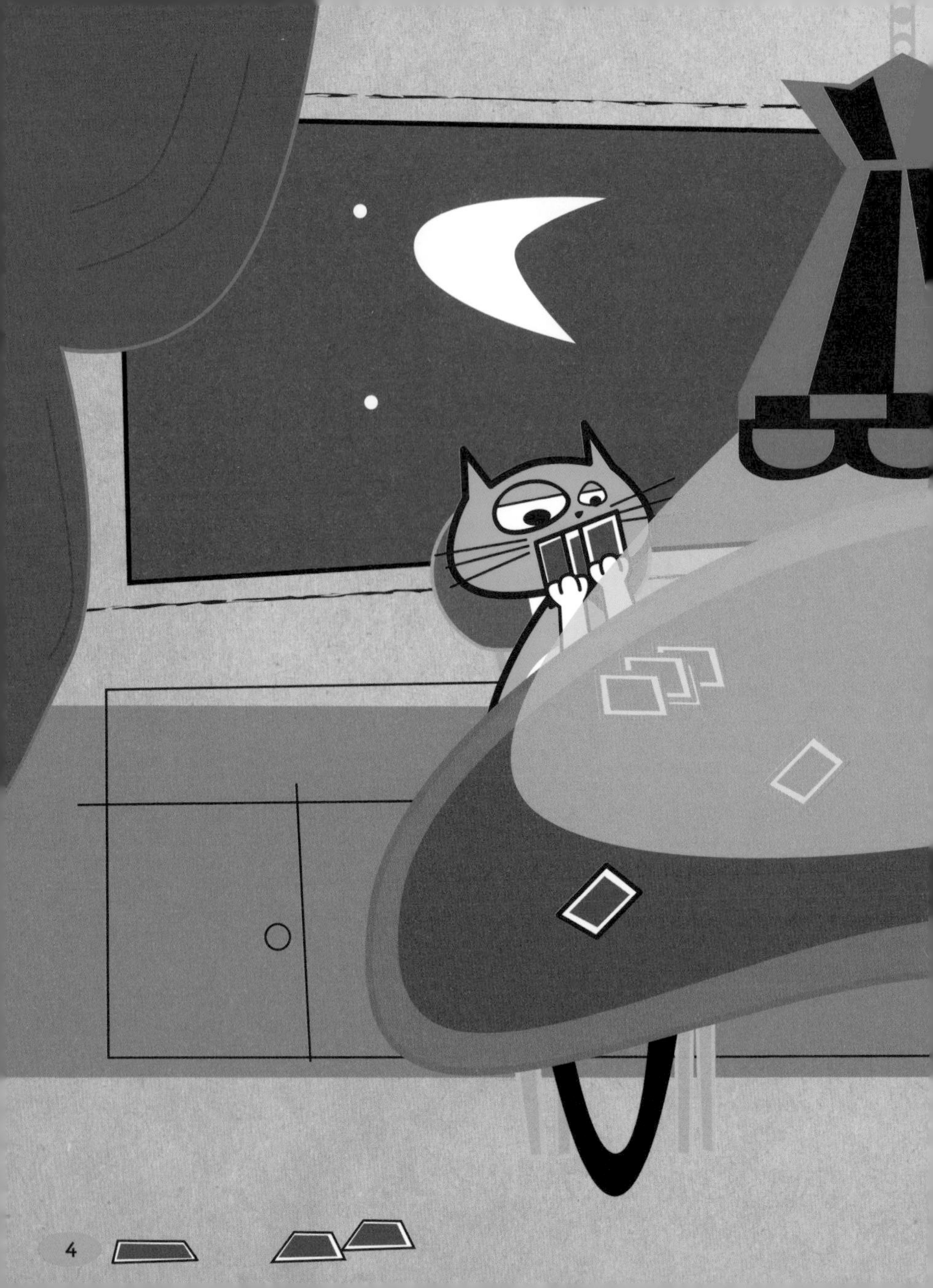

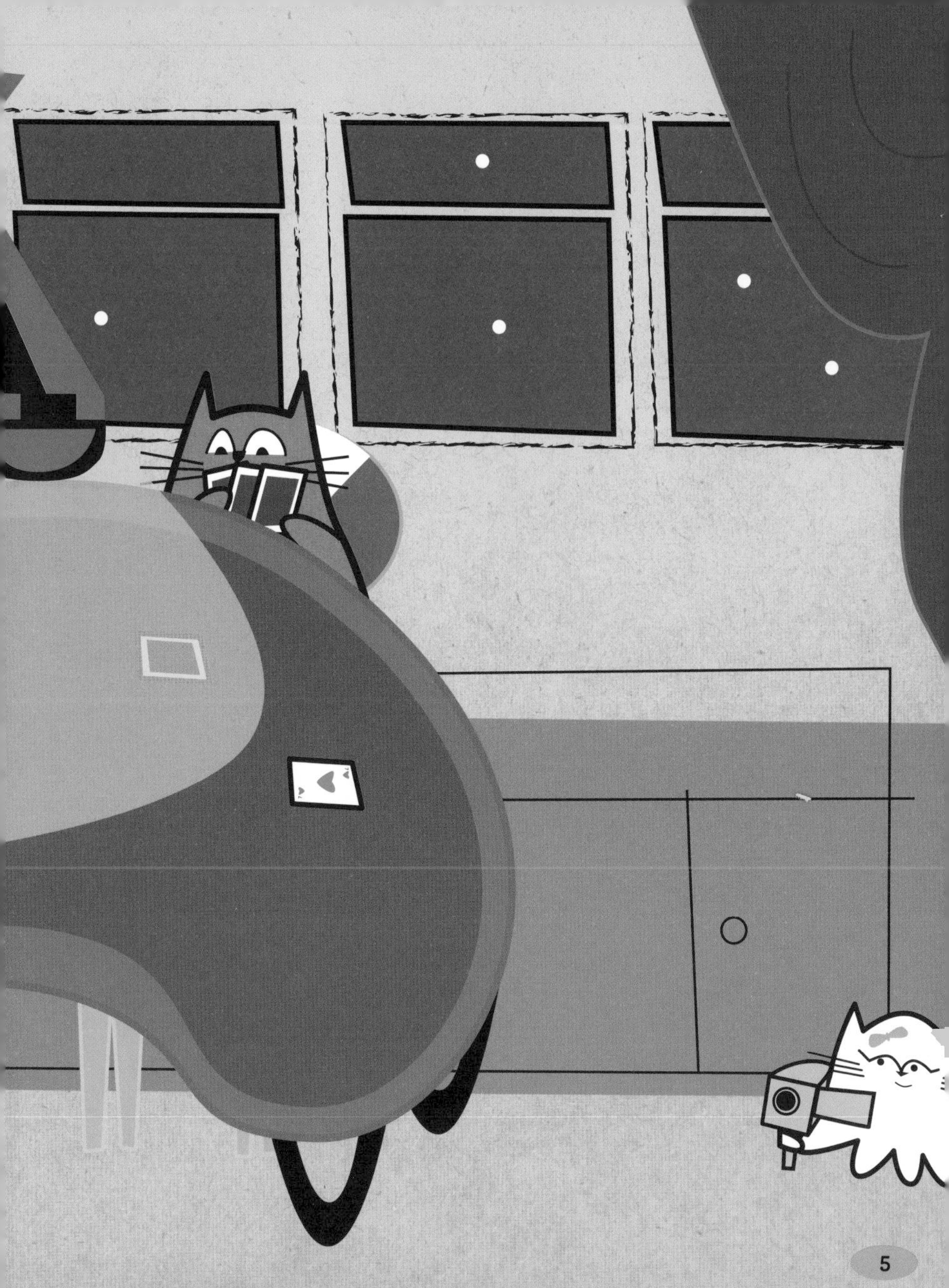

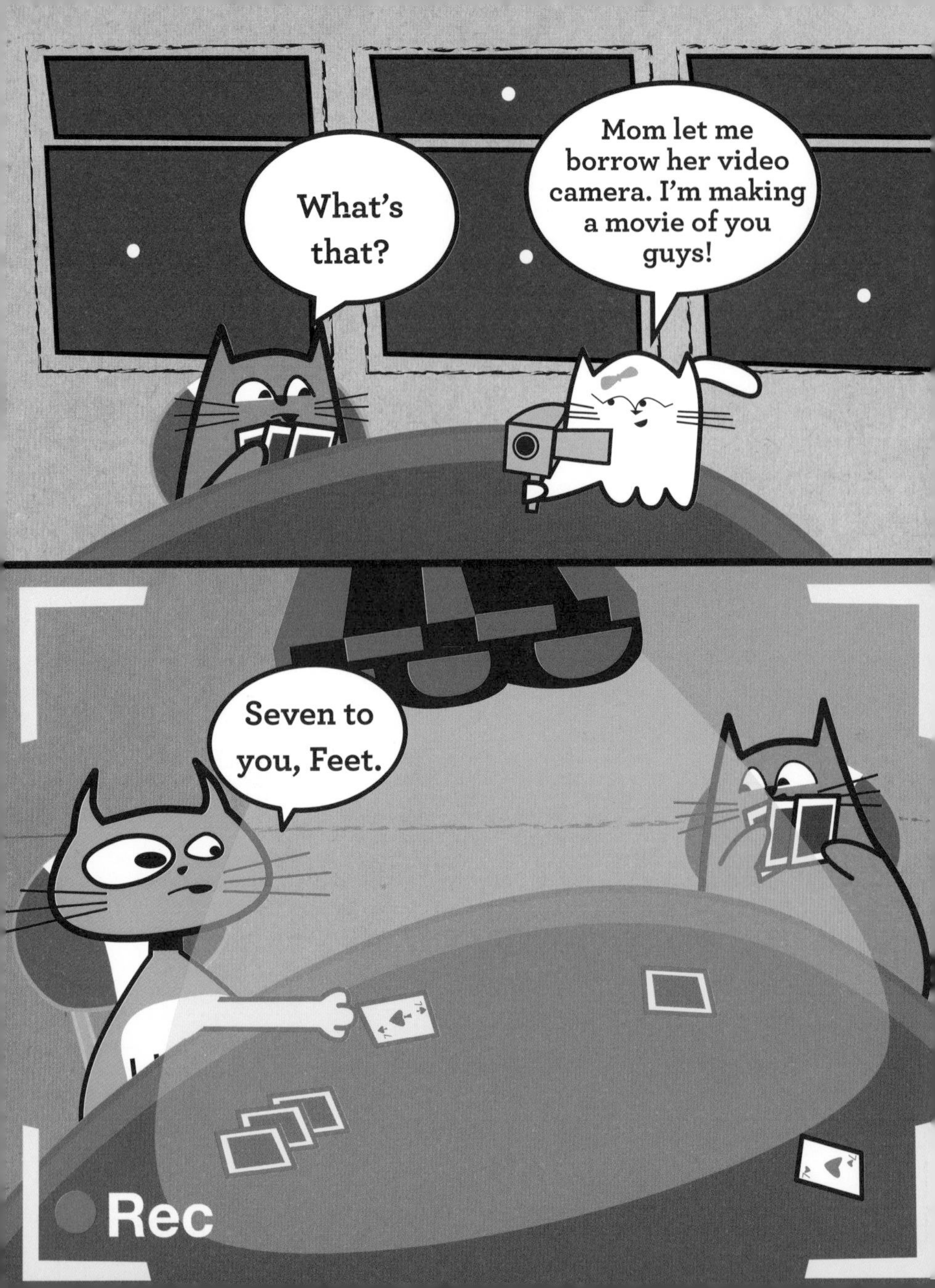
What's that?
Mom let me borrow her video camera. I'm making a movie of you guys!
Seven to you, Feet.
Rec

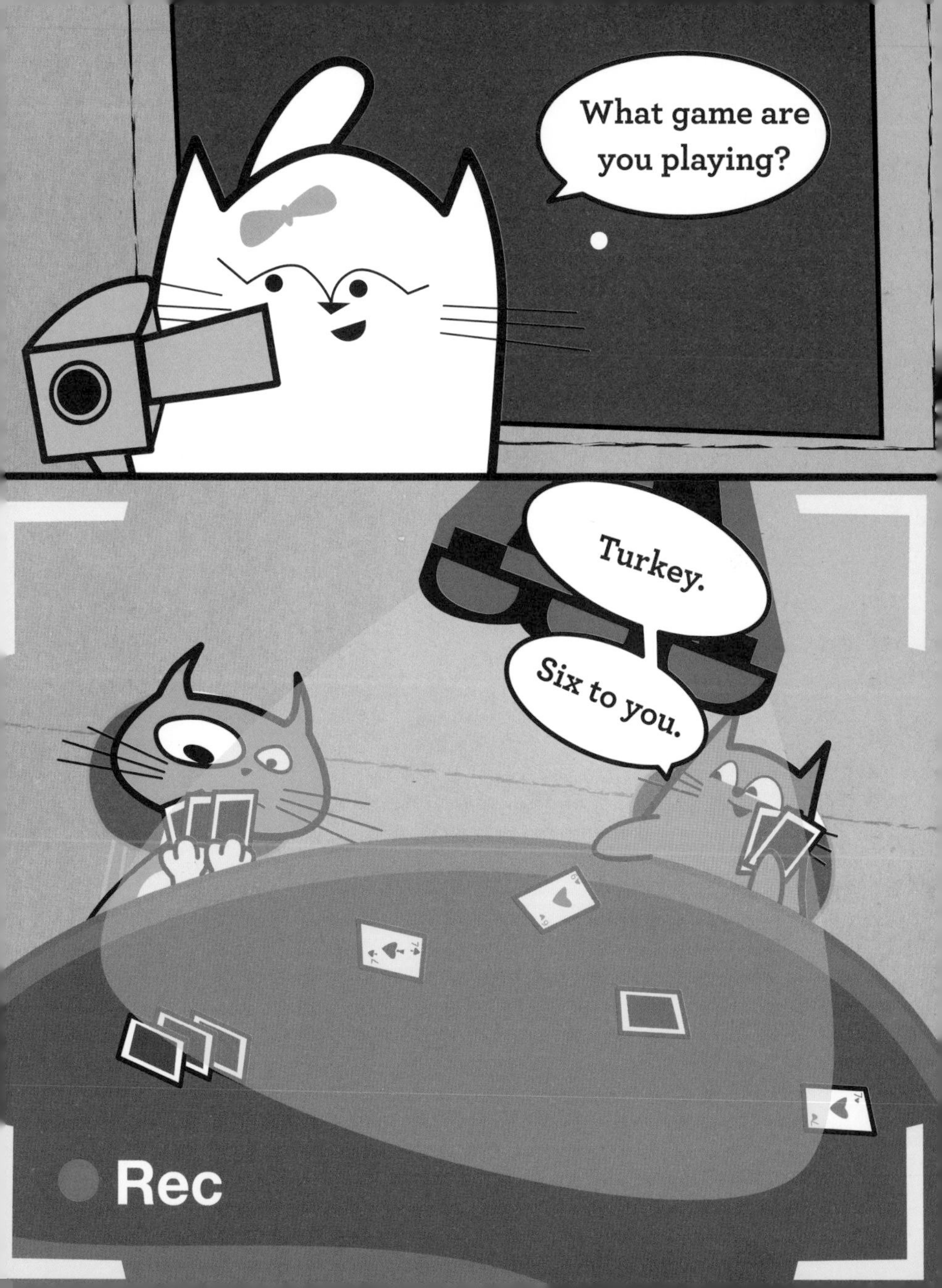
What game are you playing?
Turkey.
Six to you.
Rec

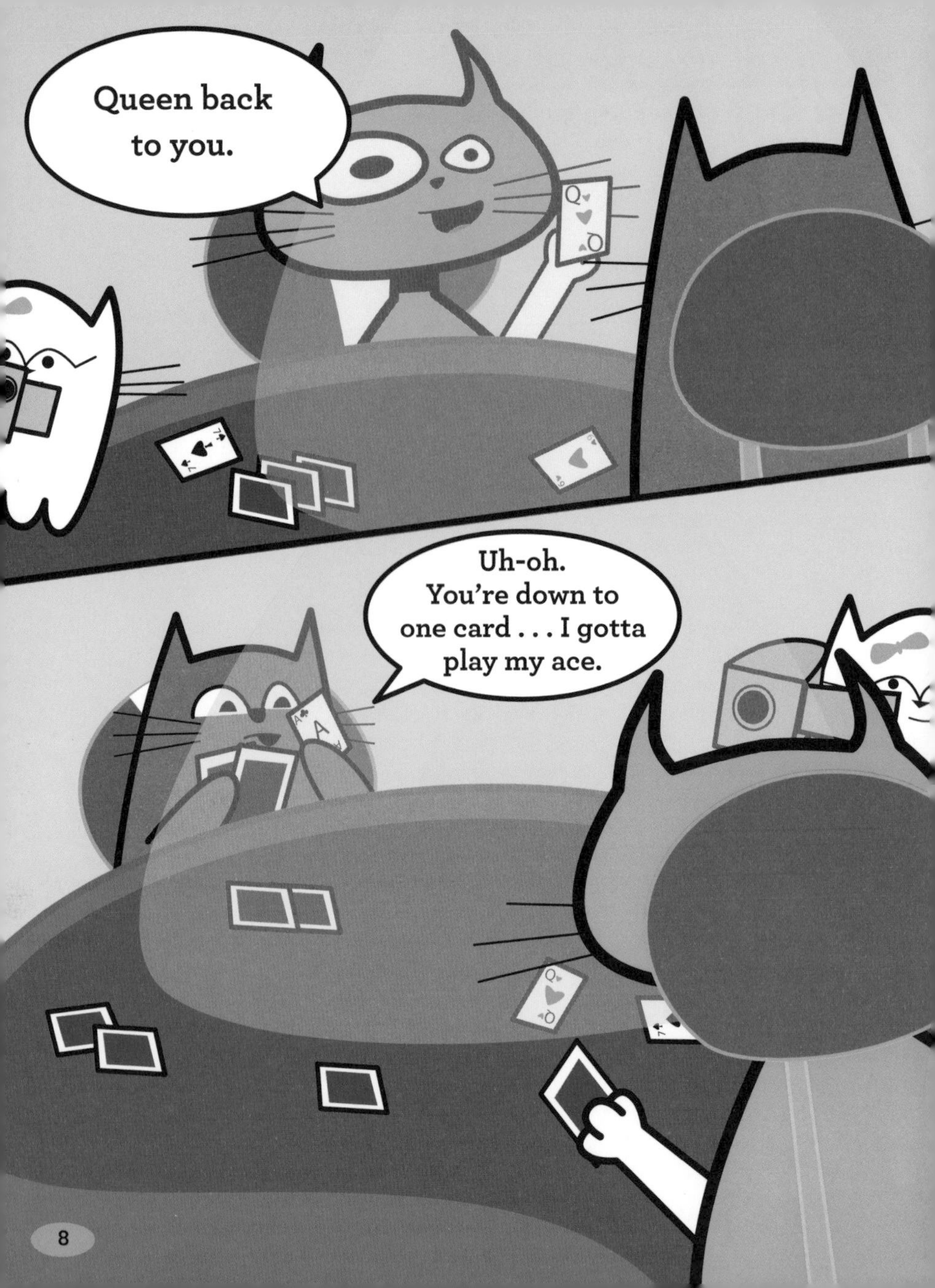
Queen back to you.
Uh-oh. You're down to one card . . . I gotta play my ace.

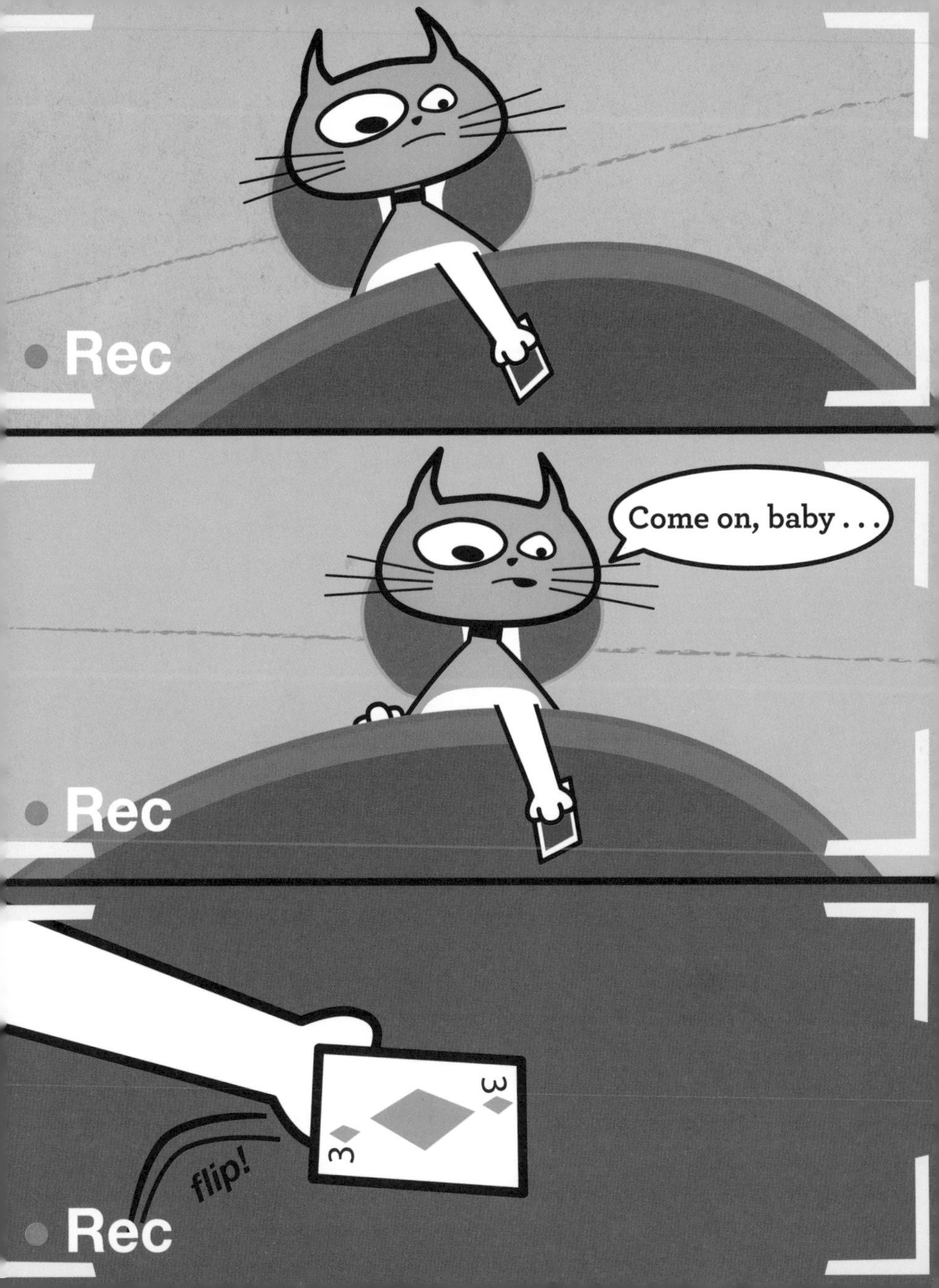
Rec
Come on, baby . . .
Rec
flip!
Rec

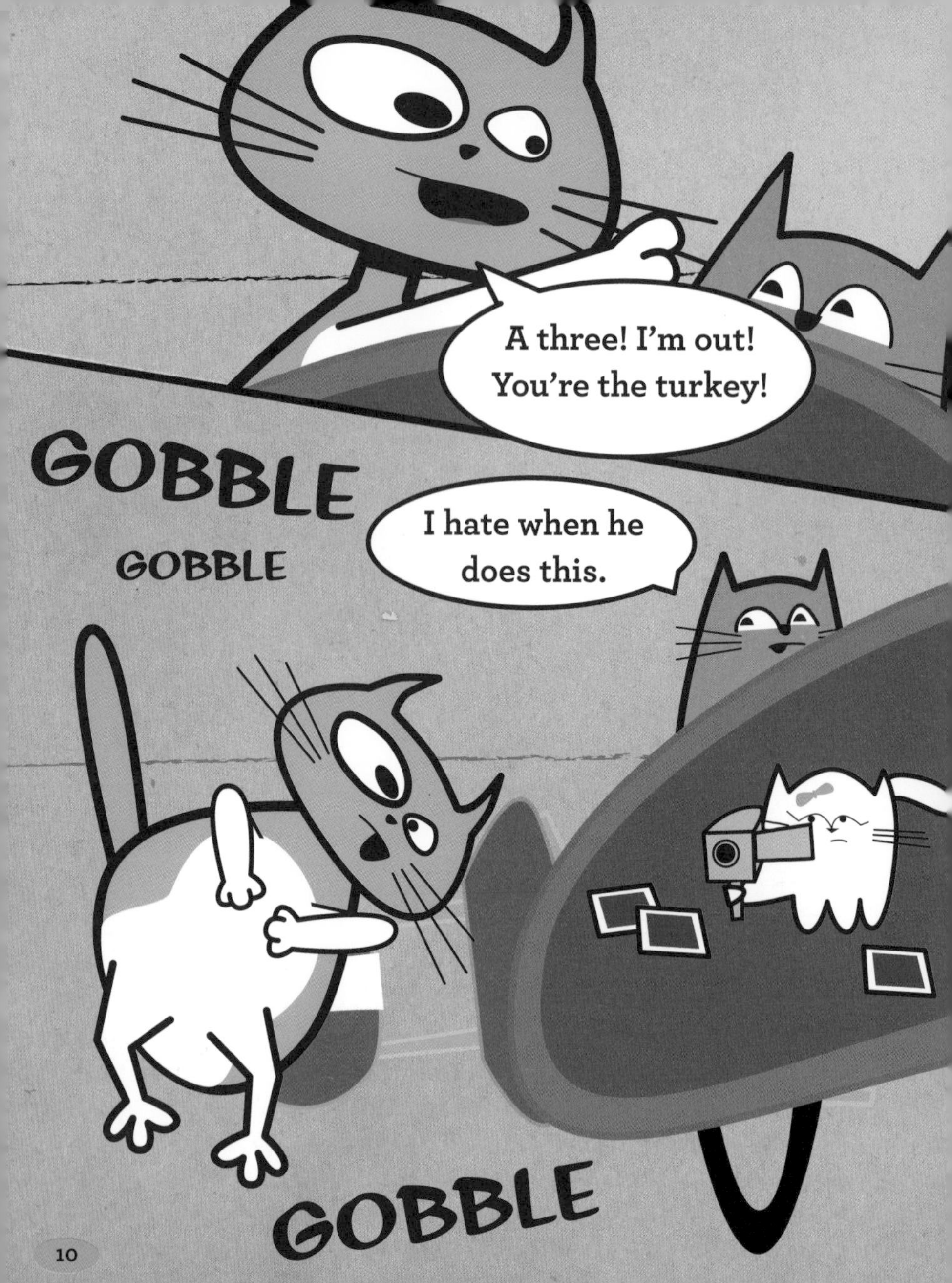
A three! I'm out!
You're the turkey!
GOBBLE
GOBBLE
I hate when he
does this.
GOBBLE

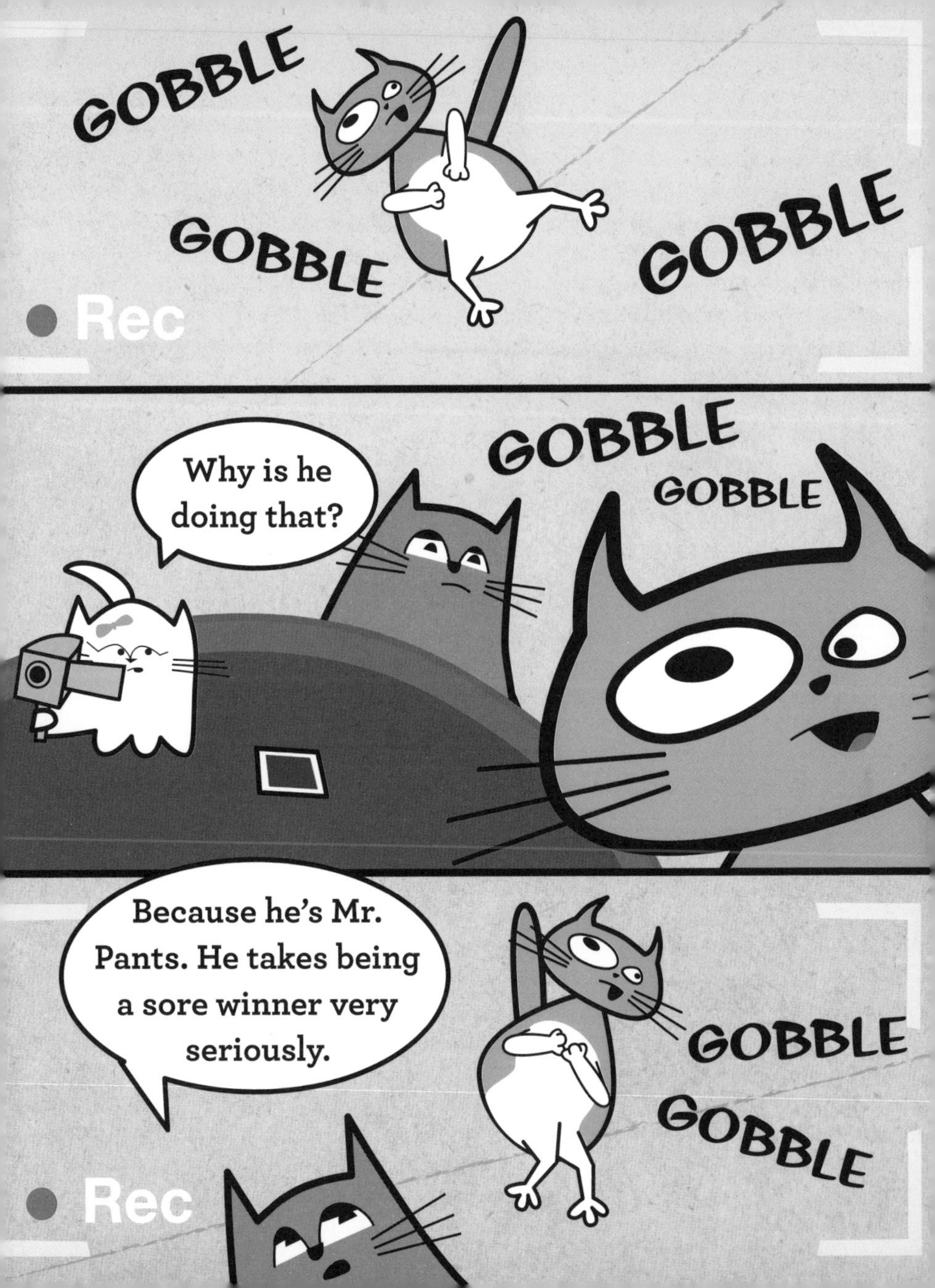
GOBBLE
GOBBLE
GOBBLE
Rec
Why is he doing that?
GOBBLE
GOBBLE
Because he's Mr. Pants. He takes being a sore winner very seriously.
GOBBLE
GOBBLE
Rec

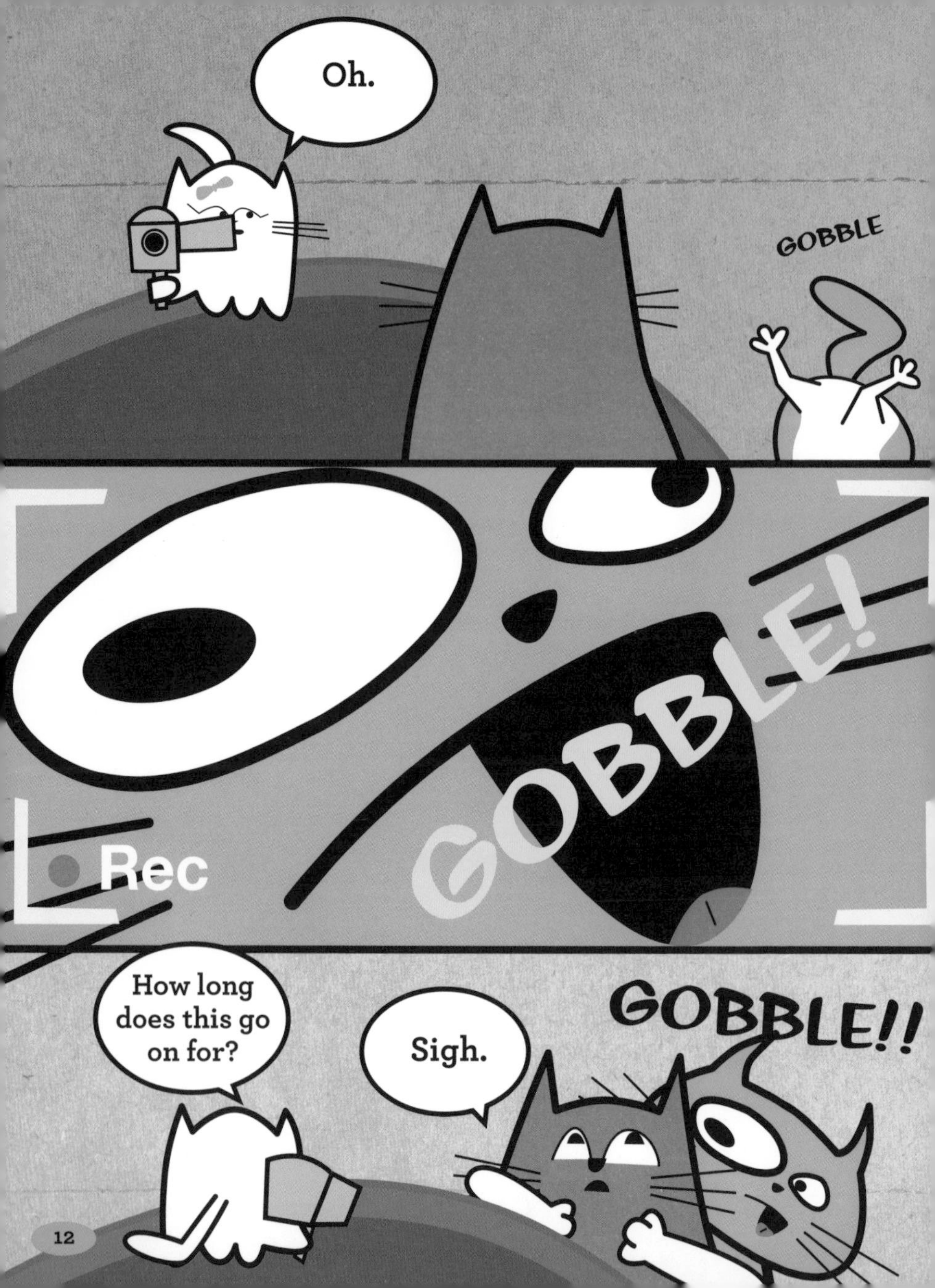

Oh.
GOBBLE
Rec
GOBBLE!
How long does this go on for?
Sigh.
GOBBLE!!

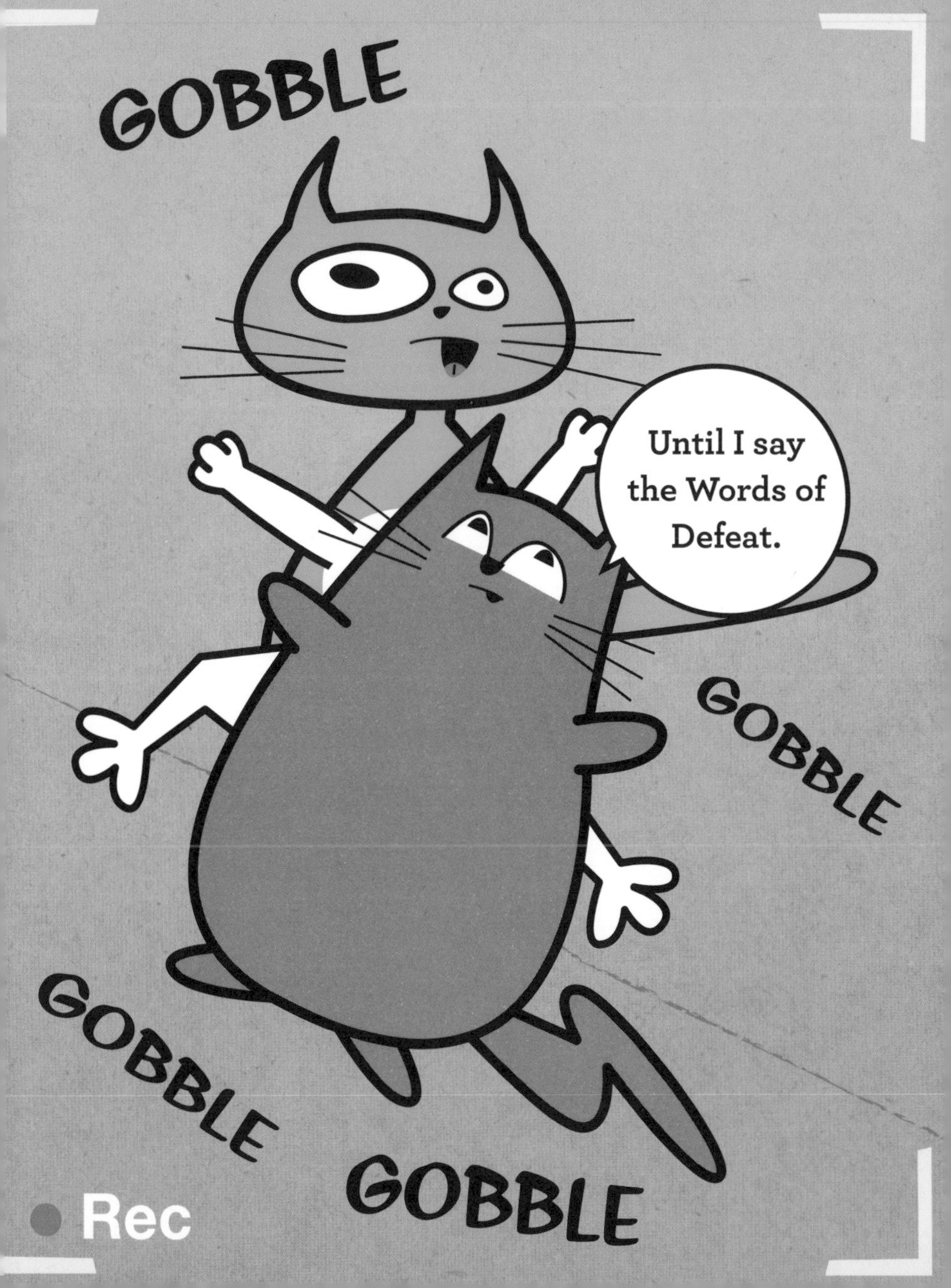
GOBBLE
Until I say the Words of Defeat.
GOBBLE
GOBBLE
GOBBLE
Rec

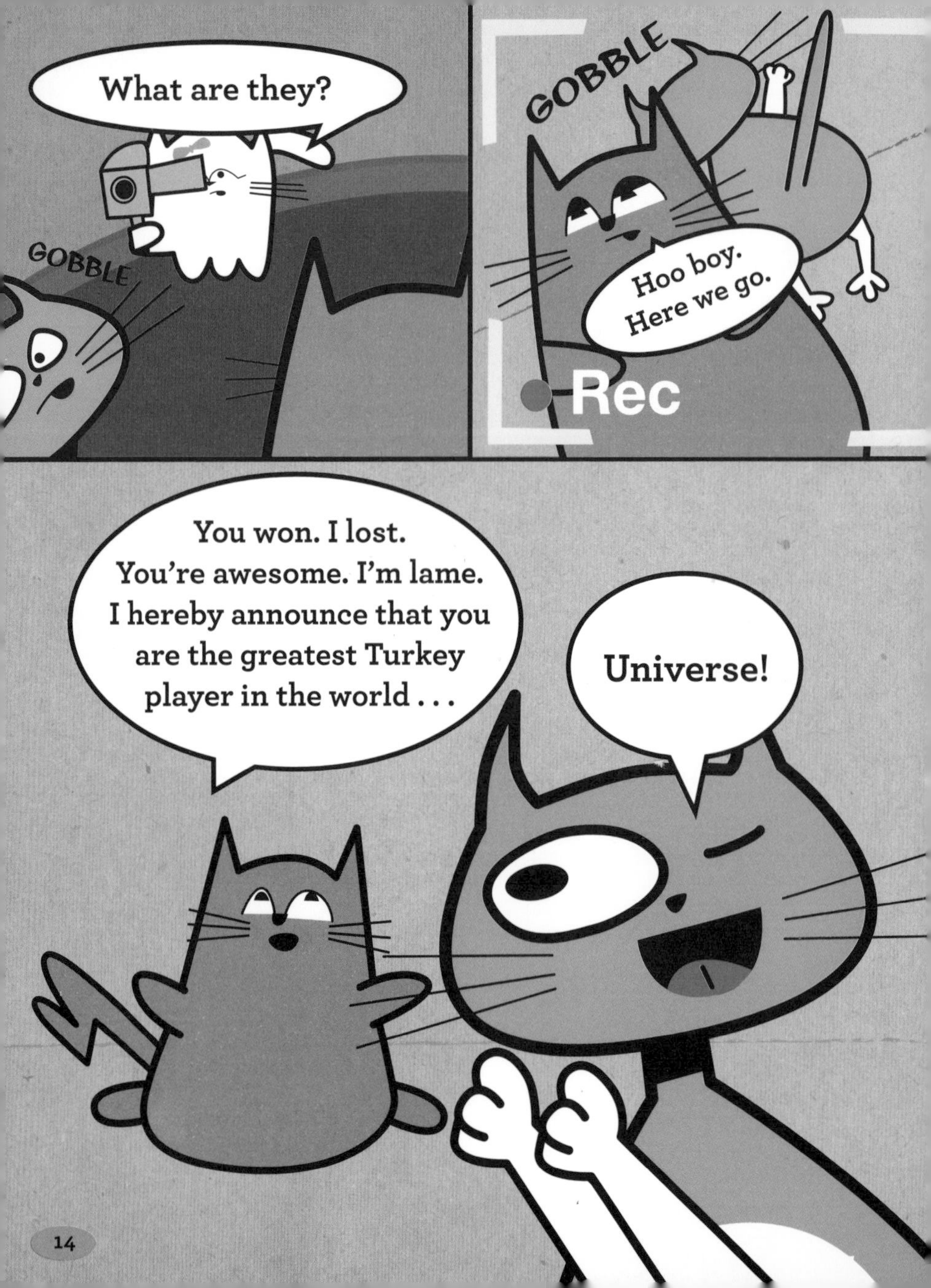
What are they?
GOBBLE
GOBBLE
GOBBLE
Hoo boy. Here we go.
Rec
You won. I lost. You're awesome. I'm lame. I hereby announce that you are the greatest Turkey player in the world . . .
Universe!

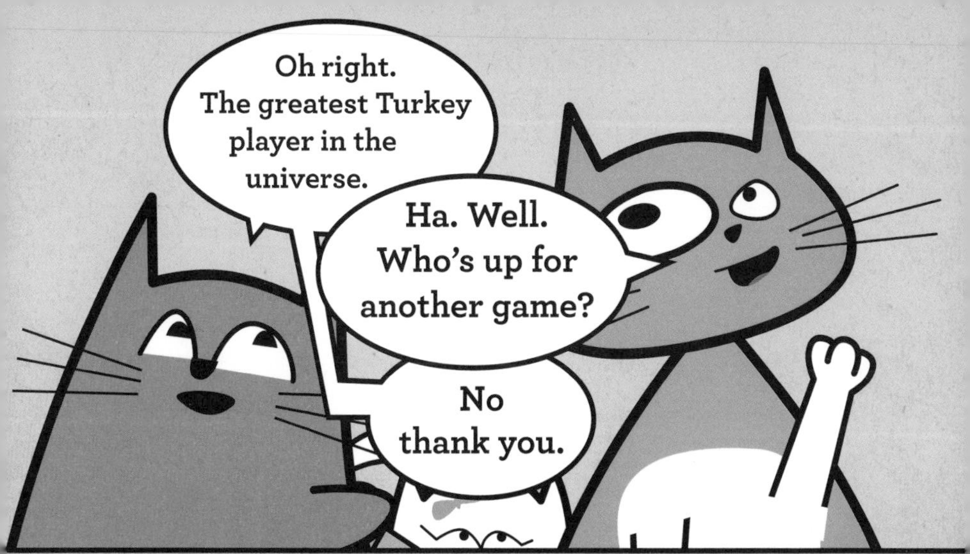
Oh right.
The greatest Turkey player in the universe.
Ha. Well.
Who's up for another game?
No
thank you.

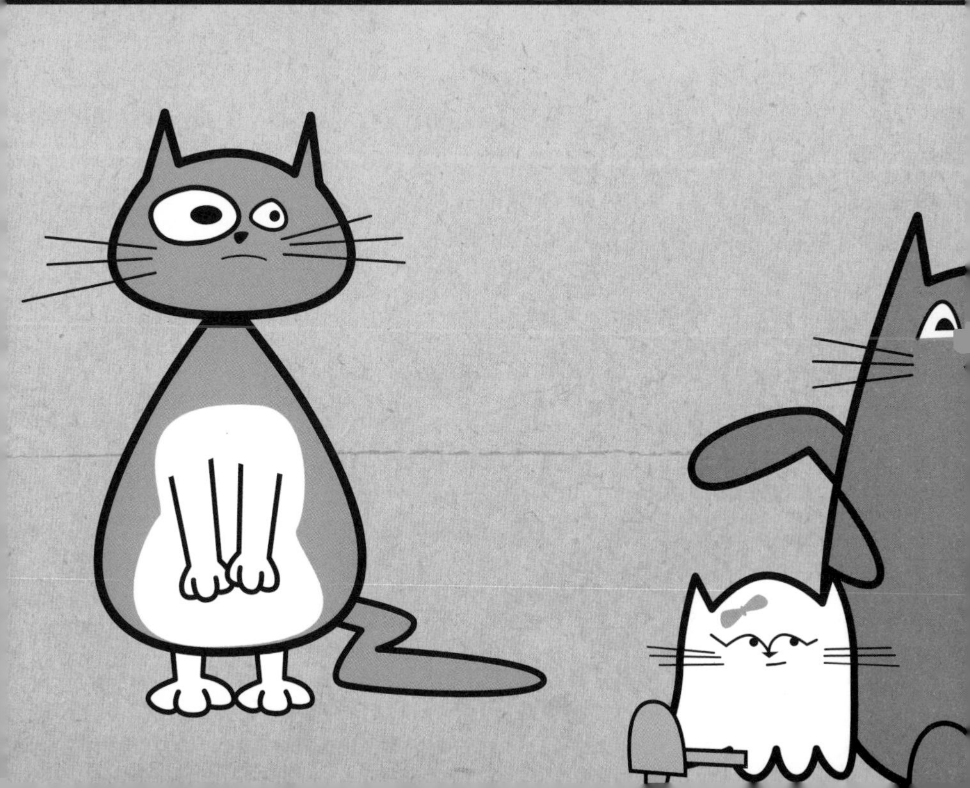

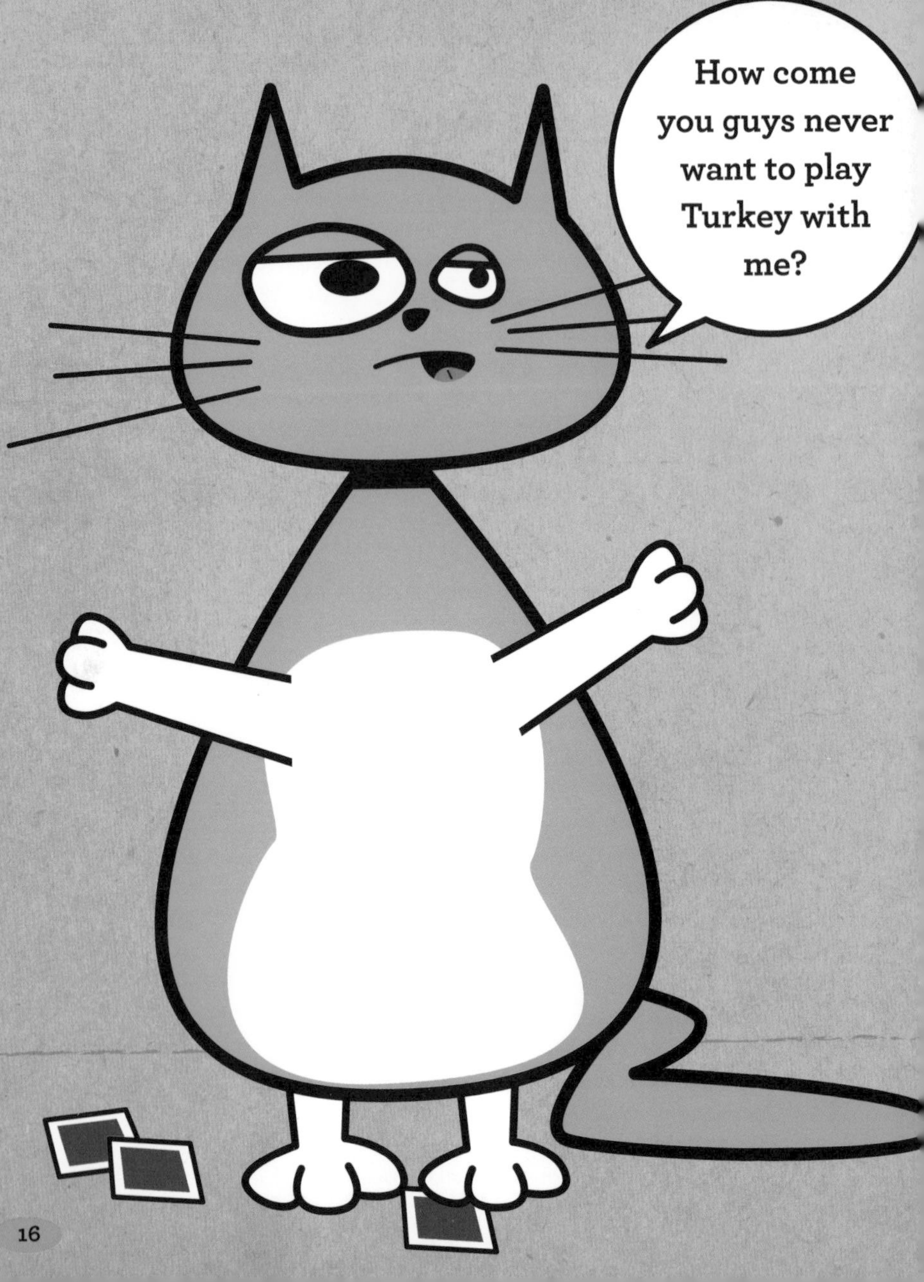
How come you guys never want to play Turkey with me?

Chapter One: THE CONTEST

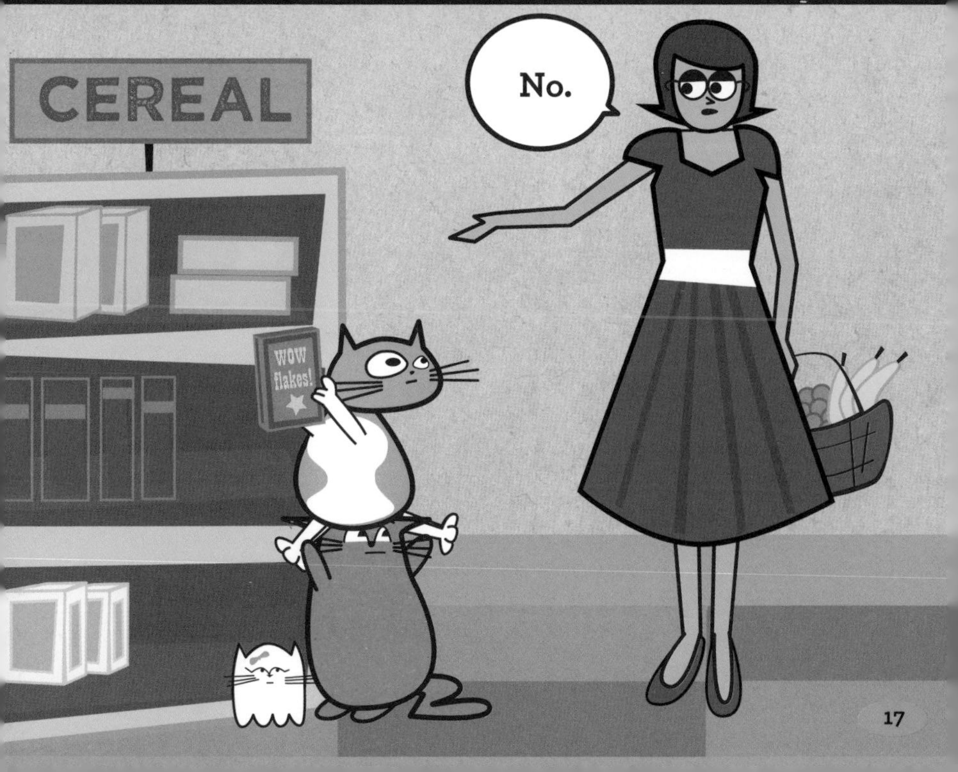
CEREAL
No.
WOW flakes!

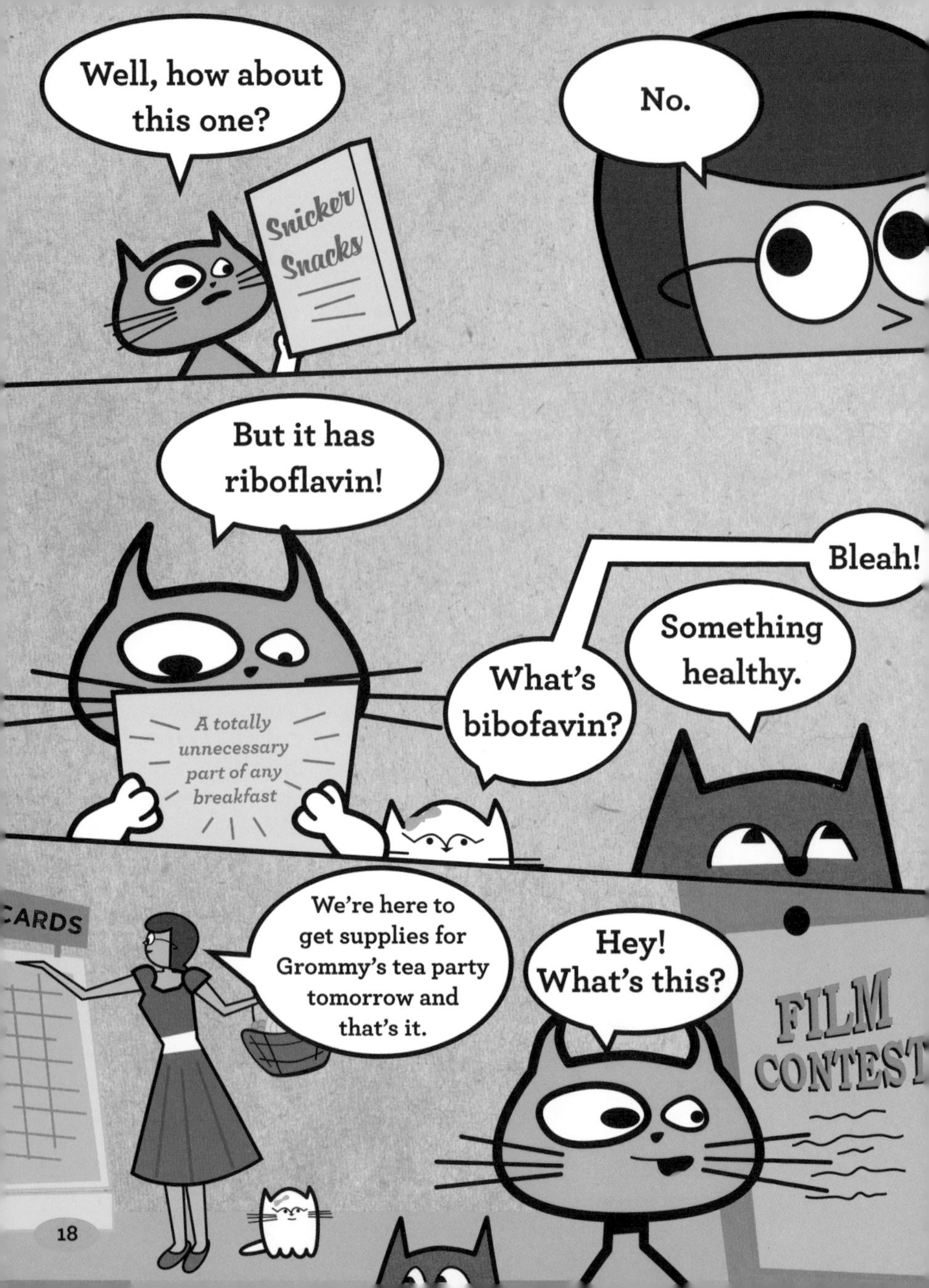
Well, how about this one?
Snicker Snacks
No.
But it has riboflavin!
A totally unnecessary part of any breakfast
What's bibofavin?
Bleah!
Something healthy.
CARDS
We're here to get supplies for Grommy's tea party tomorrow and that's it.
Hey! What's this?
FILM CONTEST

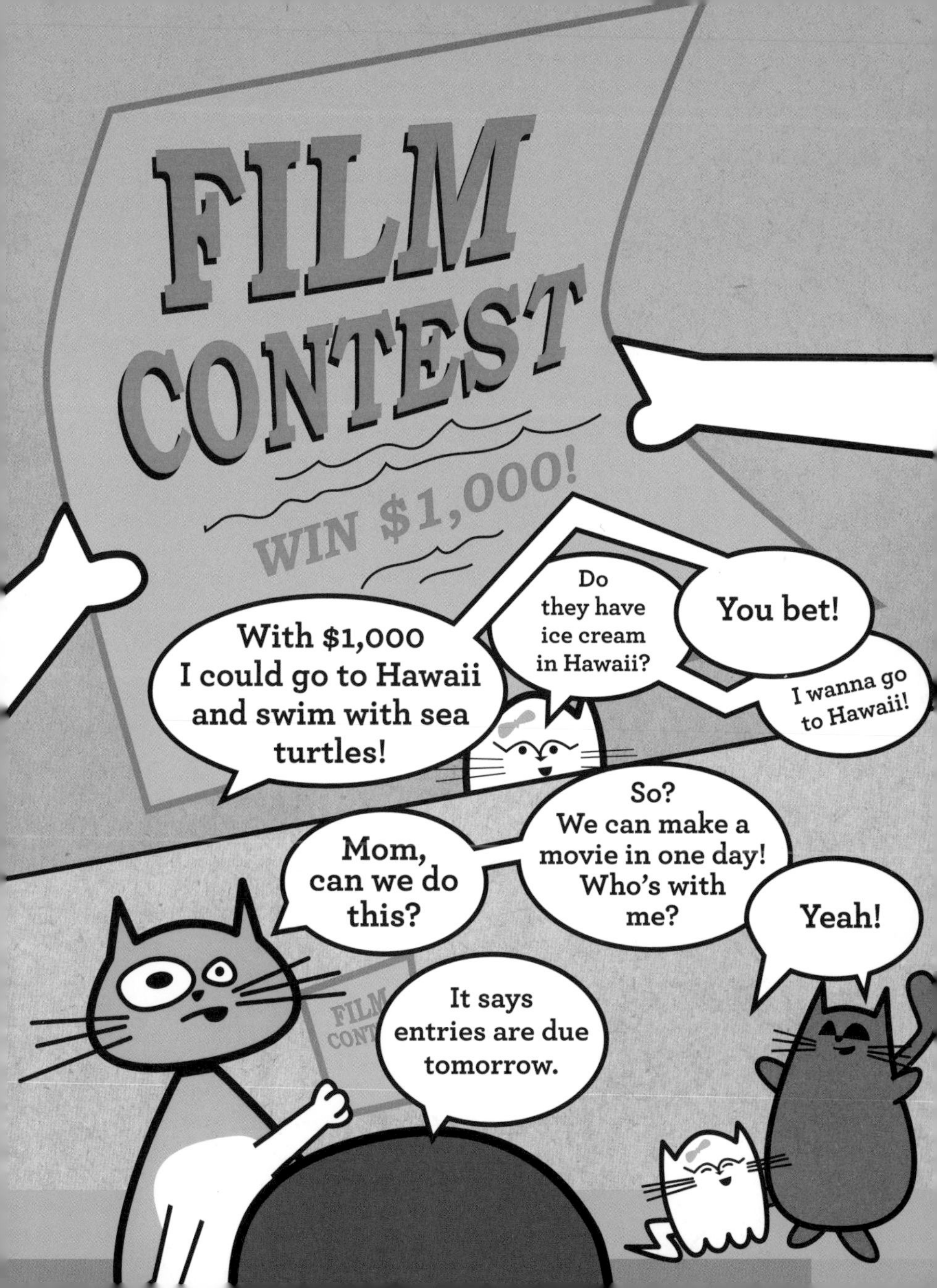
FILM CONTEST
WIN $1,000!
With $1,000 I could go to Hawaii and swim with sea turtles!
Do they have ice cream in Hawaii?
You bet!
I wanna go to Hawaii!
Mom, can we do this?
It says entries are due tomorrow.
So? We can make a movie in one day! Who's with me?
Yeah!
FILM CONT

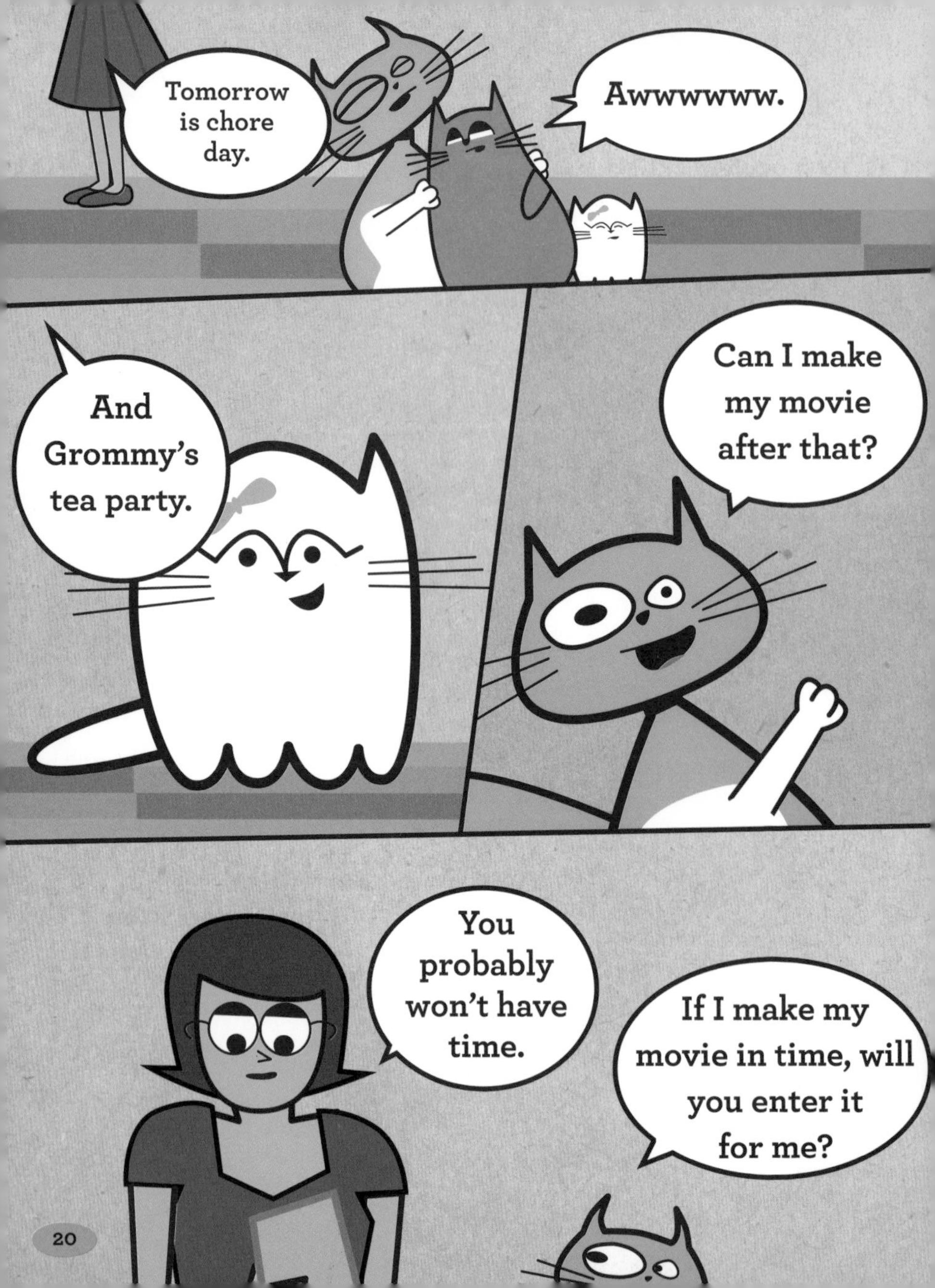

Tomorrow is chore day.
Awwwwww.
And Grommy's tea party.
Can I make my movie after that?
You probably won't have time.
If I make my movie in time, will you enter it for me?

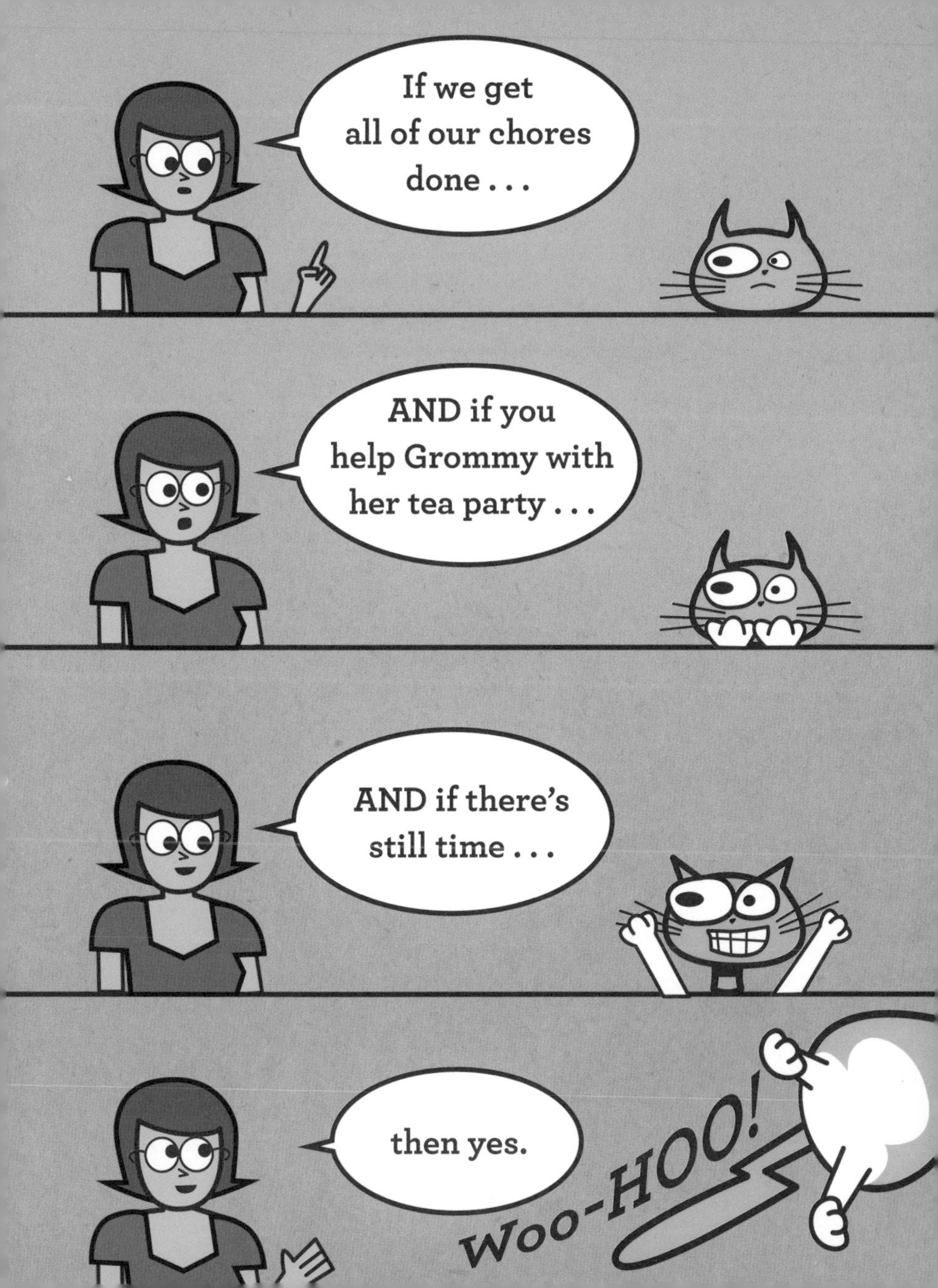
If we get all of our chores done . . .
AND if you help Grommy with her tea party . . .
AND if there's still time . . .
then yes.
Woo-HOO!

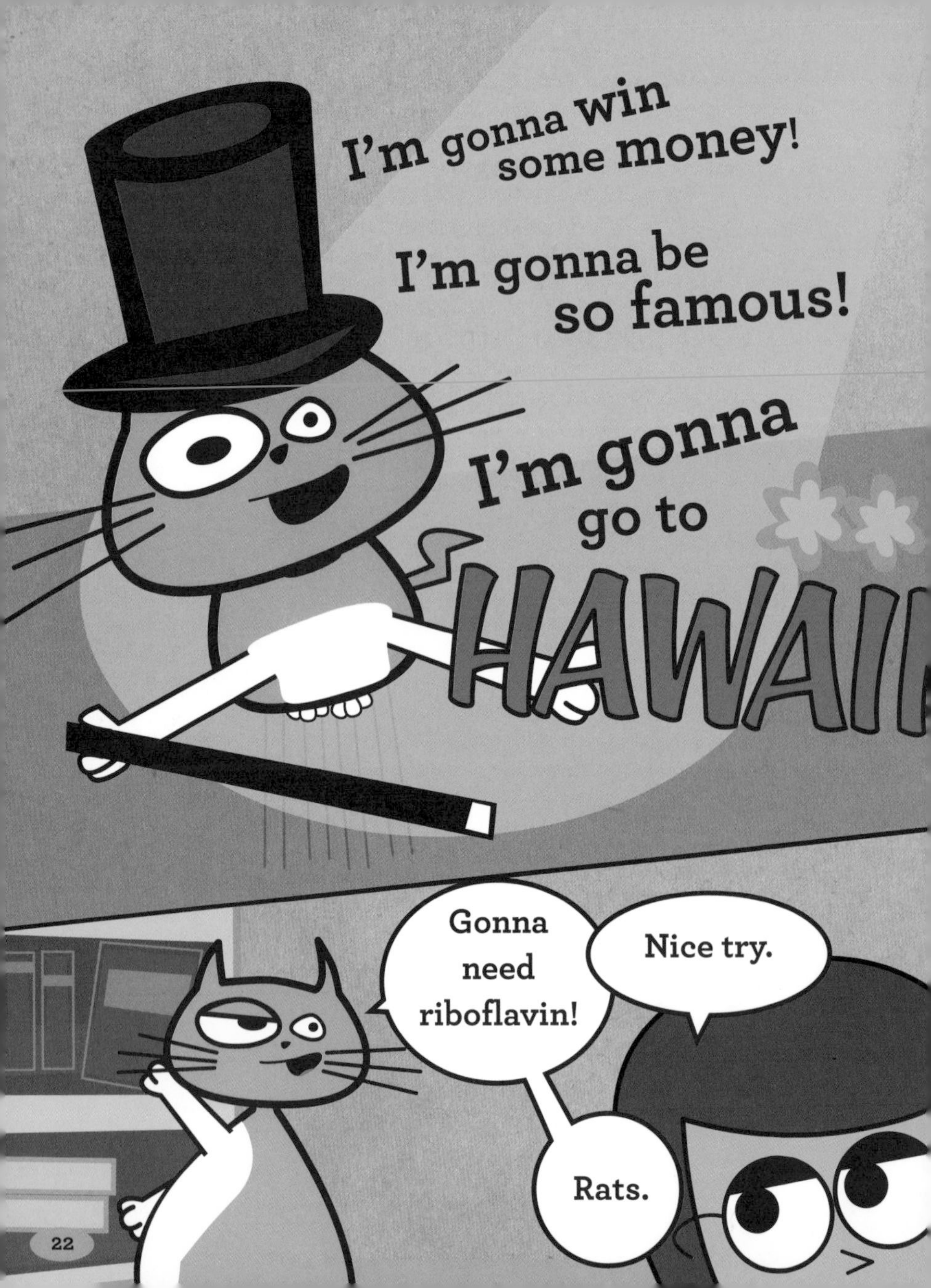
I'm gonna win some money!
I'm gonna be so famous!
I'm gonna go to
HAWAII
Gonna need riboflavin!
Nice try.
Rats.

Chapter Two:
THE HONESTLY BOMB

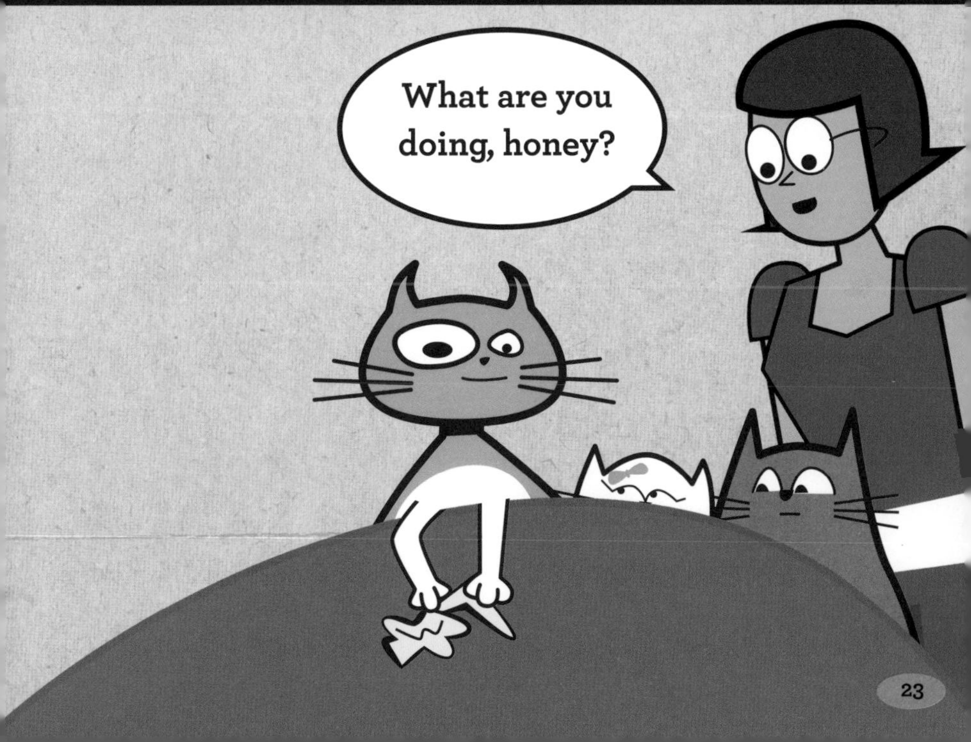
What are you doing, honey?

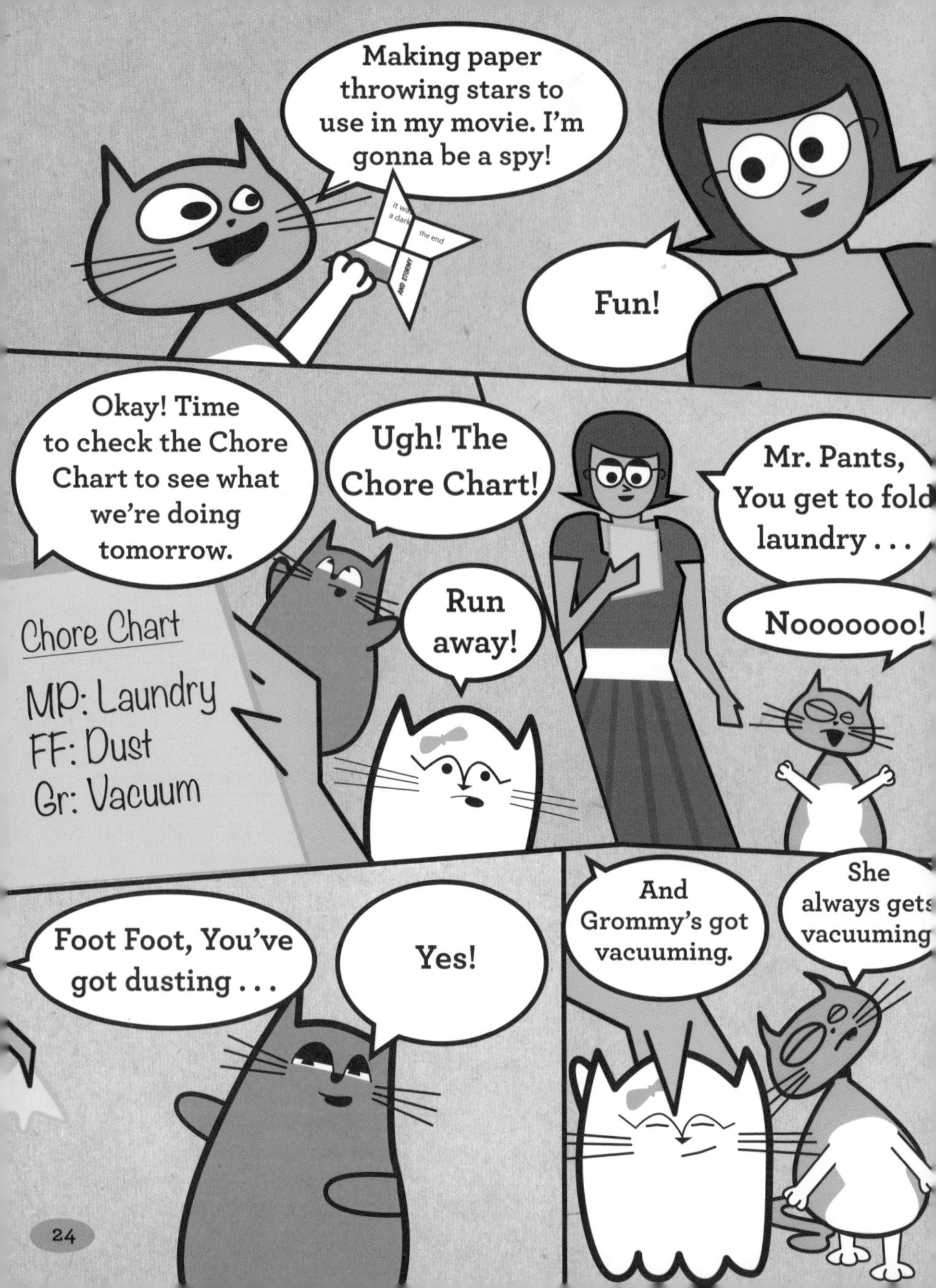
Making paper throwing stars to use in my movie. I'm gonna be a spy!
the end
AND STORMY
Fun!
Okay! Time to check the Chore Chart to see what we're doing tomorrow.
Ugh! The Chore Chart!
Chore Chart
MP: Laundry
FF: Dust
Gr: Vacuum
Run away!
Mr. Pants, You get to fold laundry . . .
Noooooooo!
Foot Foot, You've got dusting . . .
Yes!
And Grommy's got vacuuming.
She always gets vacuuming

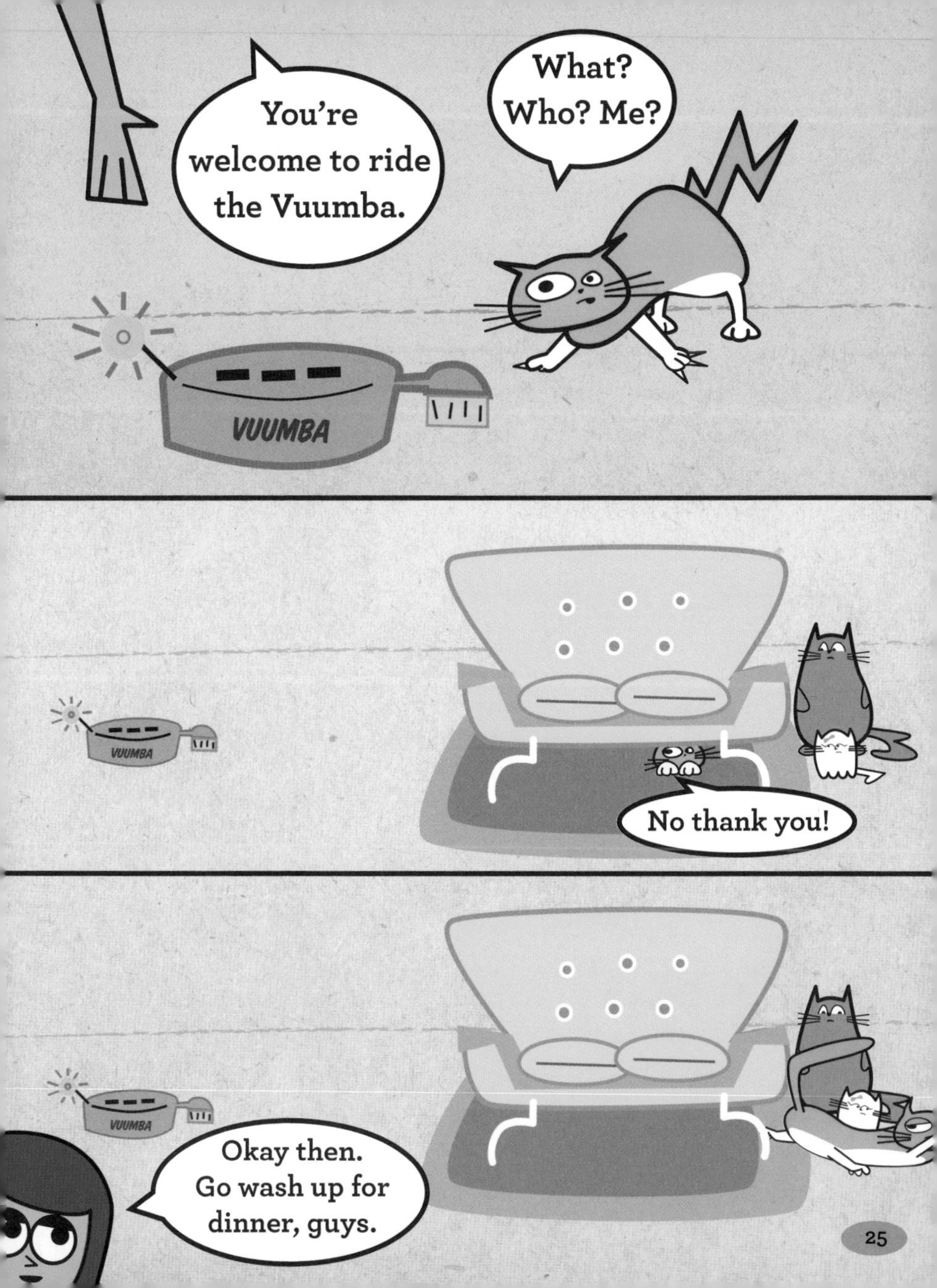
You're welcome to ride the Vuumba.
What? Who? Me?
VUUMBA
VUUMBA
No thank you!
VUUMBA
Okay then. Go wash up for dinner, guys.

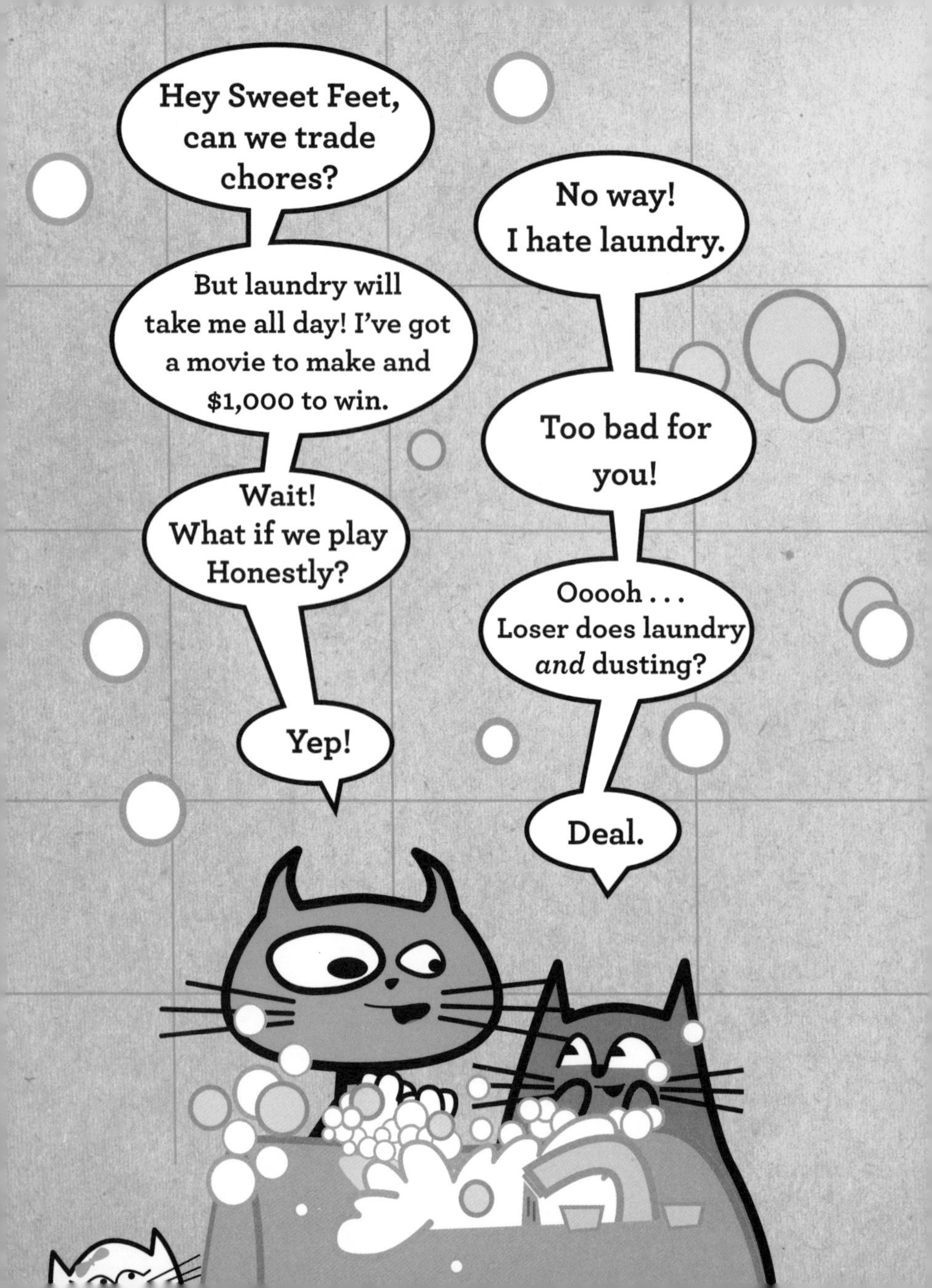
Hey Sweet Feet, can we trade chores?
No way! I hate laundry.
But laundry will take me all day! I've got a movie to make and $1,000 to win.
Too bad for you!
Wait! What if we play Honestly?
Ooooh . . . Loser does laundry *and* dusting?
Yep!
Deal.

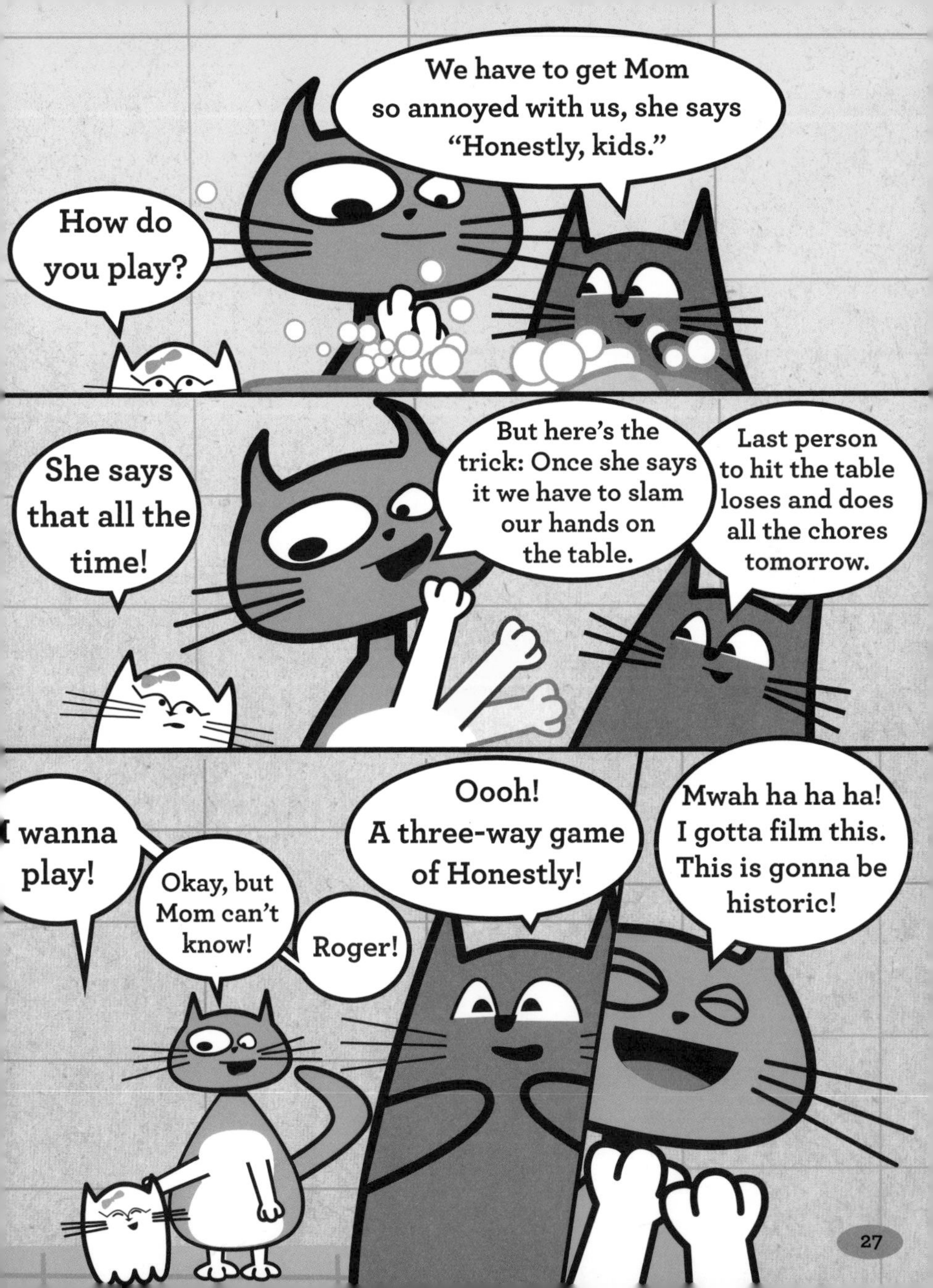
We have to get Mom so annoyed with us, she says "Honestly, kids."
How do you play?
She says that all the time!
But here's the trick: Once she says it we have to slam our hands on the table.
Last person to hit the table loses and does all the chores tomorrow.
wanna play!
Okay, but Mom can't know!
Roger!
Oooh! A three-way game of Honestly!
Mwah ha ha ha! I gotta film this. This is gonna be historic!

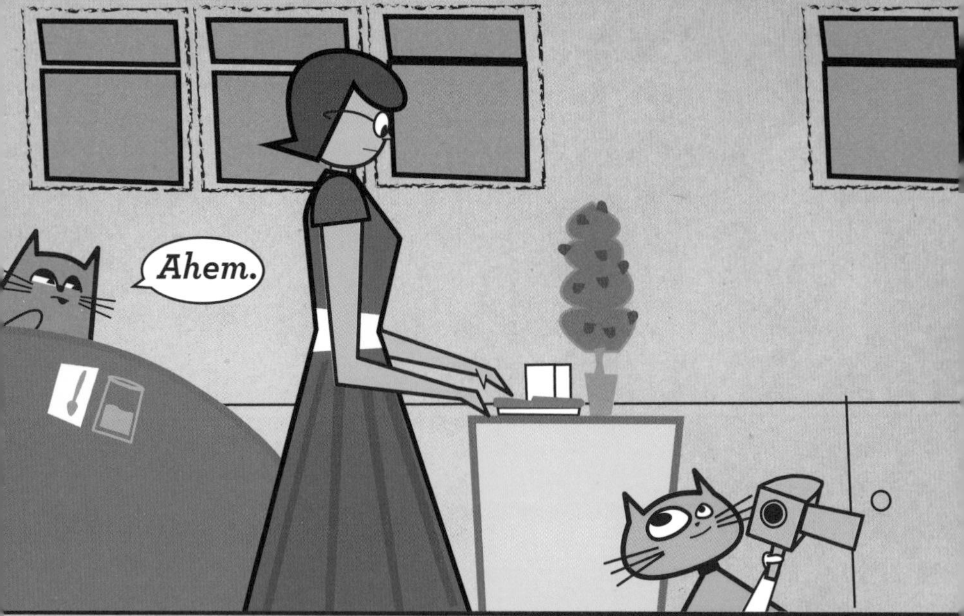
Ahem.

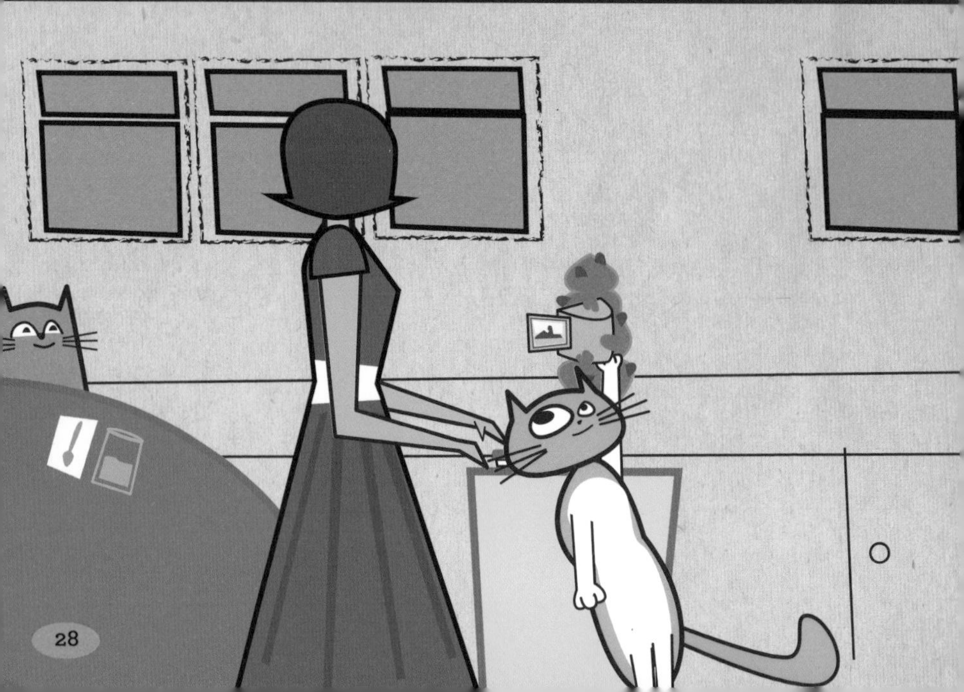

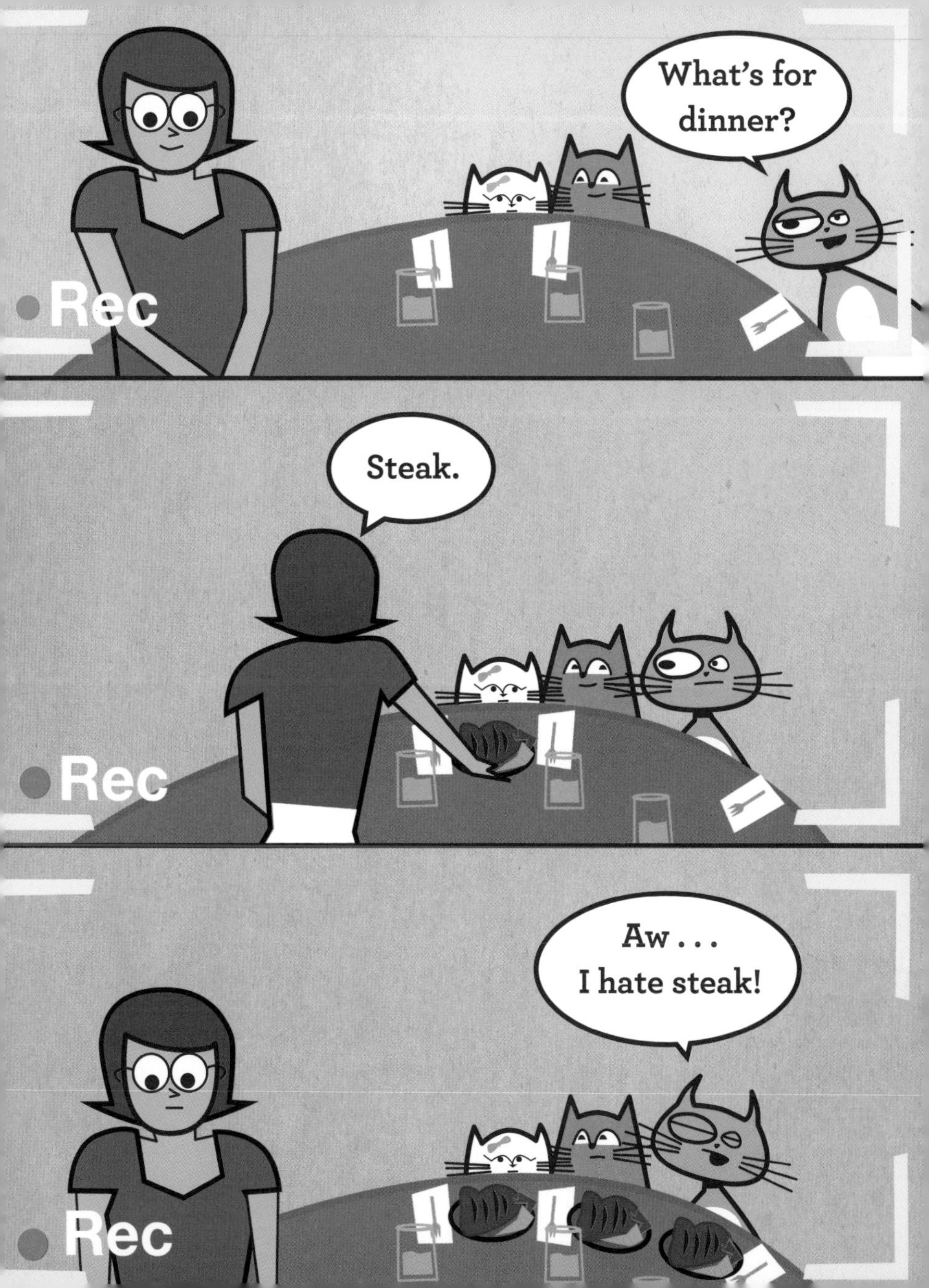
What's for dinner?
Rec
Steak.
Rec
Aw . . .
I hate steak!
Rec

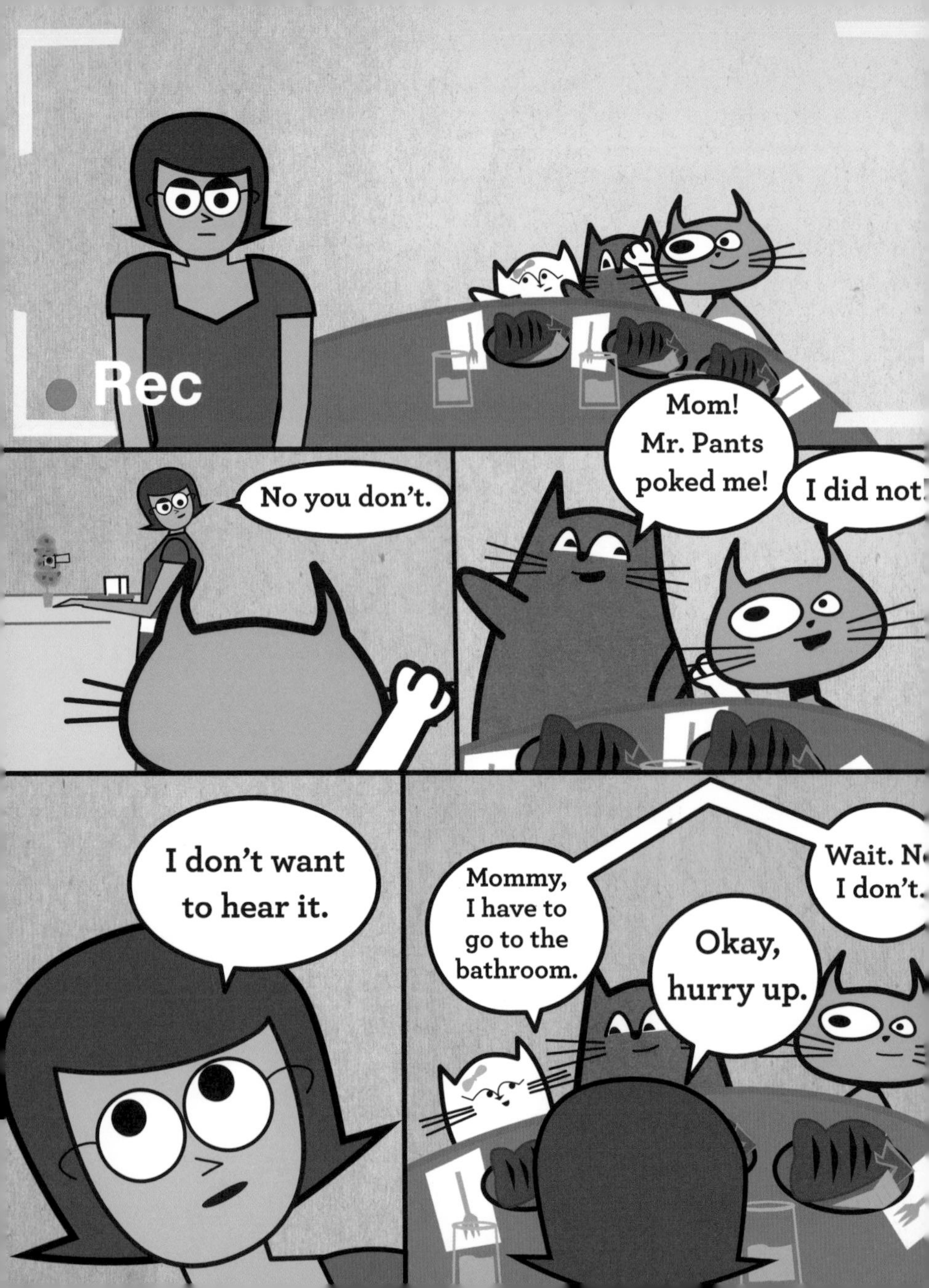
Rec
Mom! Mr. Pants poked me!
I did not!
No you don't.
I don't want to hear it.
Mommy, I have to go to the bathroom.
Wait. N
I don't.
Okay, hurry up.

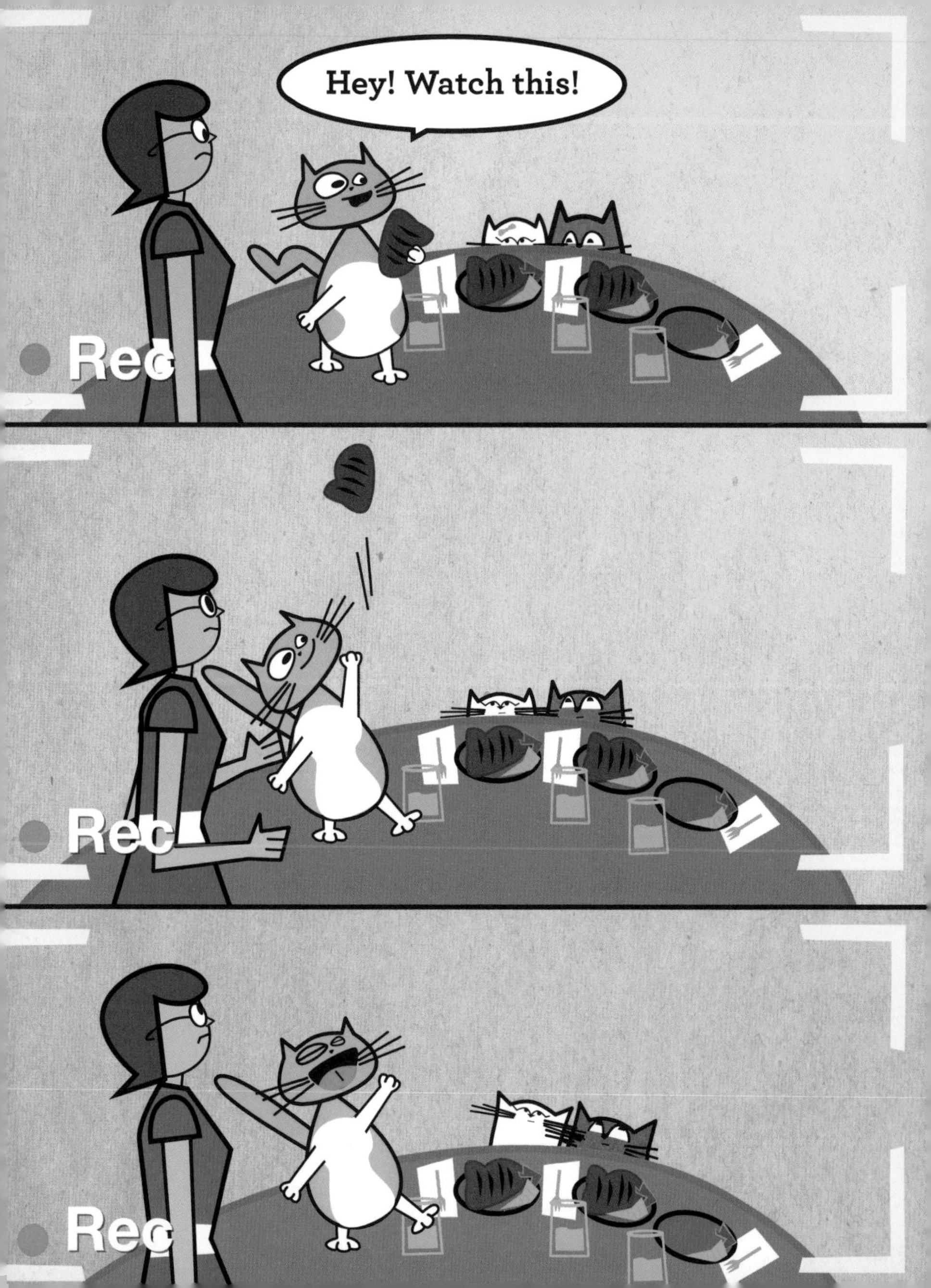
Hey! Watch this!
Rec
Rec
Rec

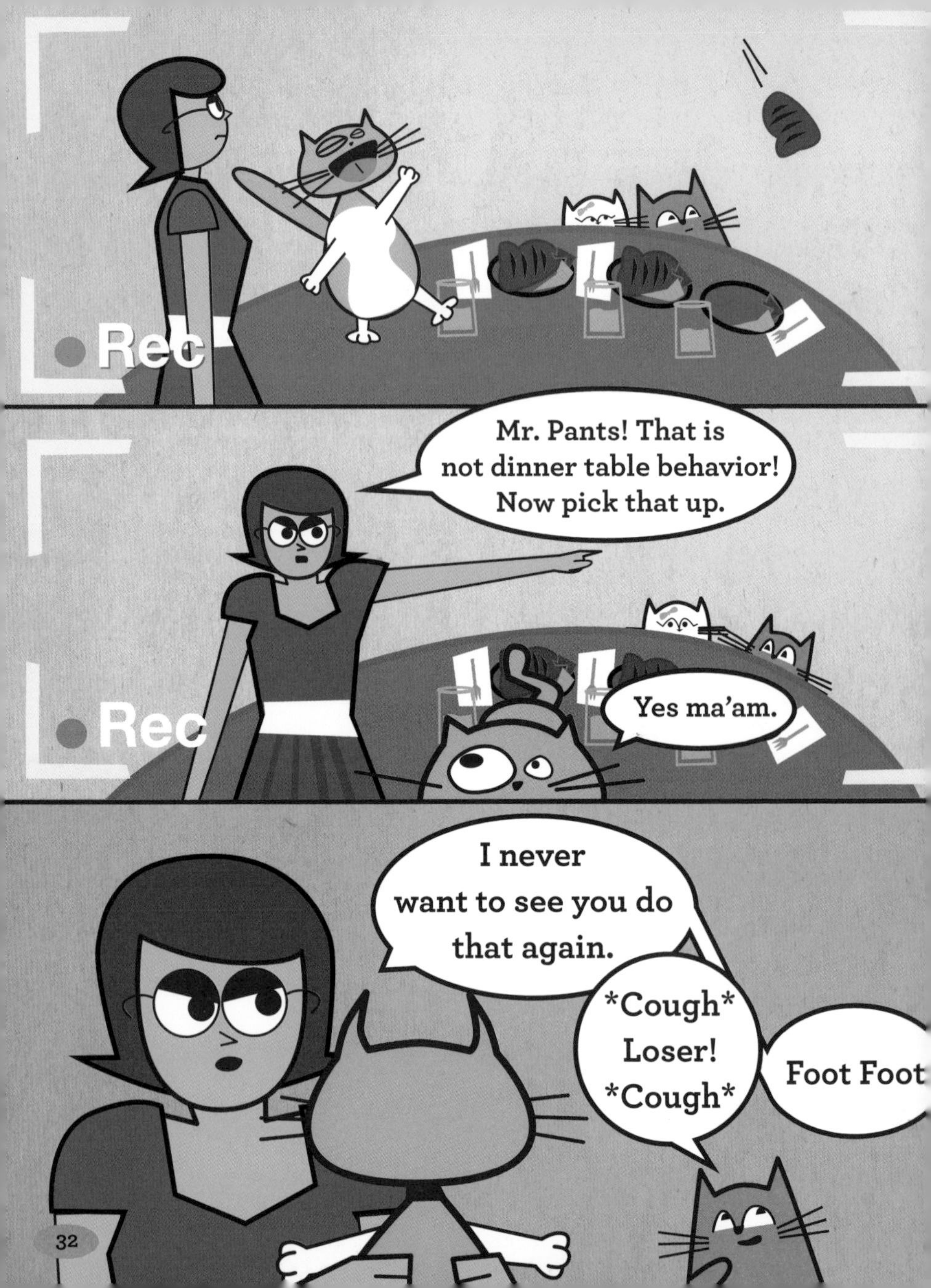
Rec
Mr. Pants! That is not dinner table behavior! Now pick that up.
Rec
Yes ma'am.
I never want to see you do that again.
Cough Loser! *Cough*
Foot Foot

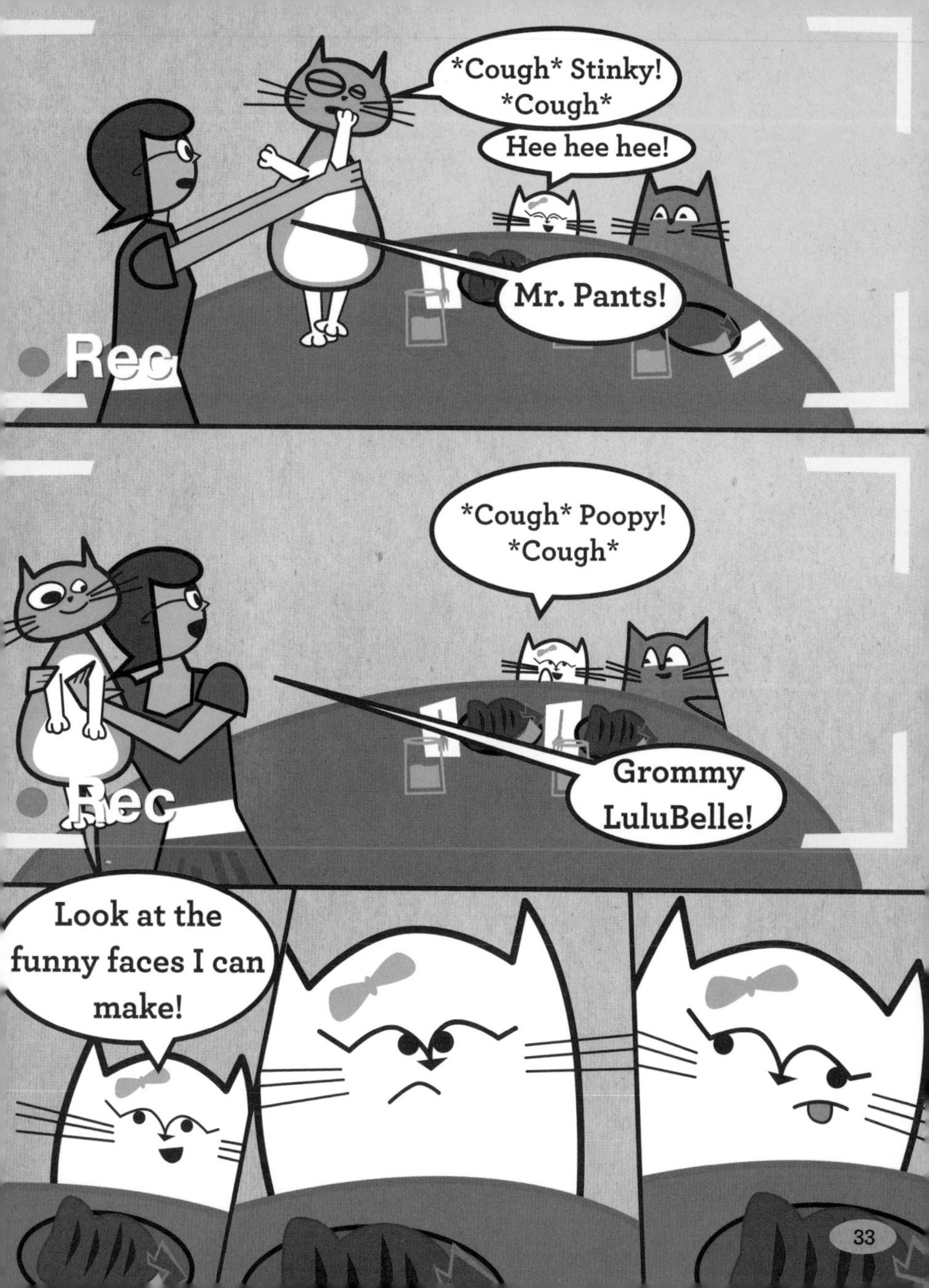
Cough Stinky! *Cough*
Hee hee hee!
Mr. Pants!
Rec
Cough Poopy! *Cough*
Grommy LuluBelle!
Rec
Look at the funny faces I can make!

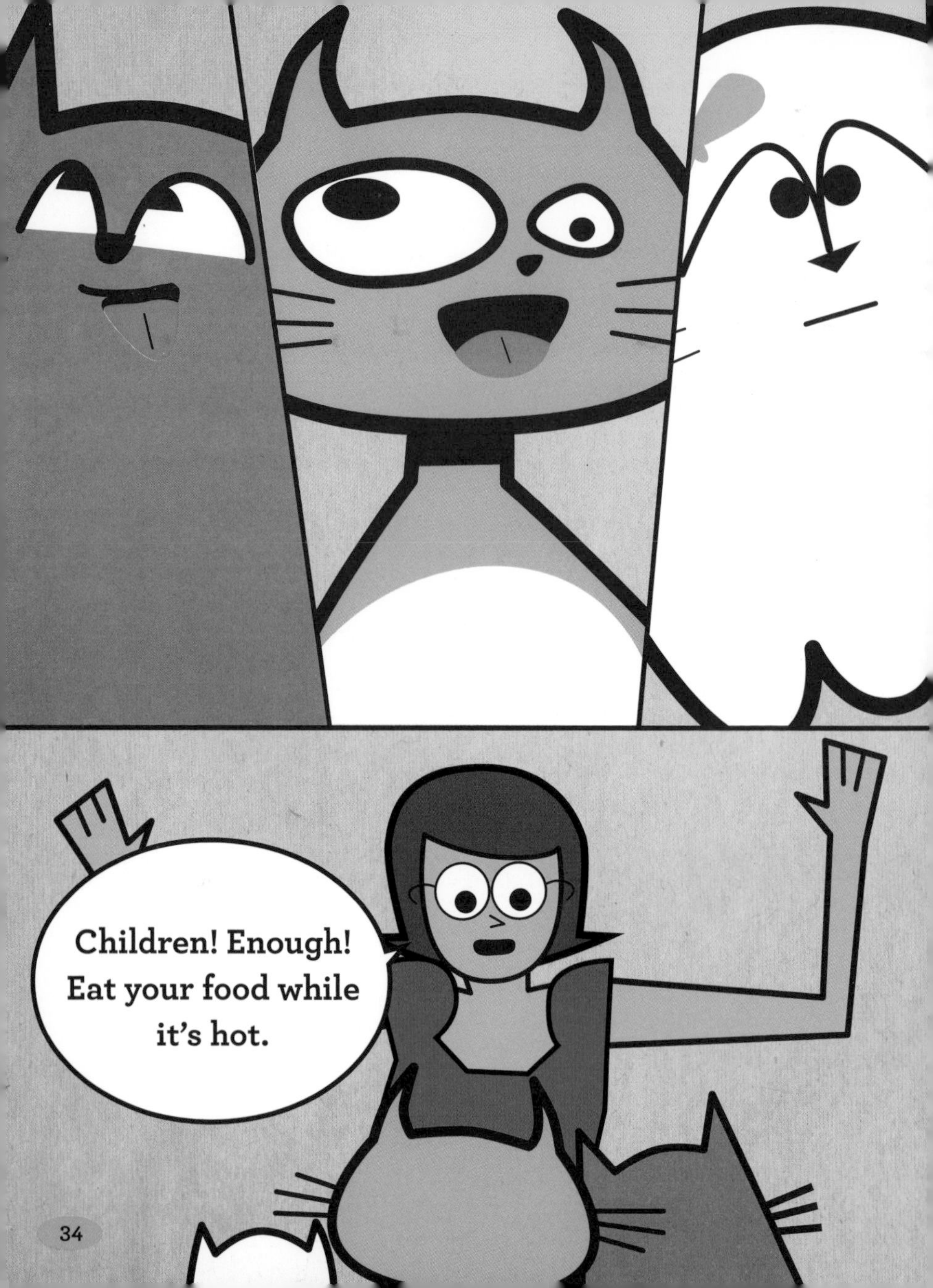
Children! Enough!
Eat your food while
it's hot.

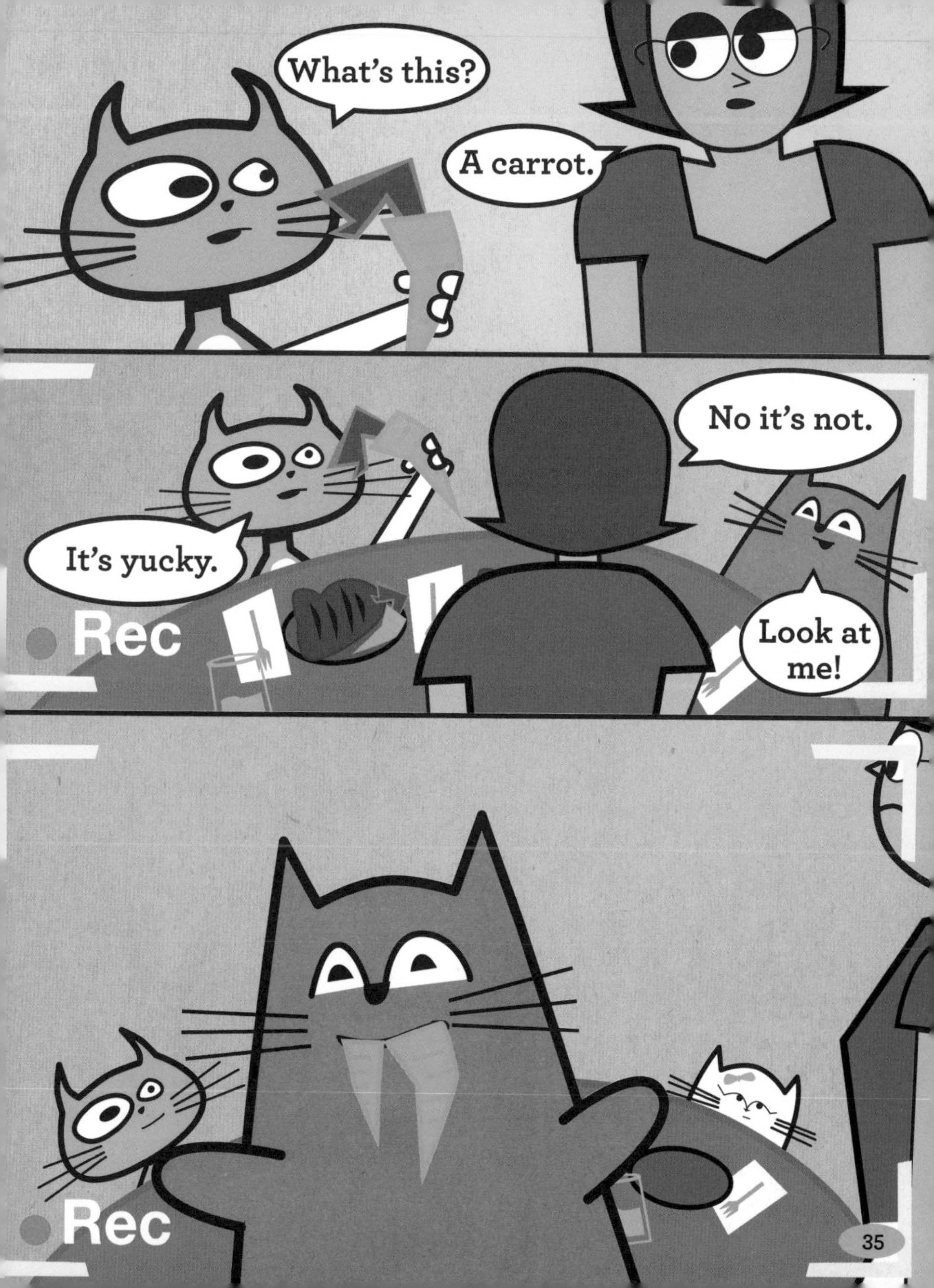
What's this?
A carrot.
No it's not.
It's yucky.
Look at me!
Rec
Rec

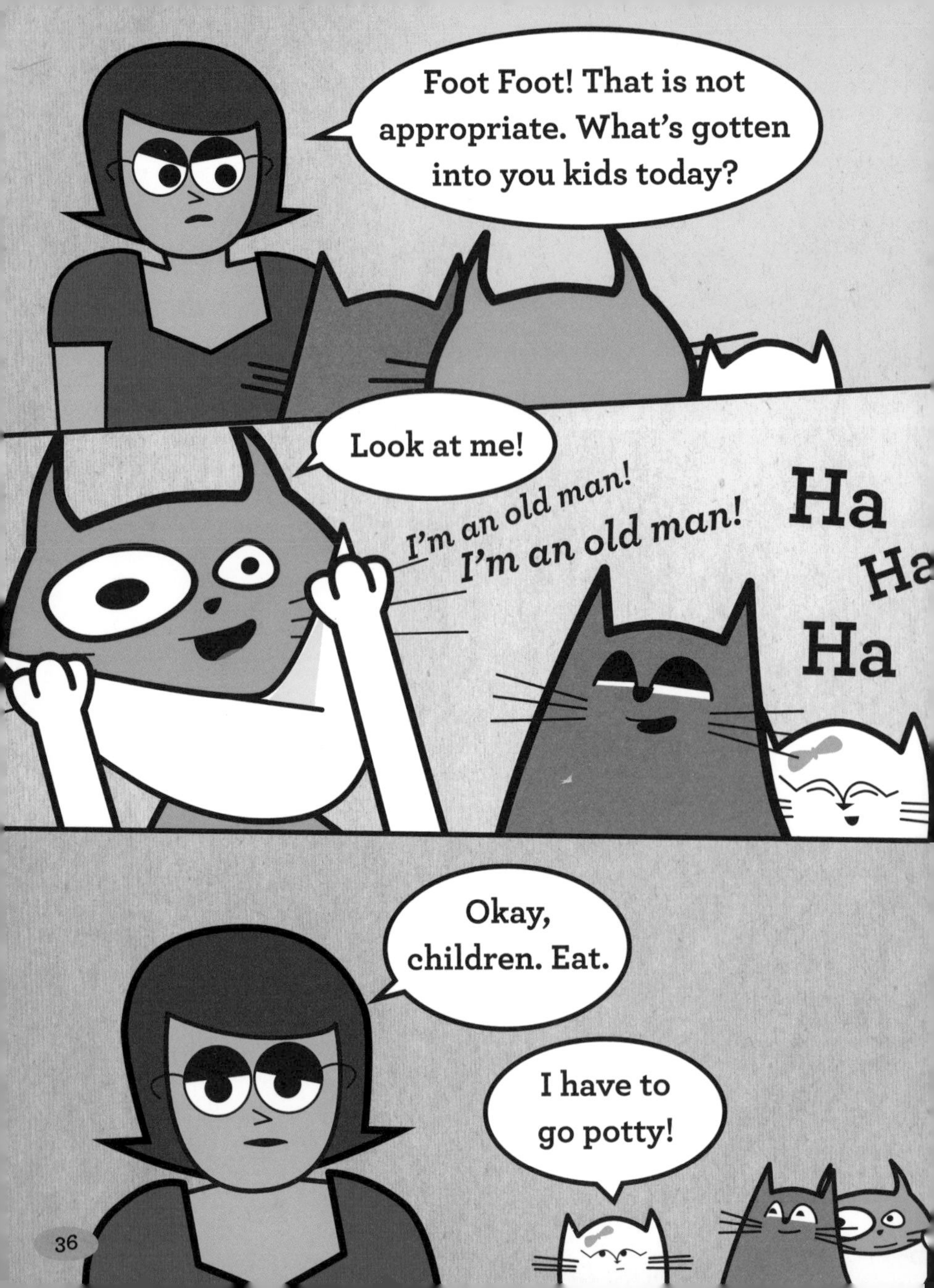
Foot Foot! That is not appropriate. What's gotten into you kids today?
Look at me!
I'm an old man!
I'm an old man!
Ha
Ha
Ha
Okay, children. Eat.
I have to go potty!

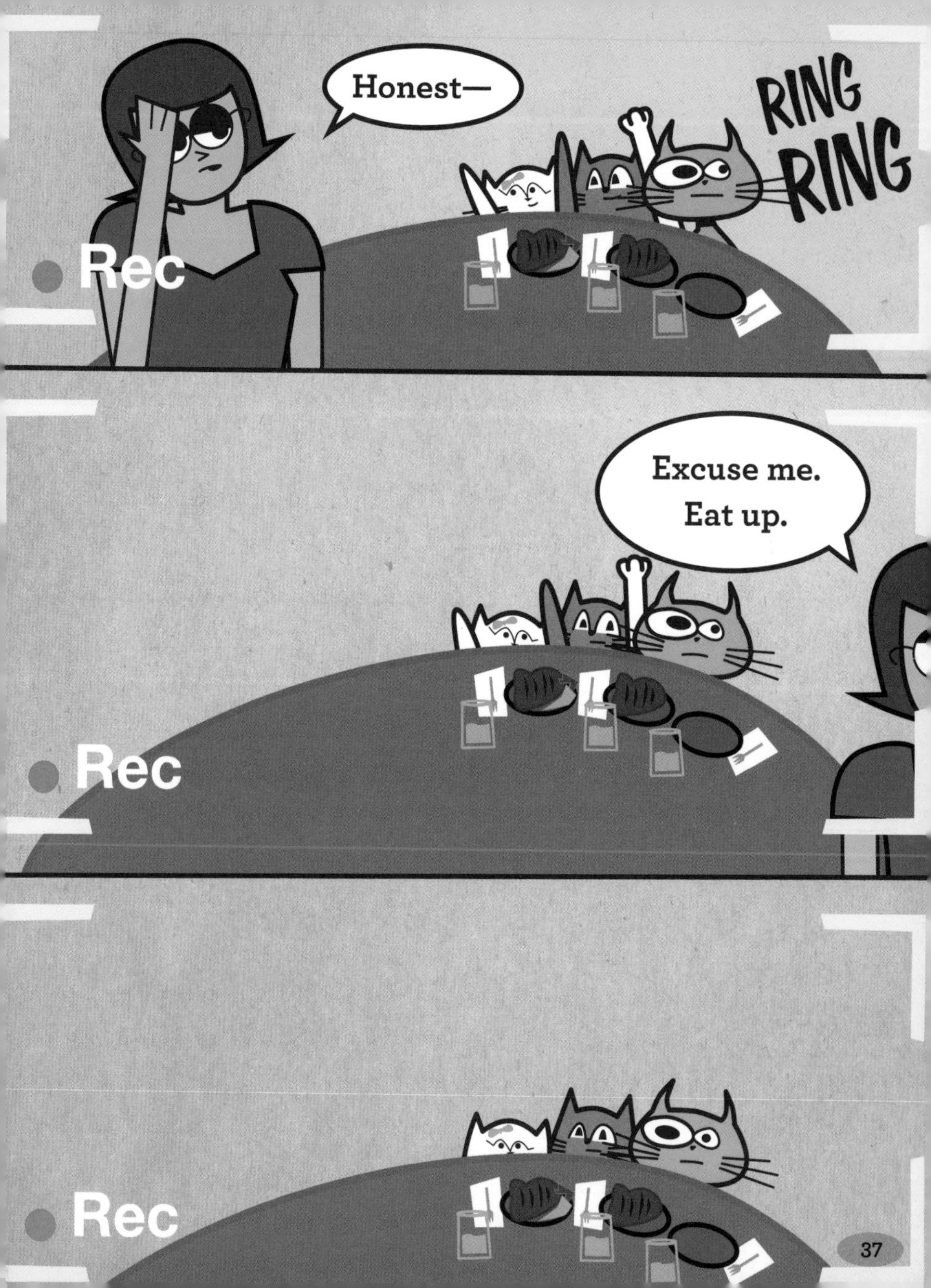
Honest—
RING RING
Rec
Excuse me.
Eat up.
Rec
Rec

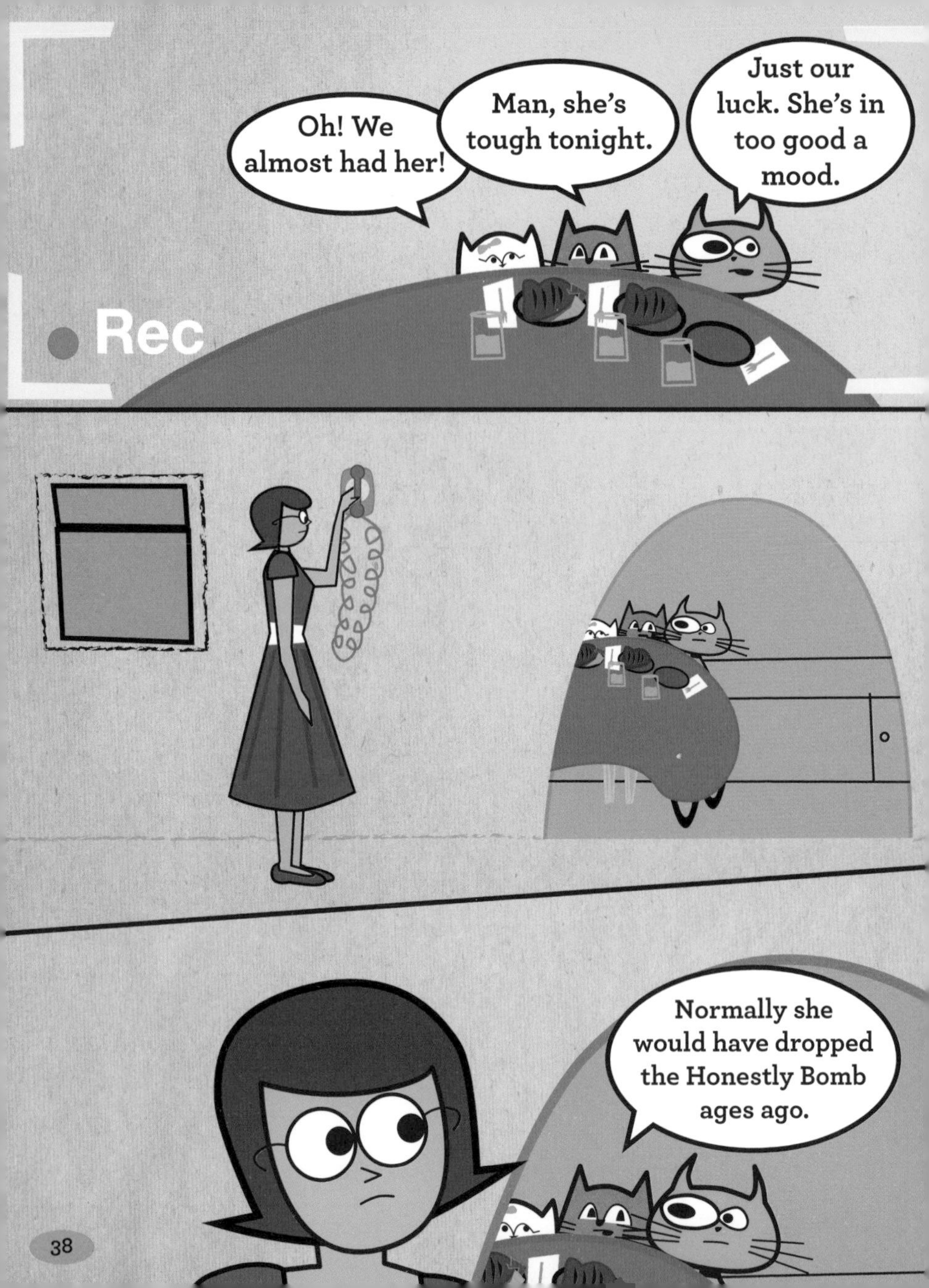
Oh! We almost had her!
Man, she's tough tonight.
Just our luck. She's in too good a mood.
Rec
Normally she would have dropped the Honestly Bomb ages ago.

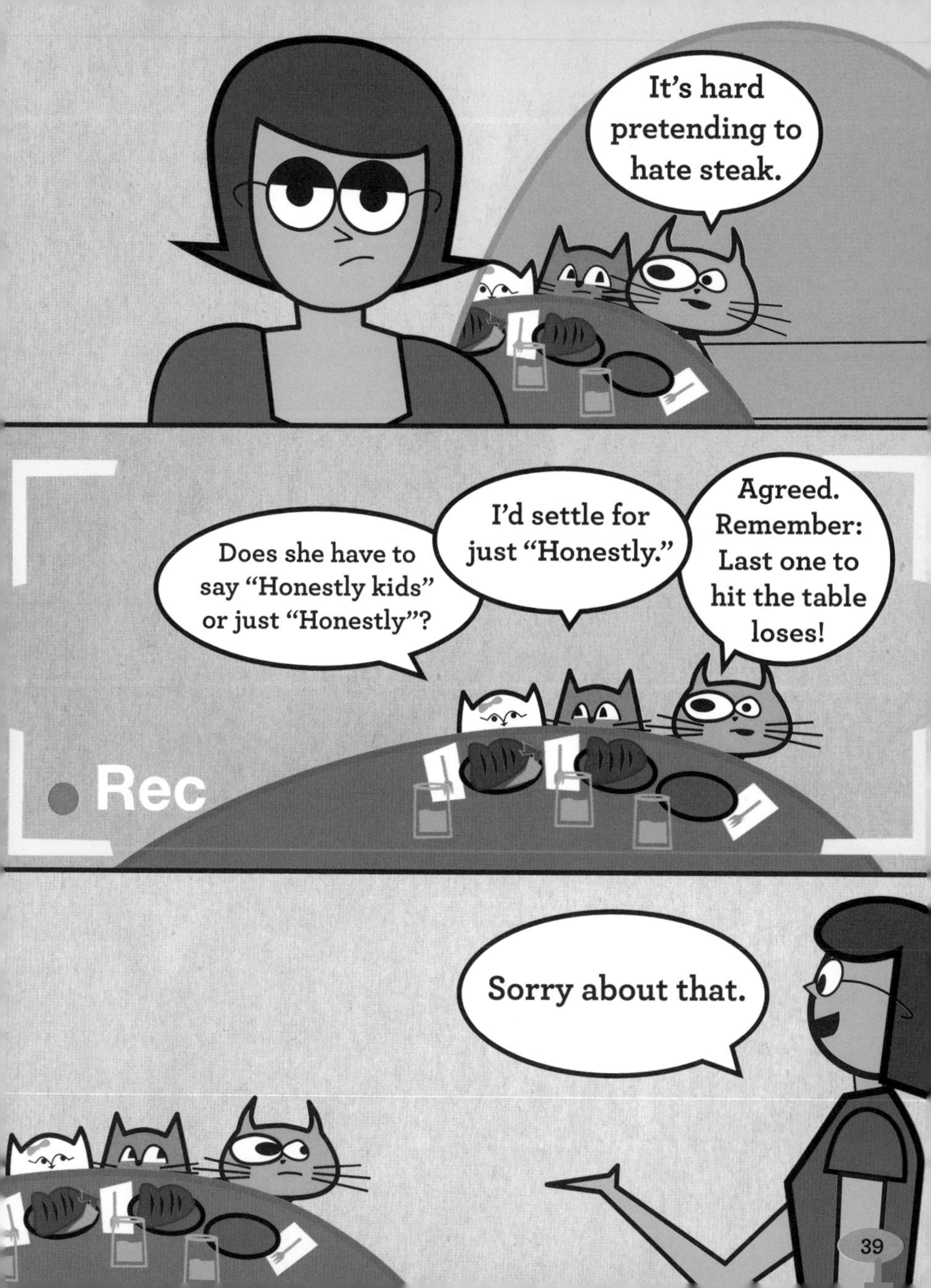
It's hard pretending to hate steak.
Does she have to say "Honestly kids" or just "Honestly"?
I'd settle for just "Honestly."
Agreed. Remember: Last one to hit the table loses!
Rec
Sorry about that.

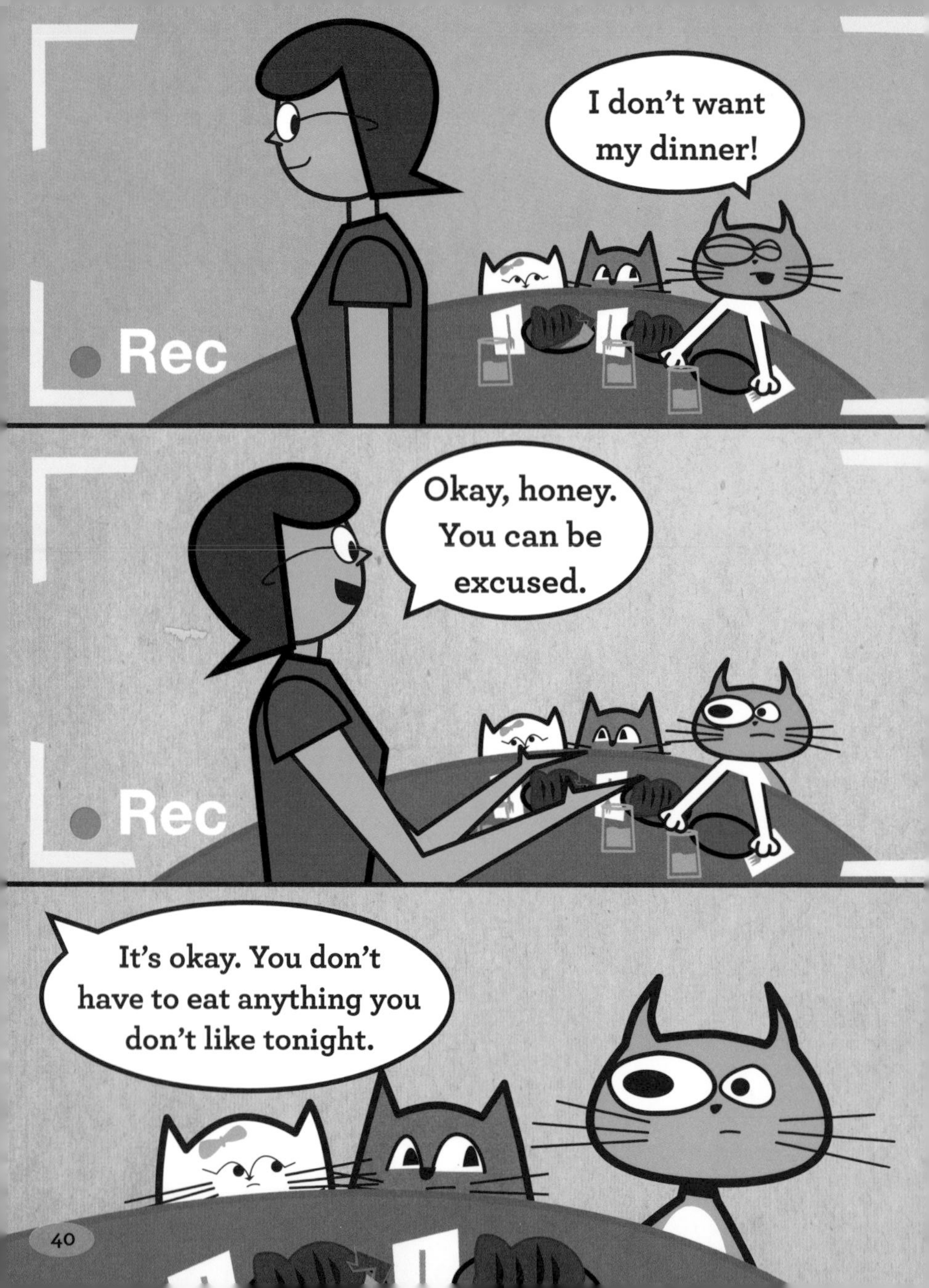
Rec
I don't want my dinner!
Rec
Okay, honey. You can be excused.
It's okay. You don't have to eat anything you don't like tonight.

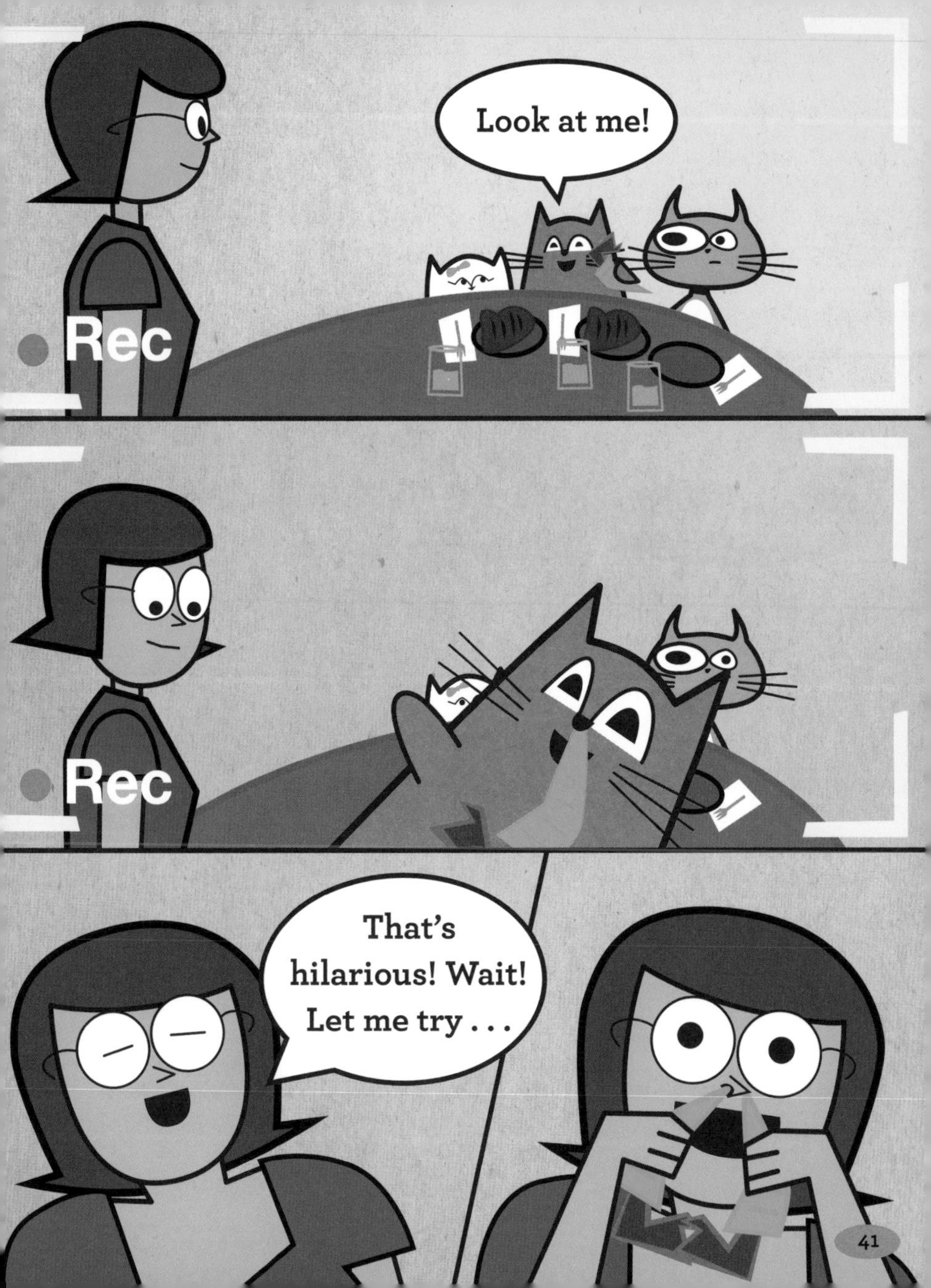
Rec
Look at me!
Rec
That's hilarious! Wait! Let me try . . .

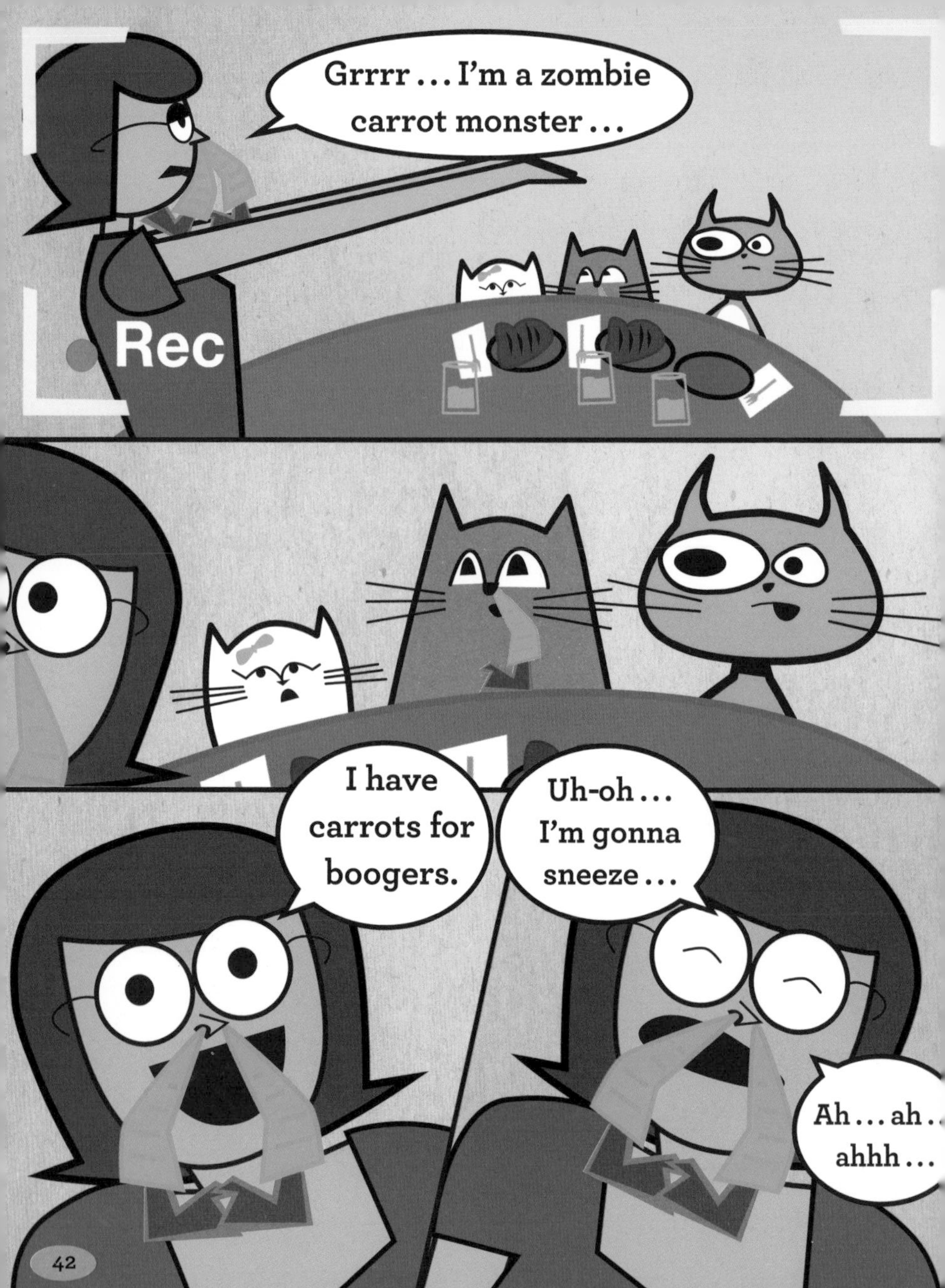
Grrrr . . . I'm a zombie carrot monster . . .
Rec
I have carrots for boogers.
Uh-oh . . . I'm gonna sneeze . . .
Ah . . . ah . . . ahhh . . .

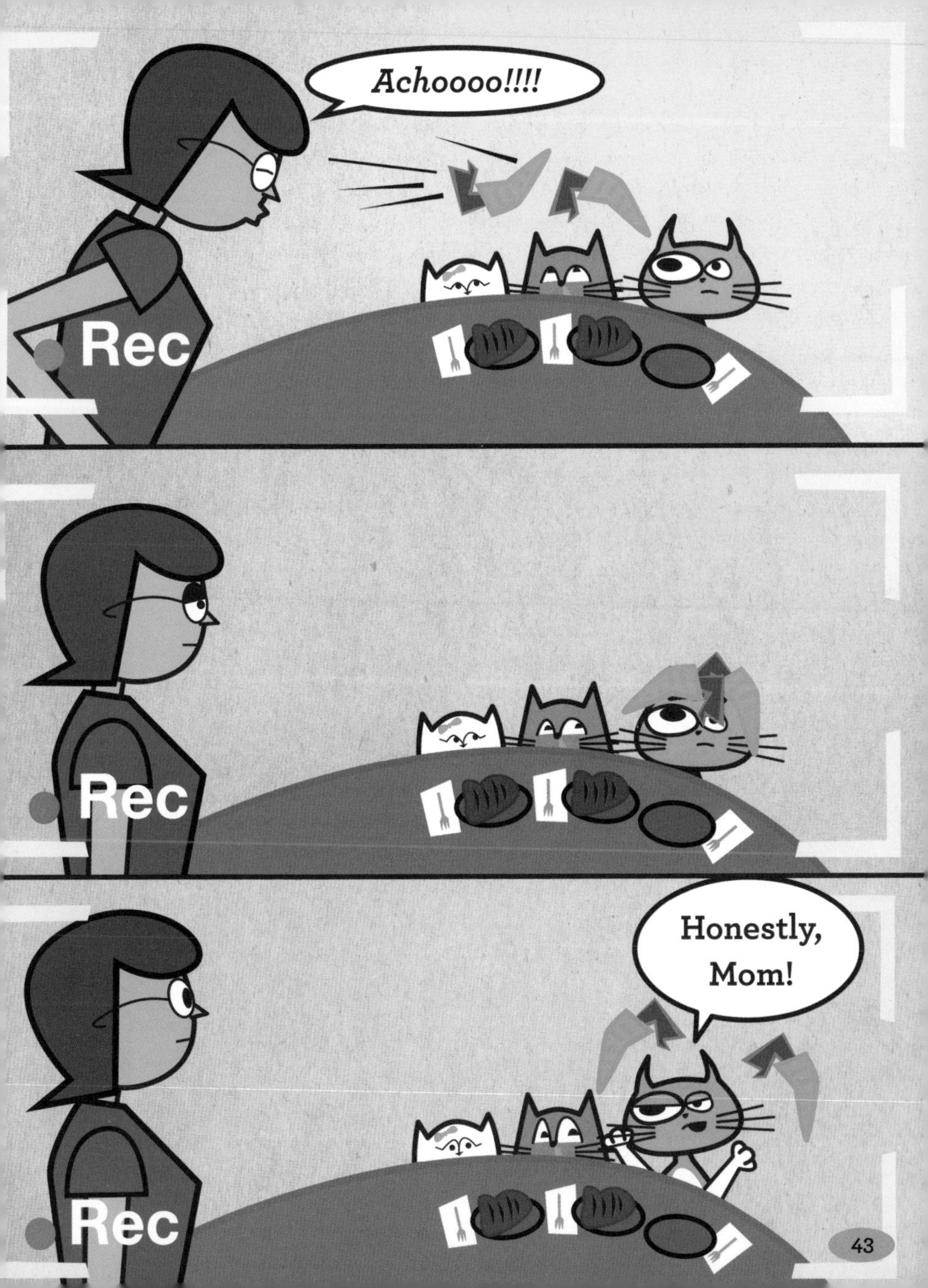
Achoooo!!!!
Rec
Rec
Honestly, Mom!
Rec

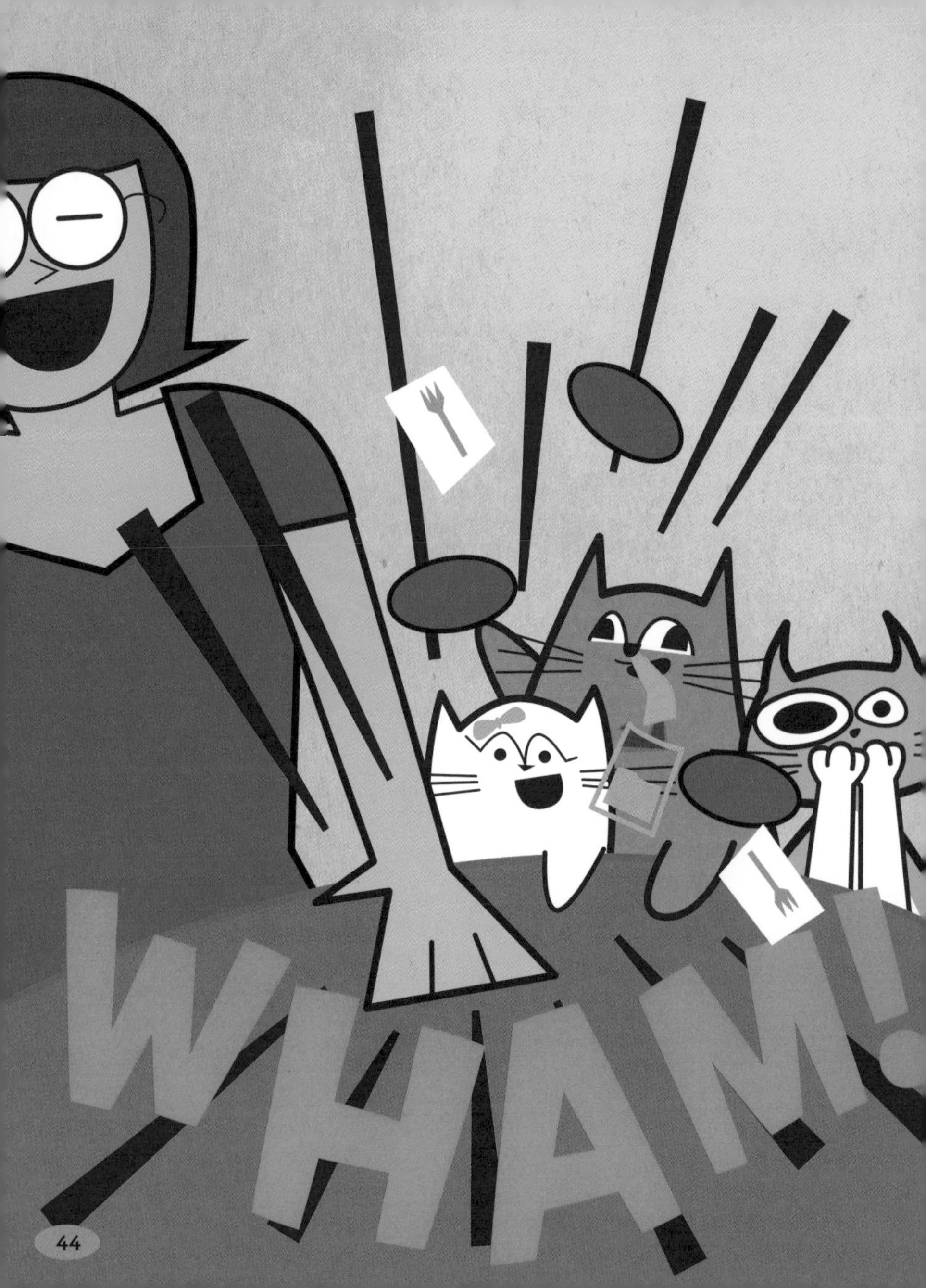
WHAM!

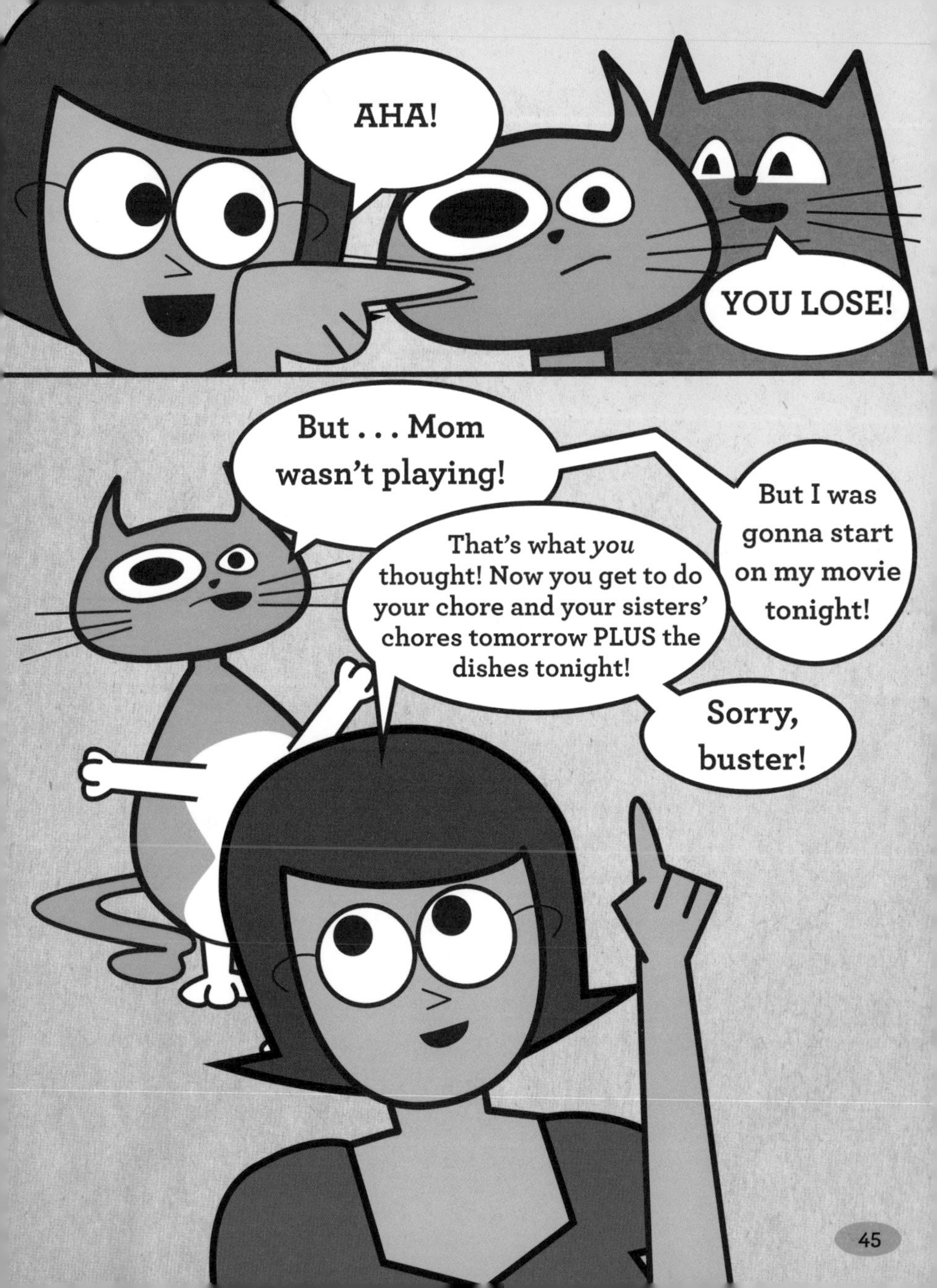
AHA!
YOU LOSE!
But . . . Mom wasn't playing!
But I was gonna start on my movie tonight!
That's what *you* thought! Now you get to do your chore and your sisters' chores tomorrow PLUS the dishes tonight!
Sorry, buster!

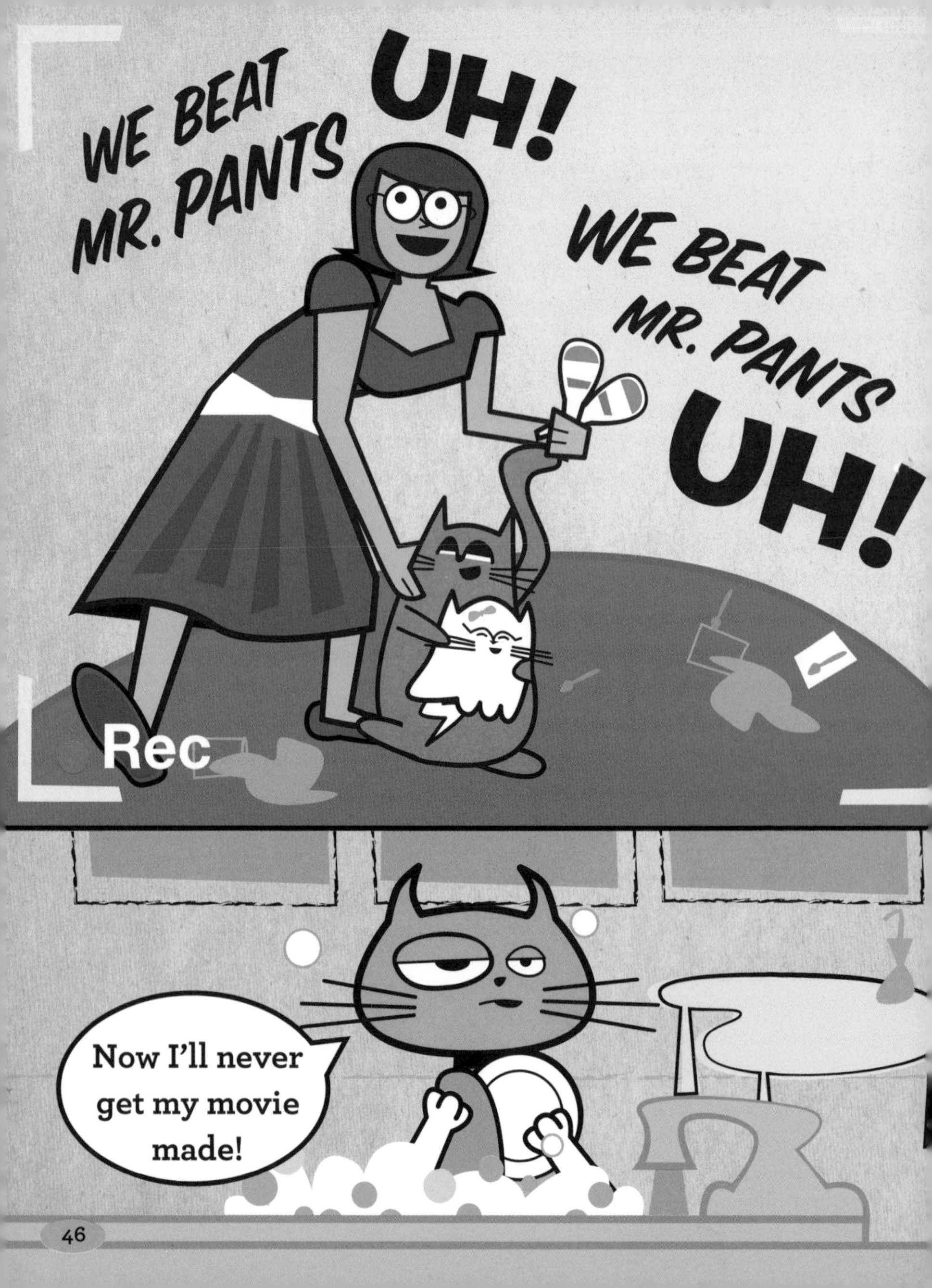
WE BEAT MR. PANTS UH!
WE BEAT MR. PANTS UH!
Rec
Now I'll never get my movie made!

Chapter Three: BUM-BUM'S VUUMBA BOOM

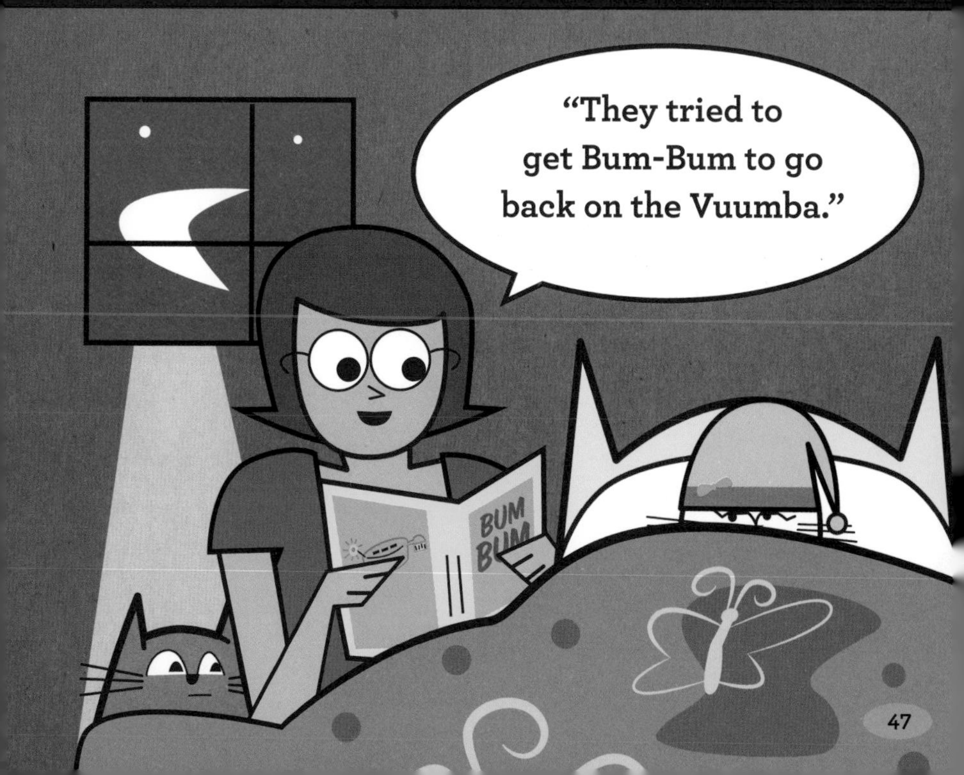

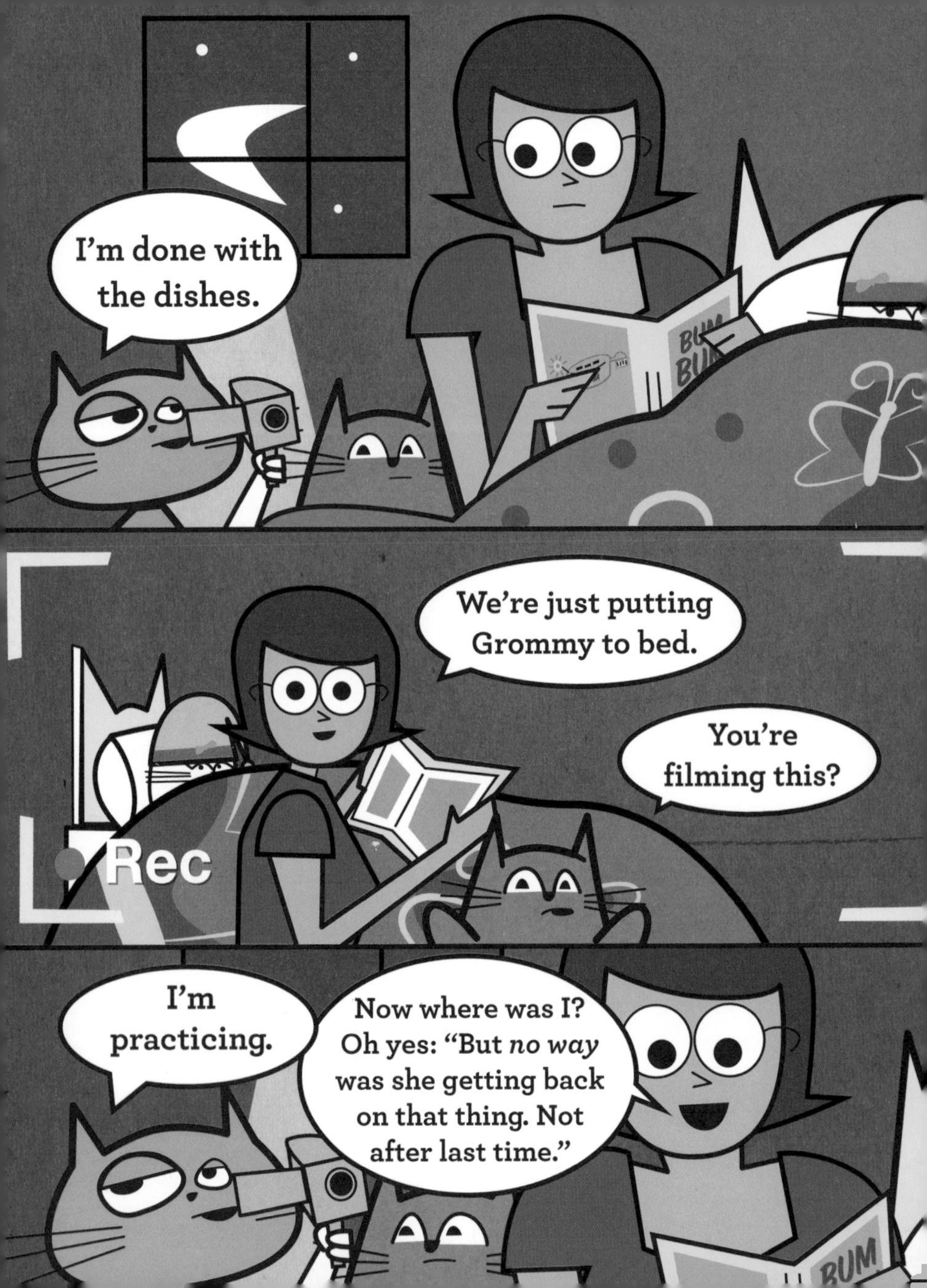
I'm done with the dishes.
BUM BUM
We're just putting Grommy to bed.
You're filming this?
Rec
I'm practicing.
Now where was I? Oh yes: "But *no way* was she getting back on that thing. Not after last time."
BUM

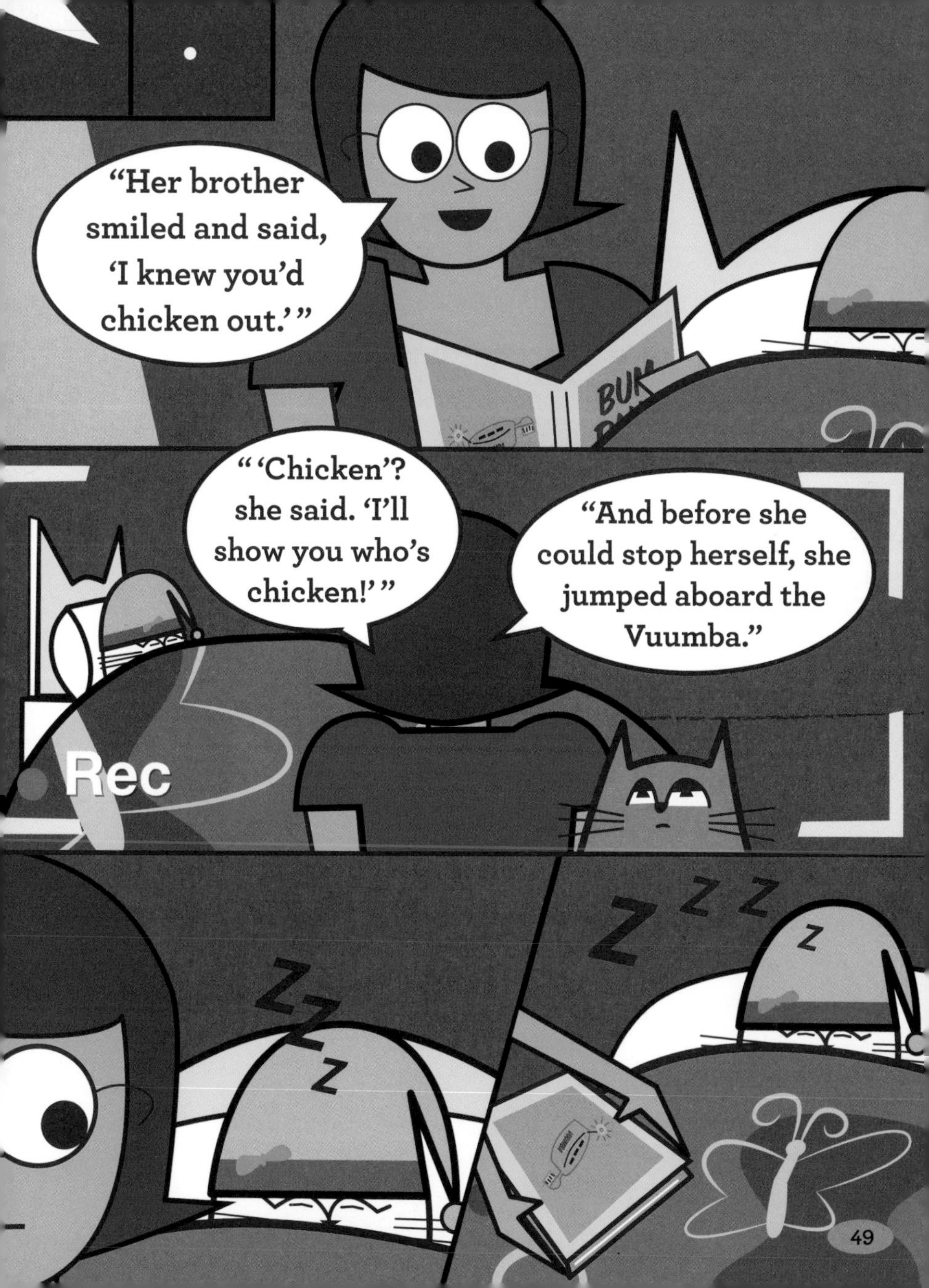
"Her brother smiled and said, 'I knew you'd chicken out.'"
"'Chicken'? she said. 'I'll show you who's chicken!'"
"And before she could stop herself, she jumped aboard the Vuumba."
Rec
Z
Z
Z
Z
Z Z Z
Z

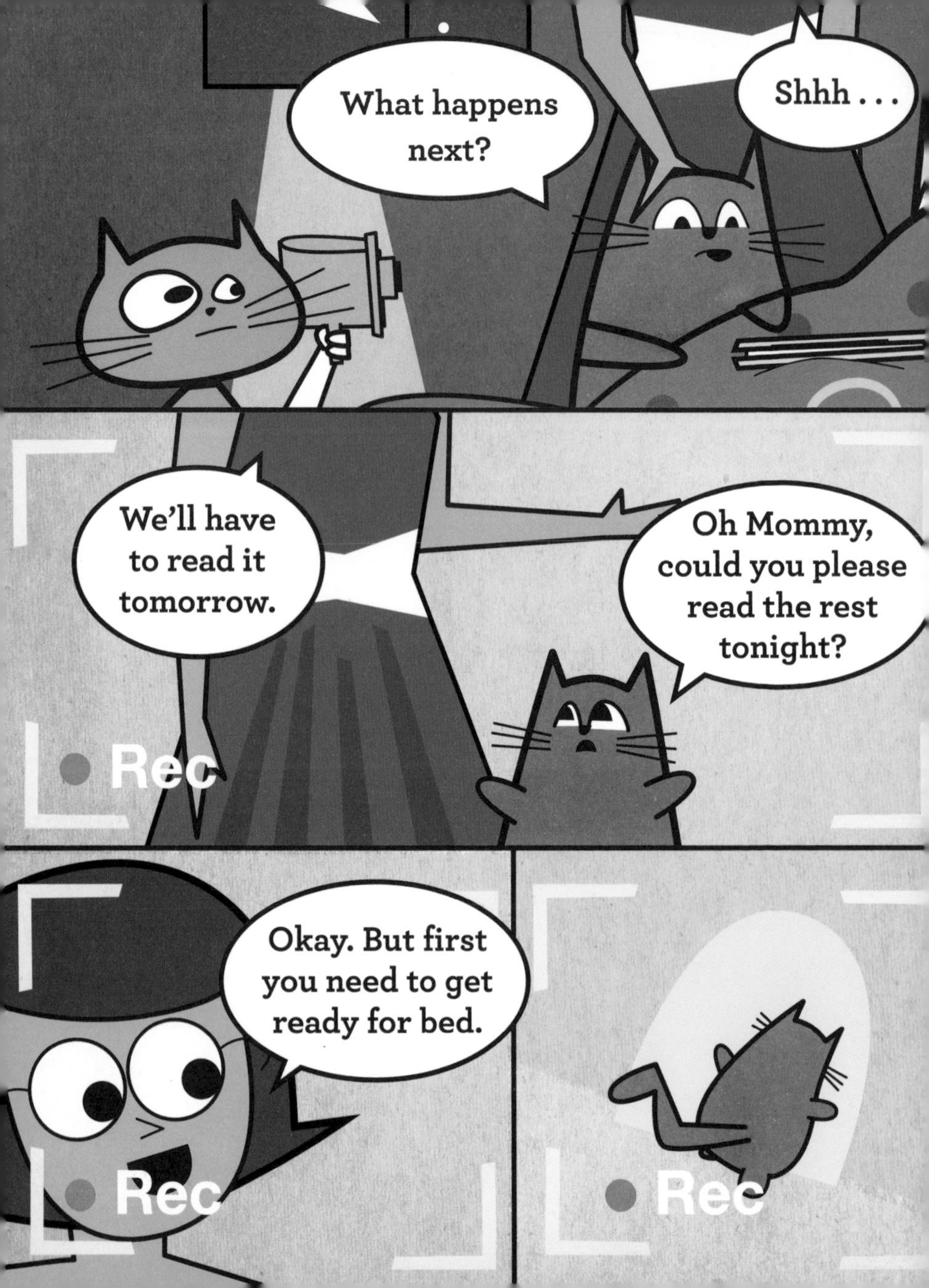
What happens next?
Shhh . . .
We'll have to read it tomorrow.
Oh Mommy, could you please read the rest tonight?
Rec
Okay. But first you need to get ready for bed.
Rec
Rec

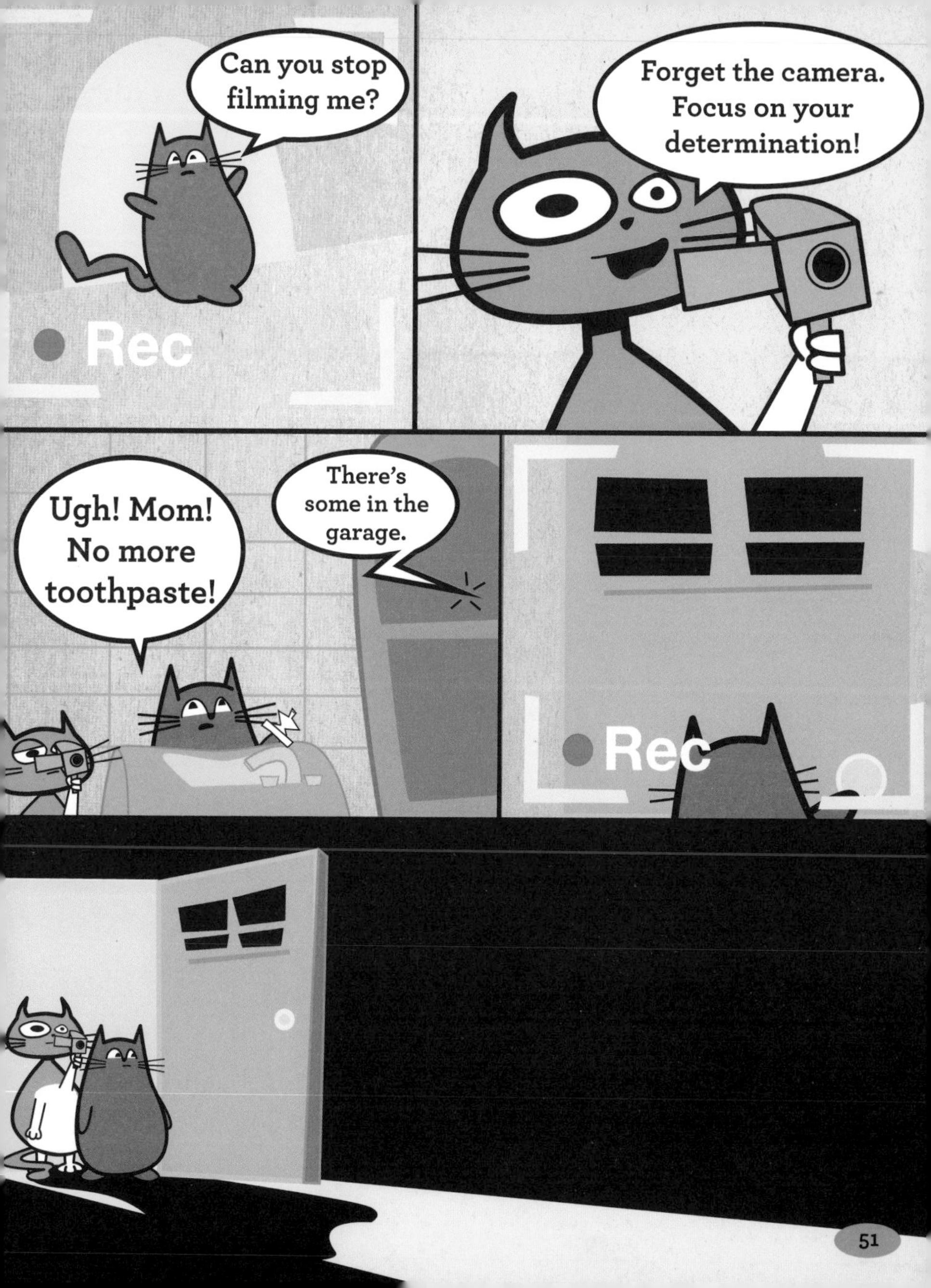
Can you stop filming me?
Rec
Forget the camera. Focus on your determination!
Ugh! Mom! No more toothpaste!
There's some in the garage.
Rec

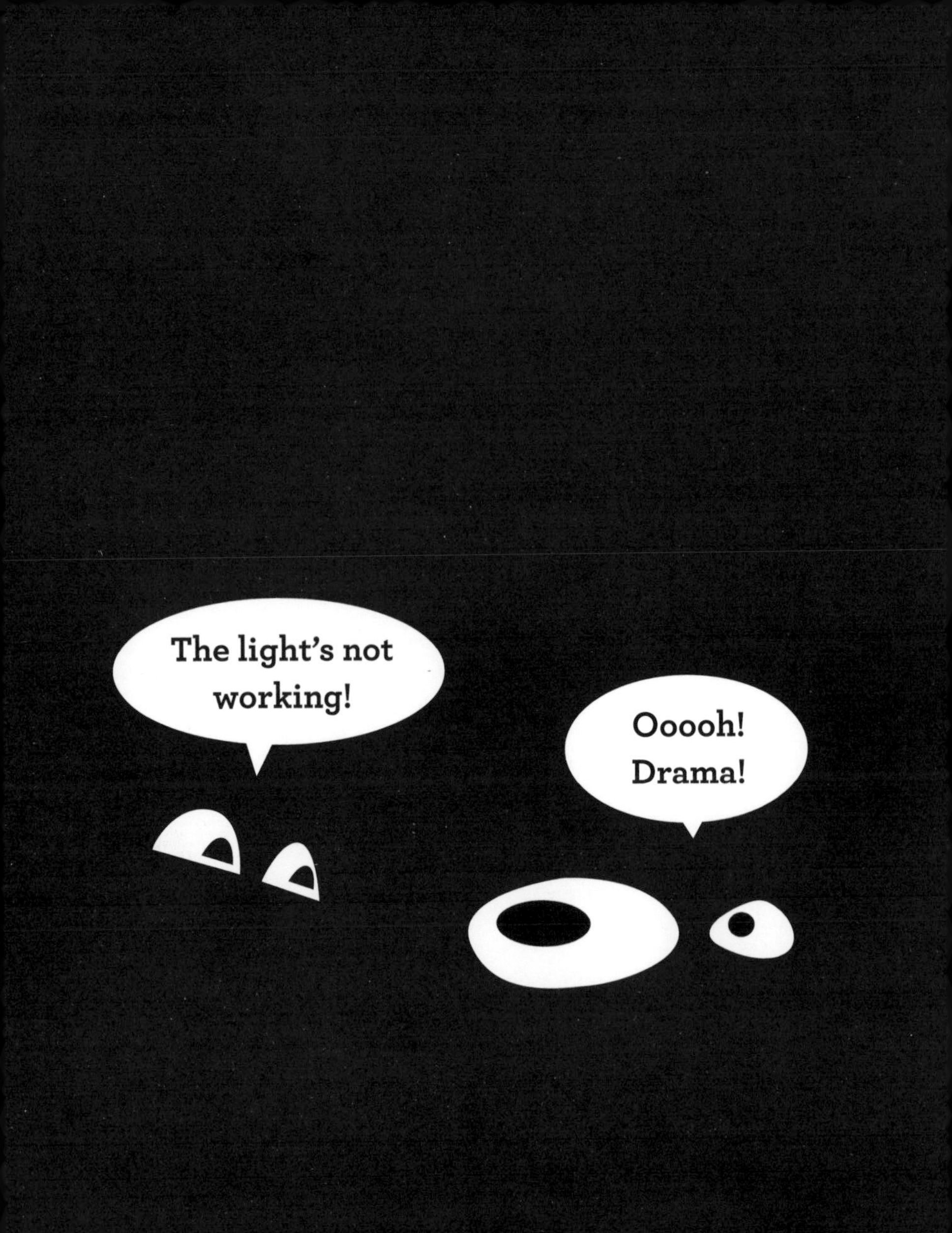
The light's not working!
Ooooh! Drama!

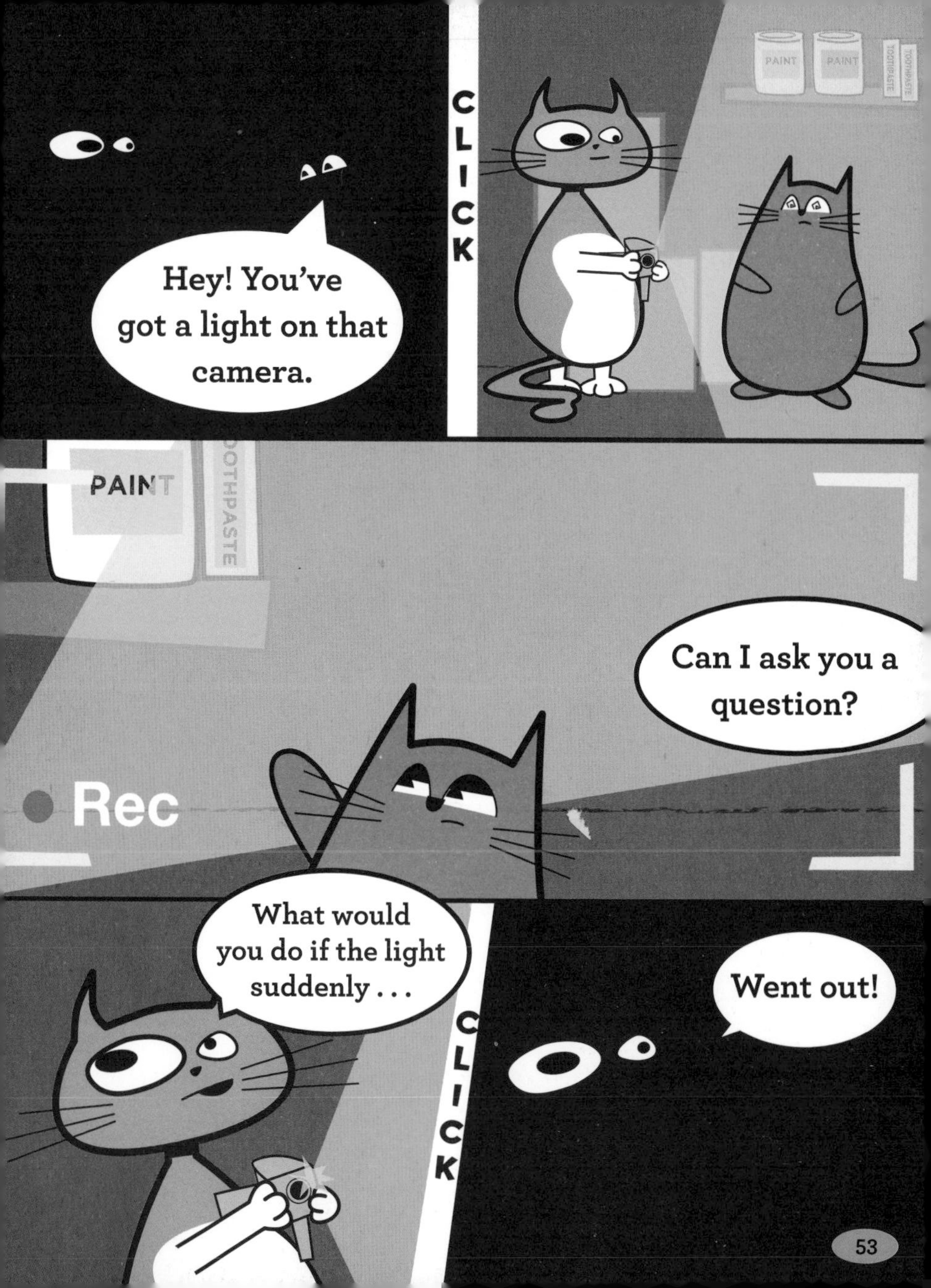
Hey! You've got a light on that camera.
CLICK
PAINT
PAINT
TOOTHPASTE
TOOTHPASTE
PAINT
TOOTHPASTE
Rec
Can I ask you a question?
What would you do if the light suddenly . . .
CLICK
Went out!

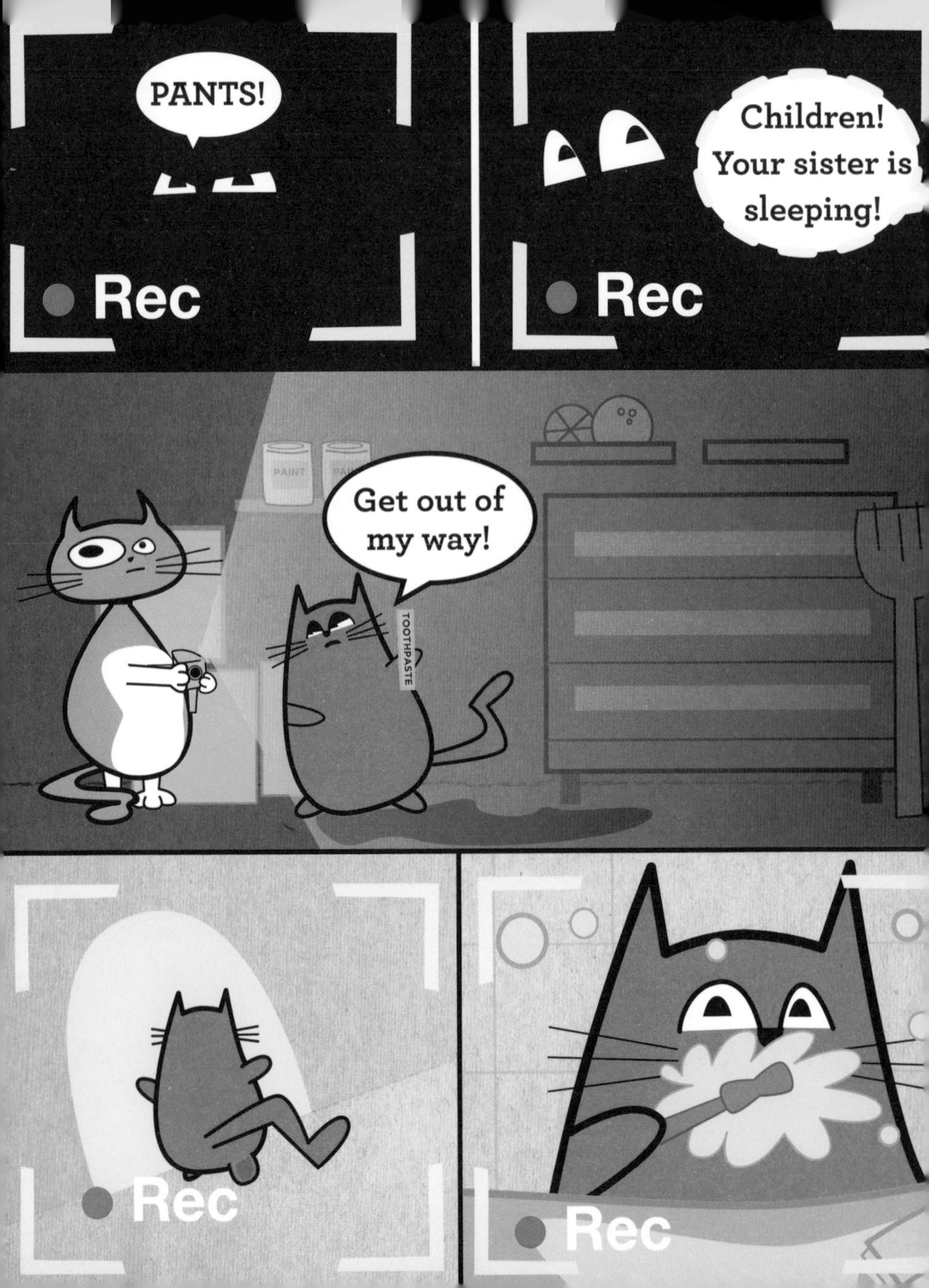
PANTS!
Rec
Children! Your sister is sleeping!
Rec
PAINT
Get out of my way!
TOOTHPASTE
Rec
Rec

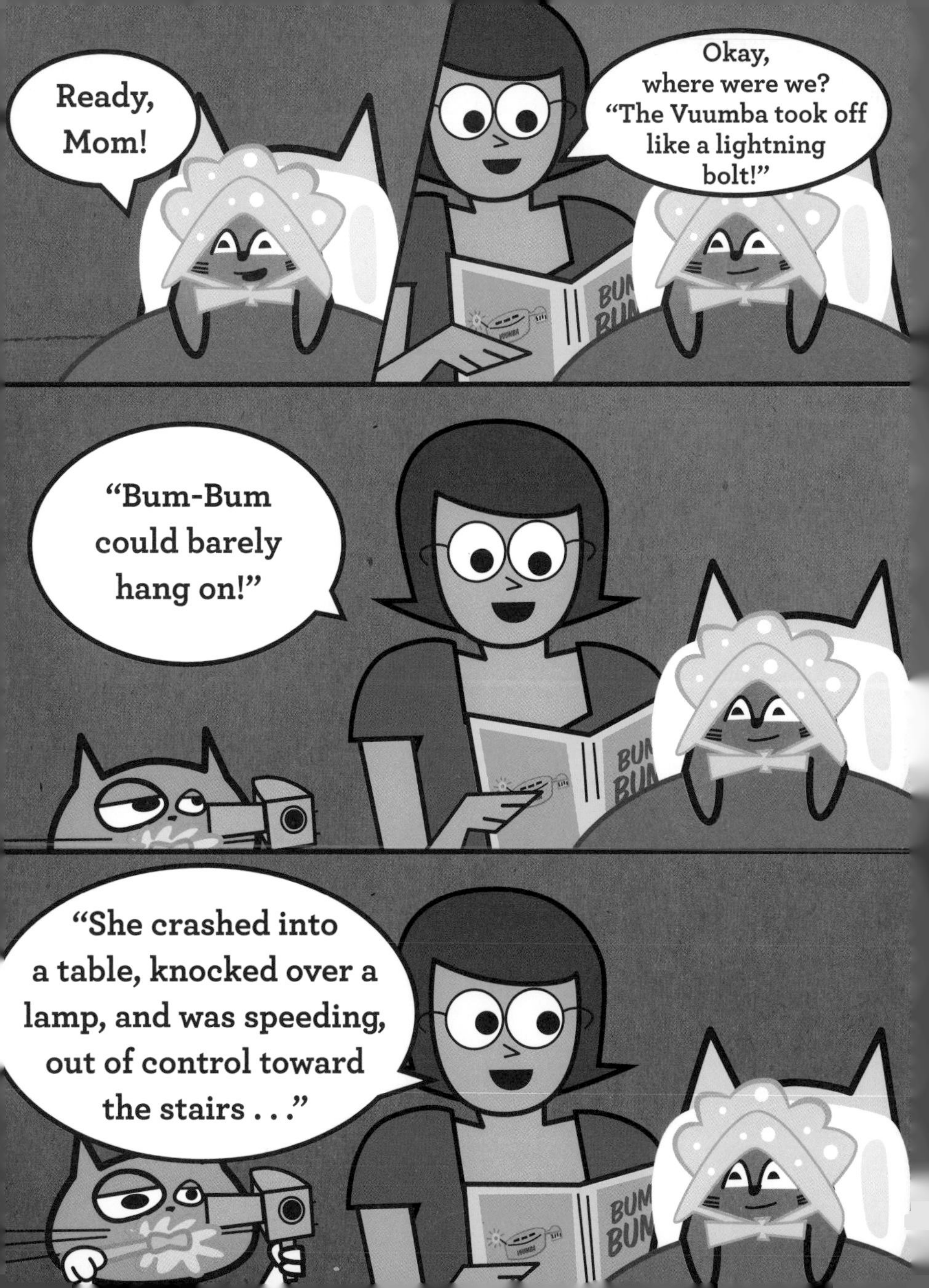
Ready, Mom!
Okay, where were we? "The Vuumba took off like a lightning bolt!"
"Bum-Bum could barely hang on!"
"She crashed into a table, knocked over a lamp, and was speeding, out of control toward the stairs . . ."

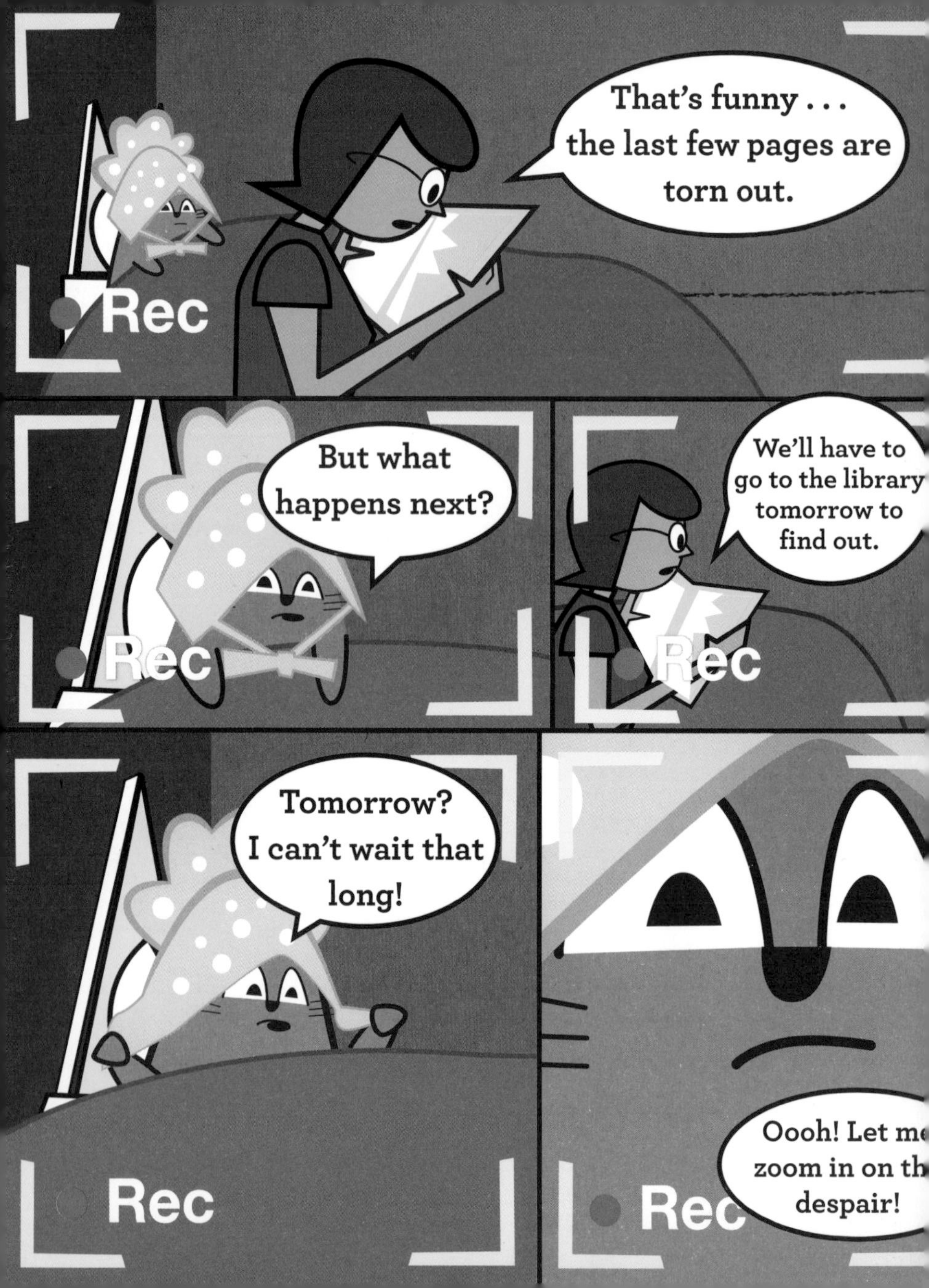

Rec
That's funny . . .
the last few pages are
torn out.
But what
happens next?
Rec
We'll have to
go to the library
tomorrow to
find out.
Rec
Tomorrow?
I can't wait that
long!
Rec
Oooh! Let m
zoom in on th
despair!
Rec

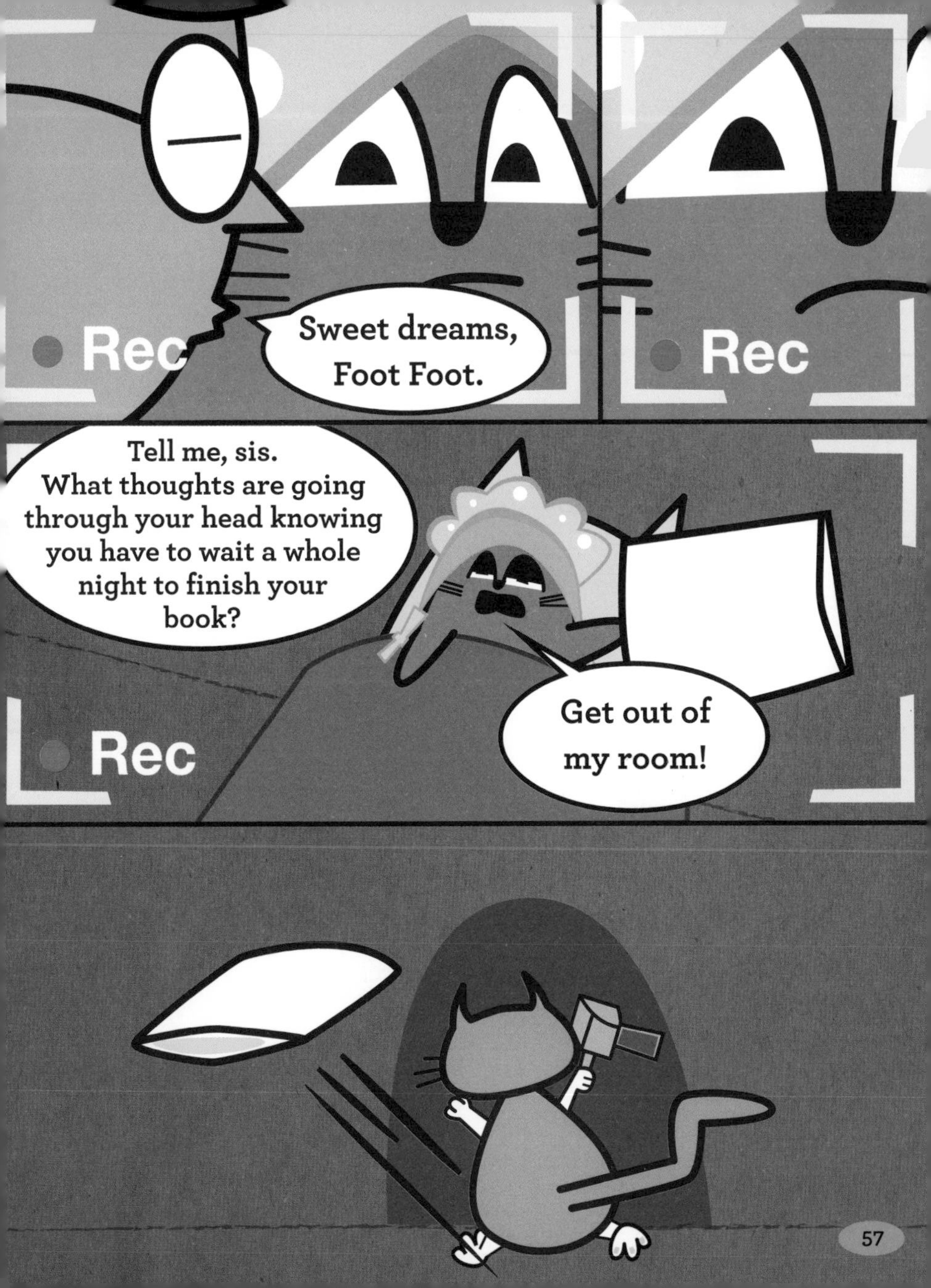
Rec
Sweet dreams, Foot Foot.
Rec
Tell me, sis. What thoughts are going through your head knowing you have to wait a whole night to finish your book?
Get out of my room!
Rec

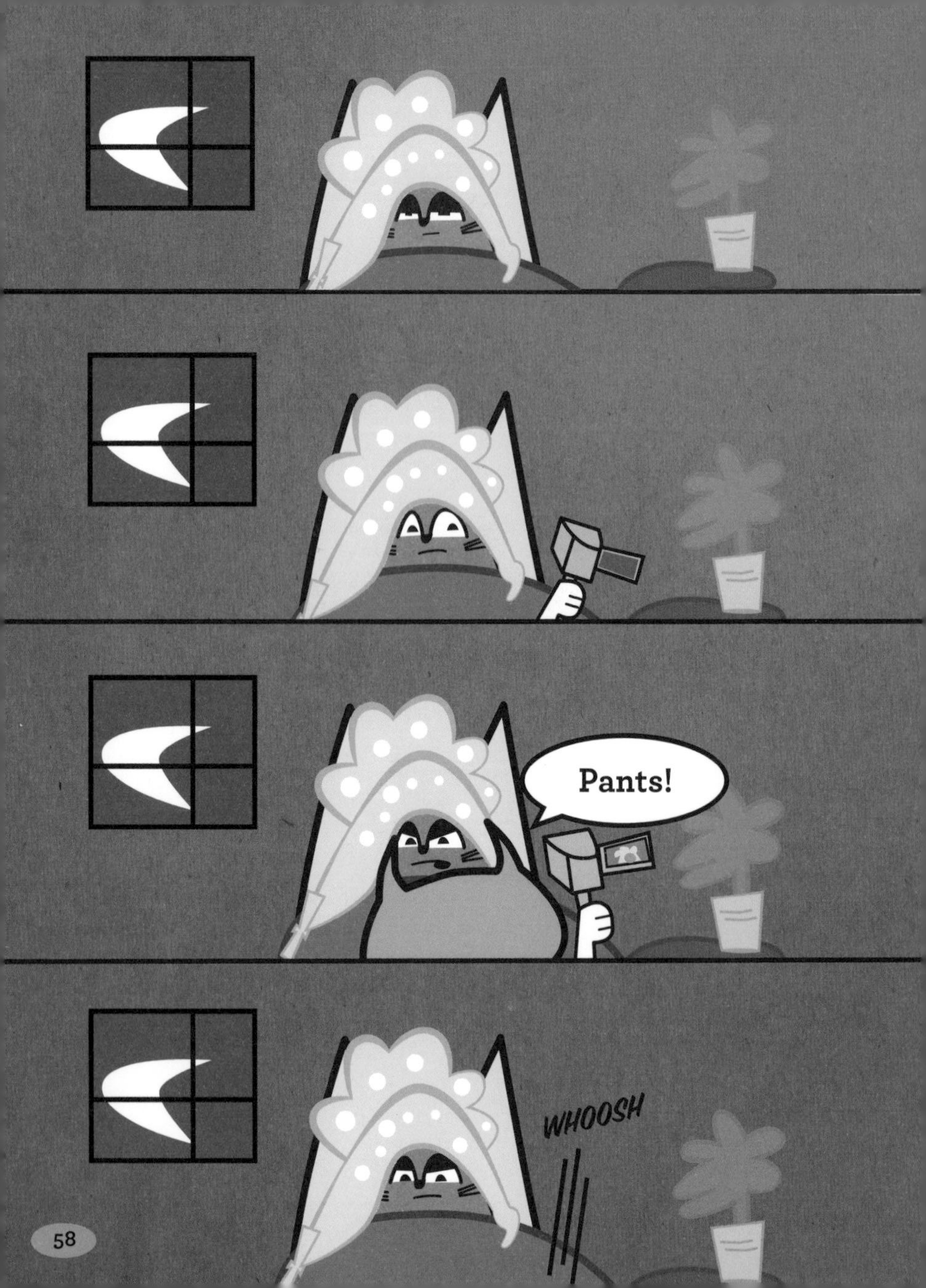
Pants!
WHOOSH

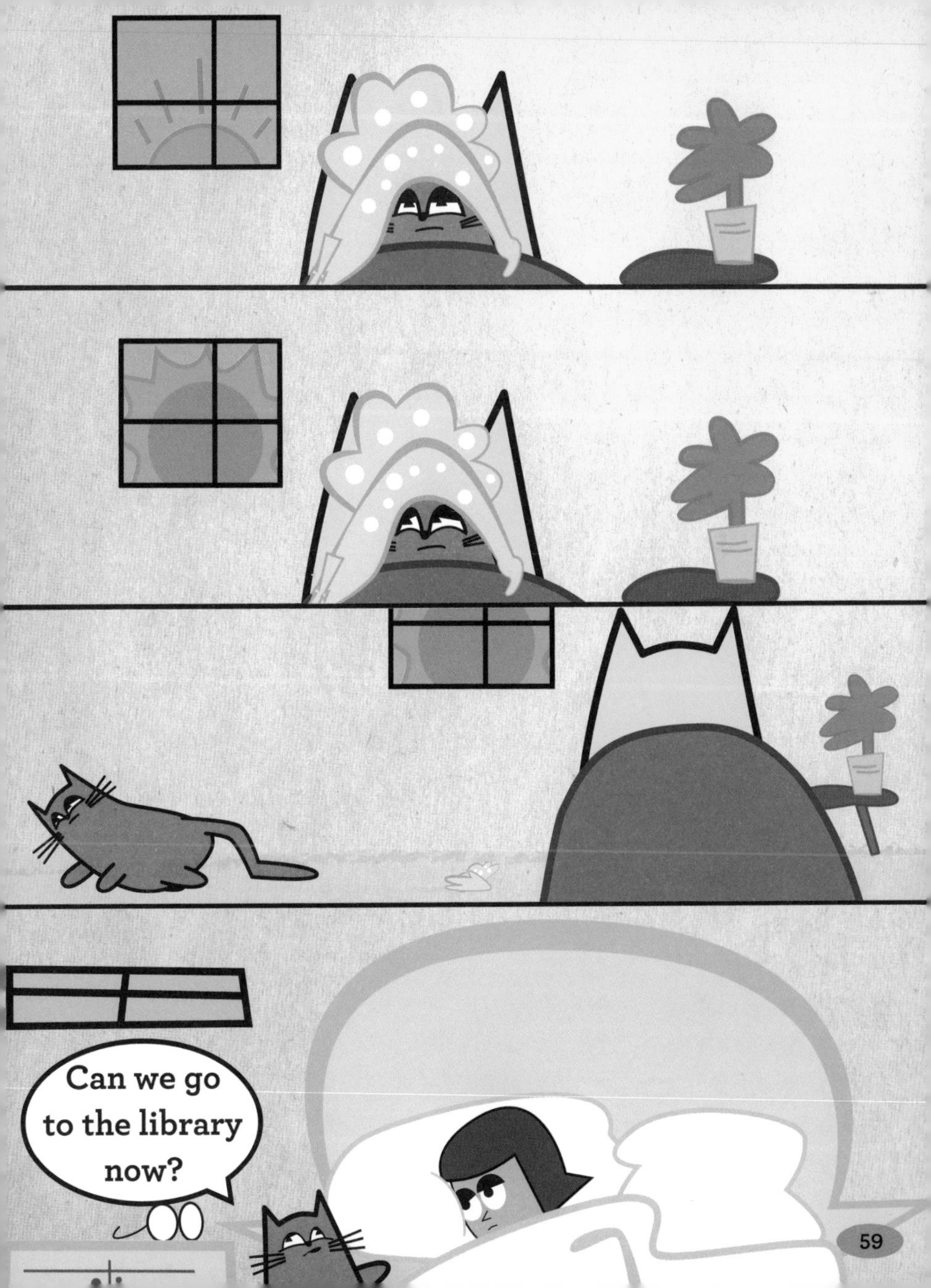
Can we go to the library now?

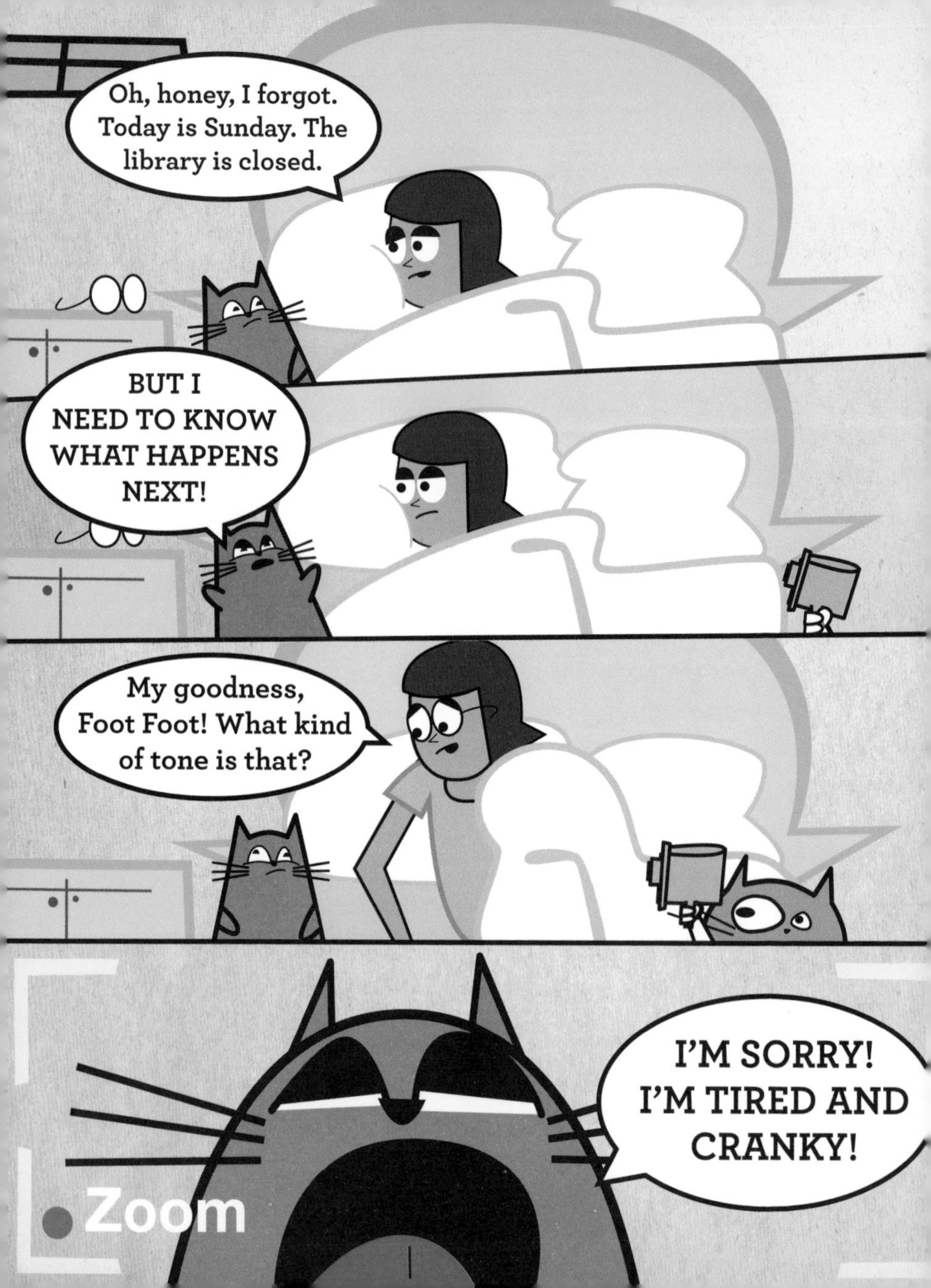
Oh, honey, I forgot. Today is Sunday. The library is closed.
BUT I NEED TO KNOW WHAT HAPPENS NEXT!
My goodness, Foot Foot! What kind of tone is that?
I'M SORRY! I'M TIRED AND CRANKY!
Zoom

61

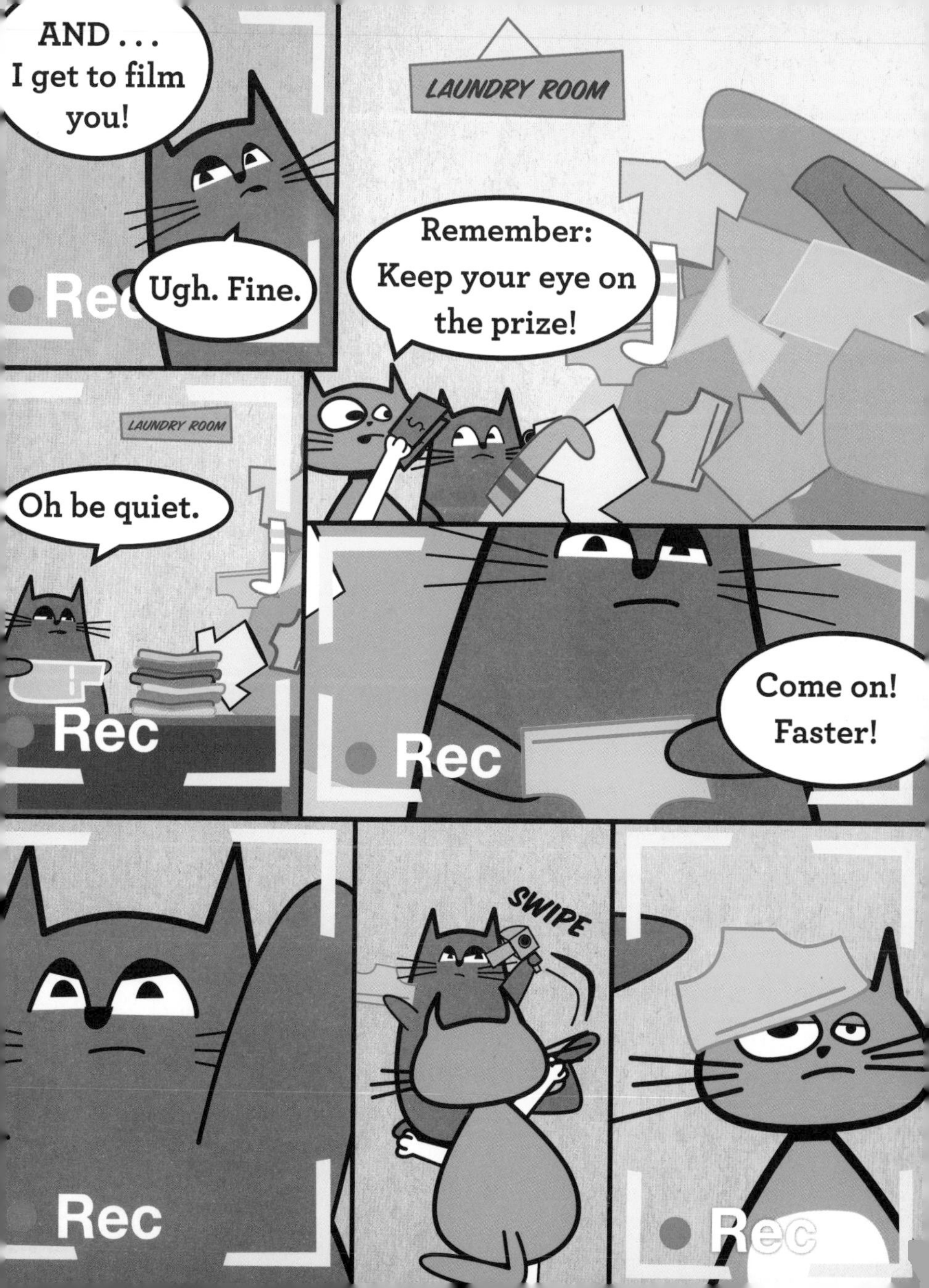
AND . . . I get to film you!
Rec
Ugh. Fine.
LAUNDRY ROOM
Remember: Keep your eye on the prize!
LAUNDRY ROOM
Oh be quiet.
Rec
Rec
Come on! Faster!
Rec
SWIPE
Rec

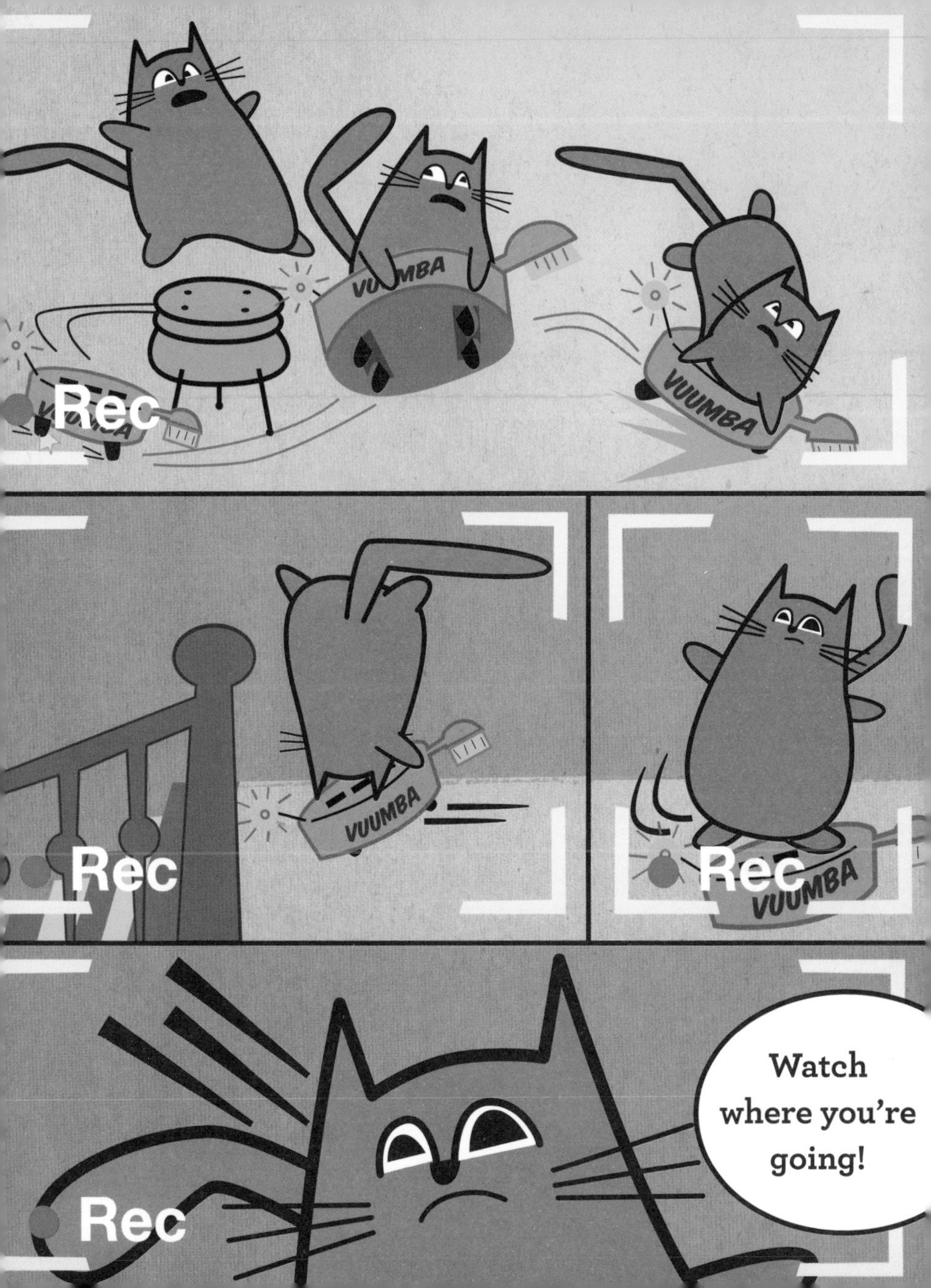
VUUMBA
Rec
VUUMBA
VUUMBA
Rec
VUUMBA
Rec
VUUMBA
Rec
Rec
Watch where you're going!

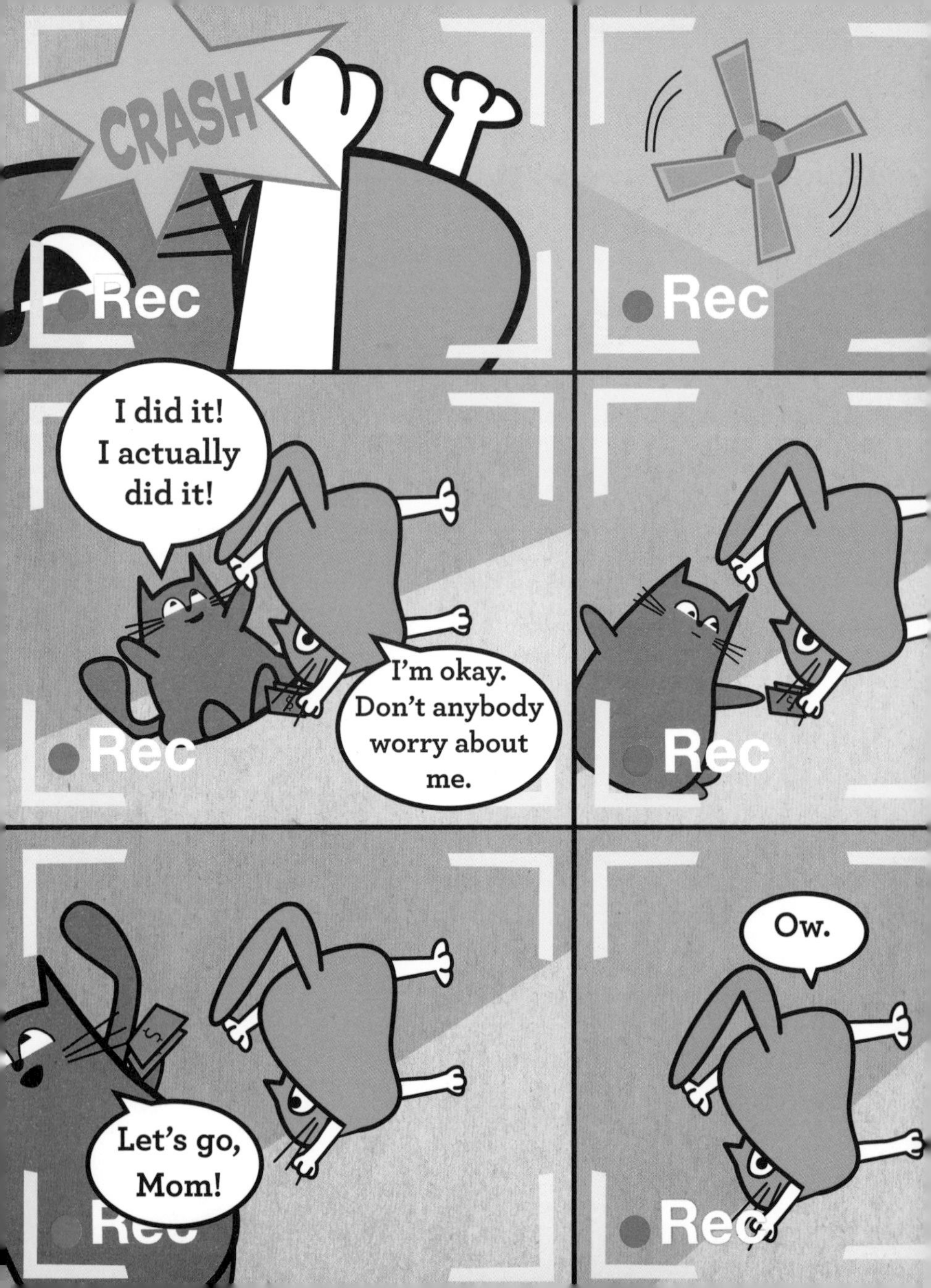
CRASH
Rec
Rec
I did it! I actually did it!
I'm okay. Don't anybody worry about me.
Rec
Rec
Let's go, Mom!
Ow.
Rec

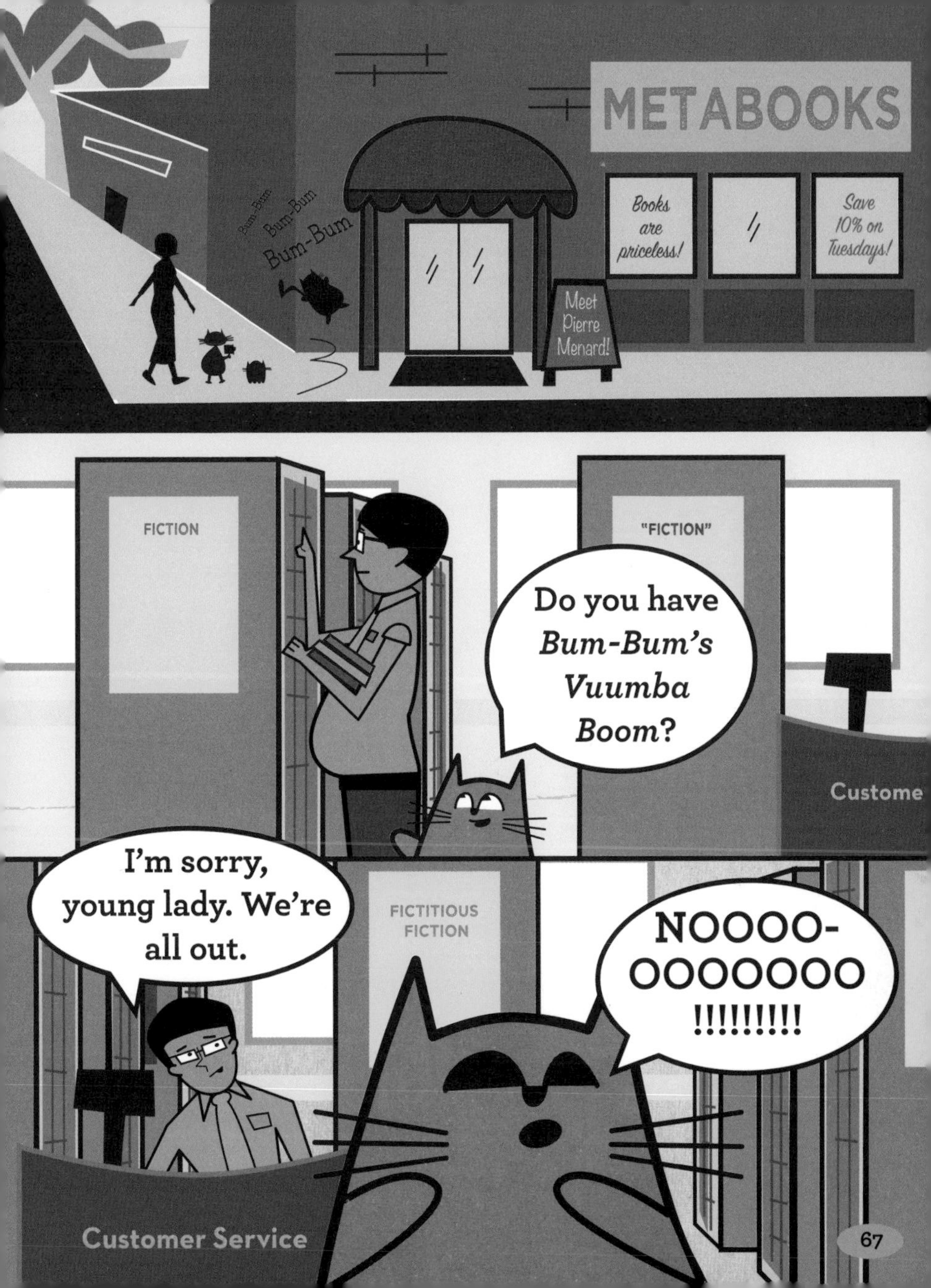
Bum-Bum
Bum-Bum
Bum-Bum
METABOOKS
Books are priceless!
Save 10% on Tuesdays!
Meet Pierre Menard!
FICTION
"FICTION"
Do you have *Bum-Bum's Vuumba Boom*?
Custome
I'm sorry, young lady. We're all out.
FICTITIOUS FICTION
NOOOO-OOOOOOO !!!!!!!!!
Customer Service

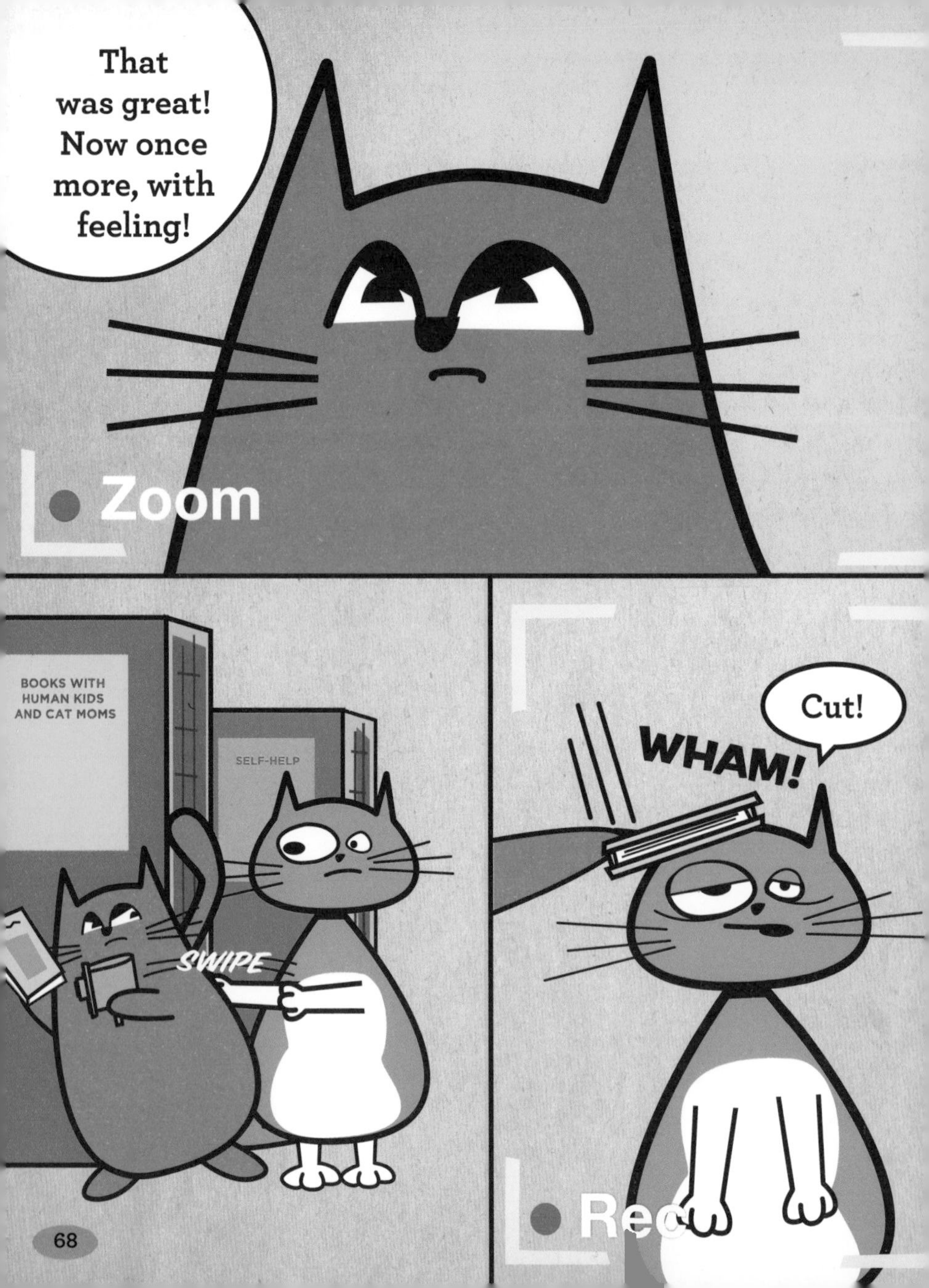
That was great! Now once more, with feeling!
Zoom
BOOKS WITH HUMAN KIDS AND CAT MOMS
SELF-HELP
SWIPE
Cut!
WHAM!
Rec

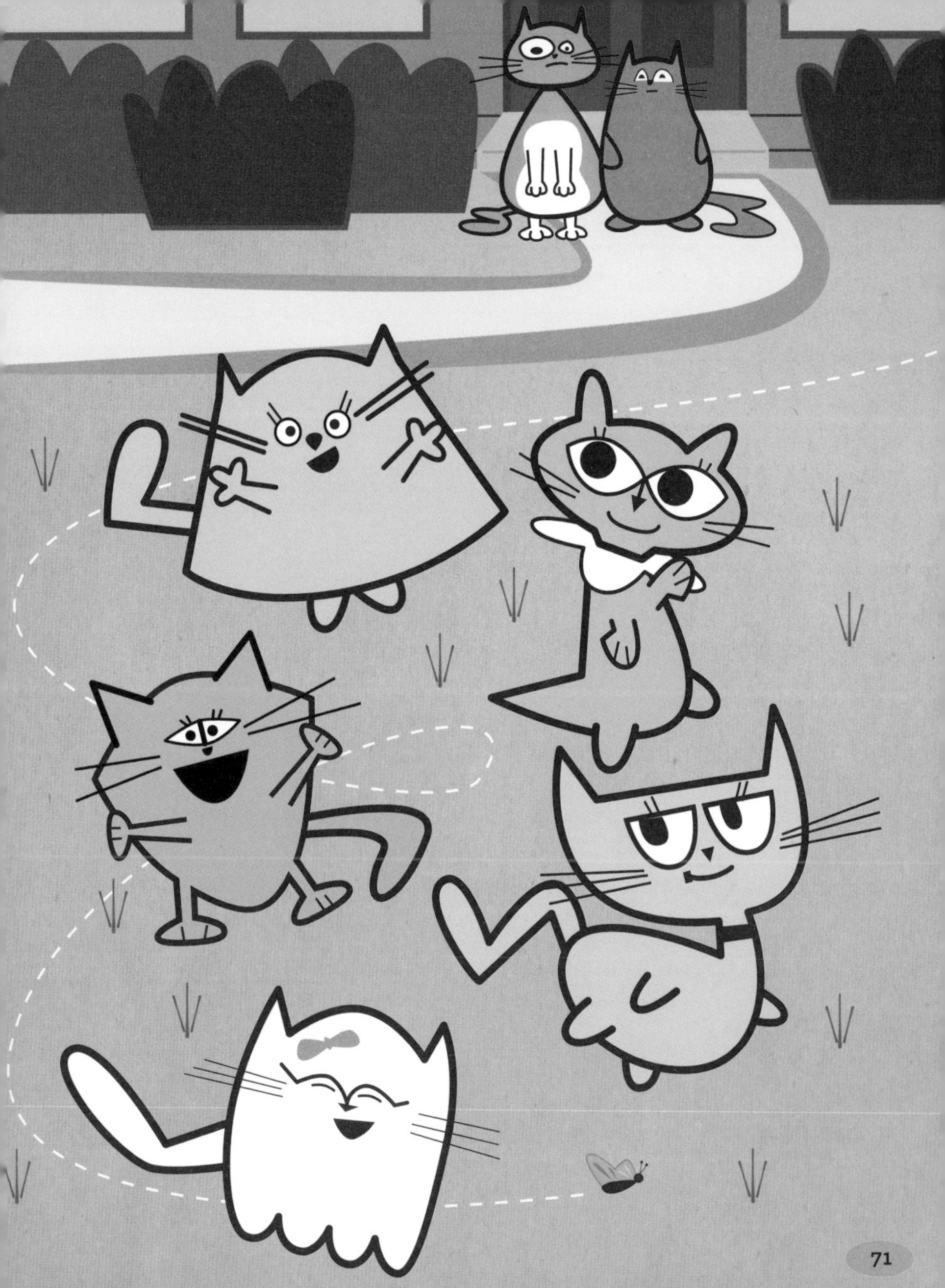

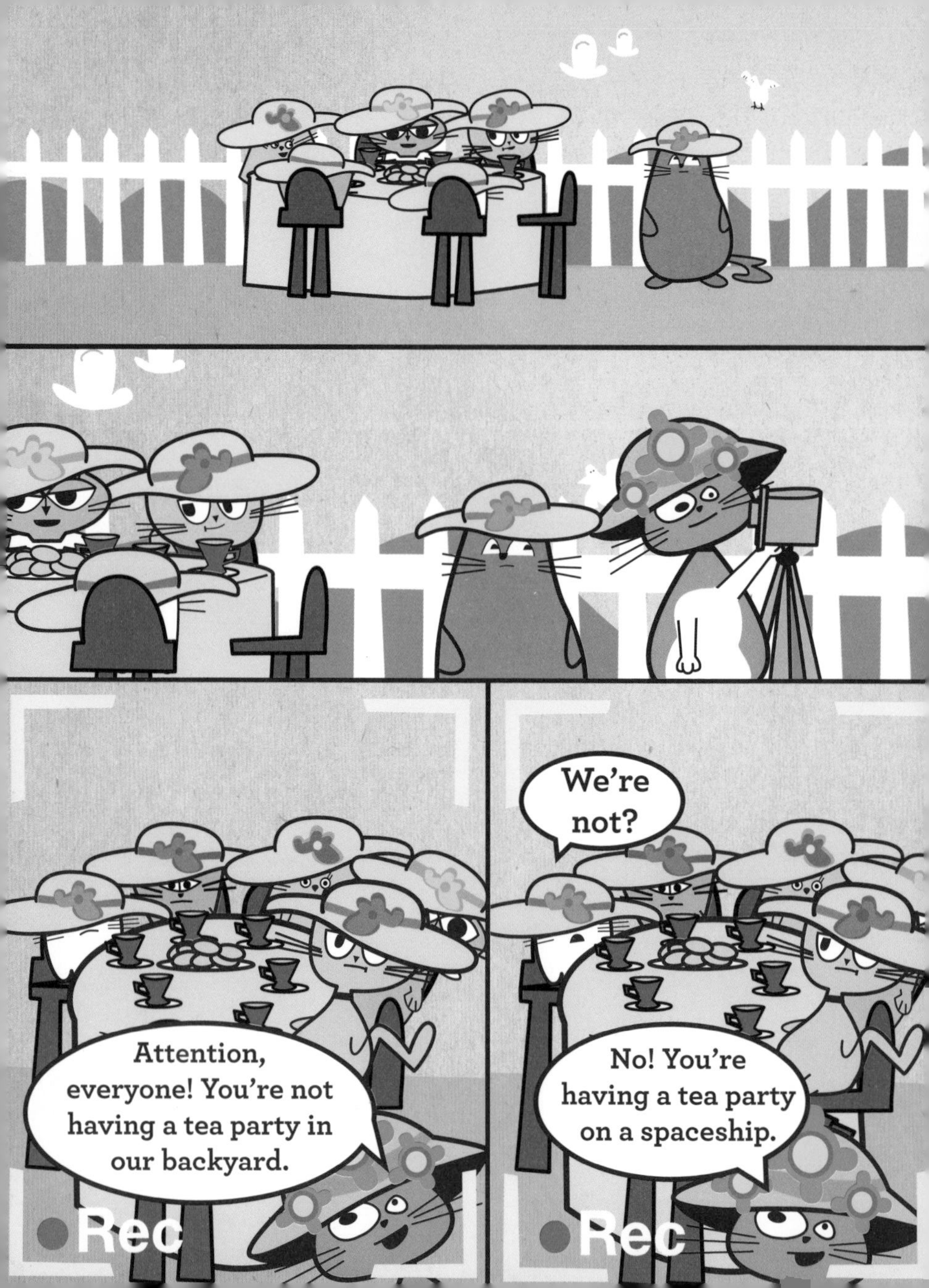
Attention, everyone! You're not having a tea party in our backyard.
Rec
We're not?
No! You're having a tea party on a spaceship.
Rec

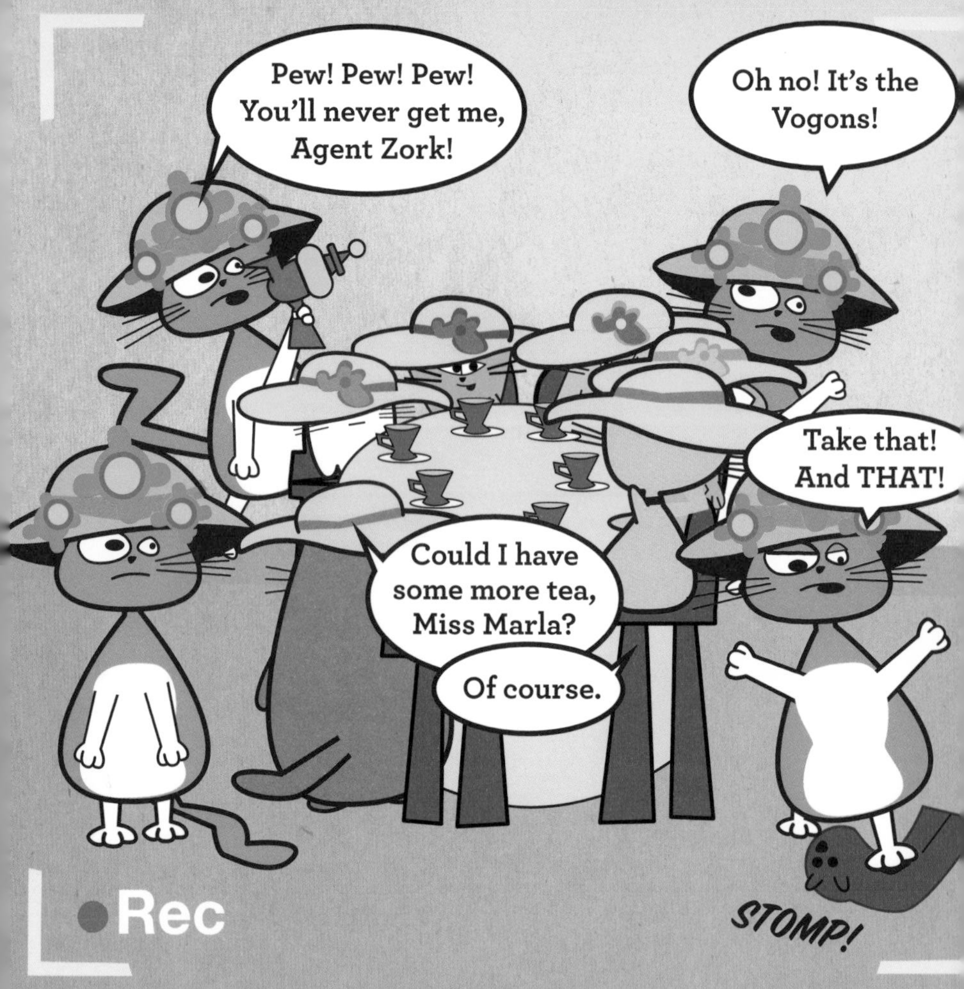
Pew! Pew! Pew! You'll never get me, Agent Zork!
Oh no! It's the Vogons!
Take that! And THAT!
Could I have some more tea, Miss Marla?
Of course.
Rec
STOMP!

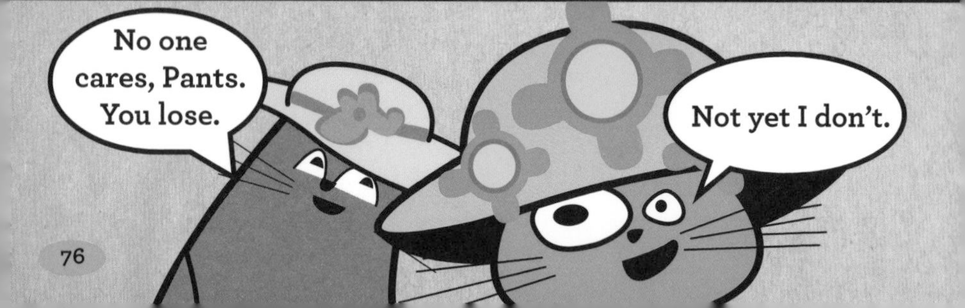
No one cares, Pants. You lose.
Not yet I don't.

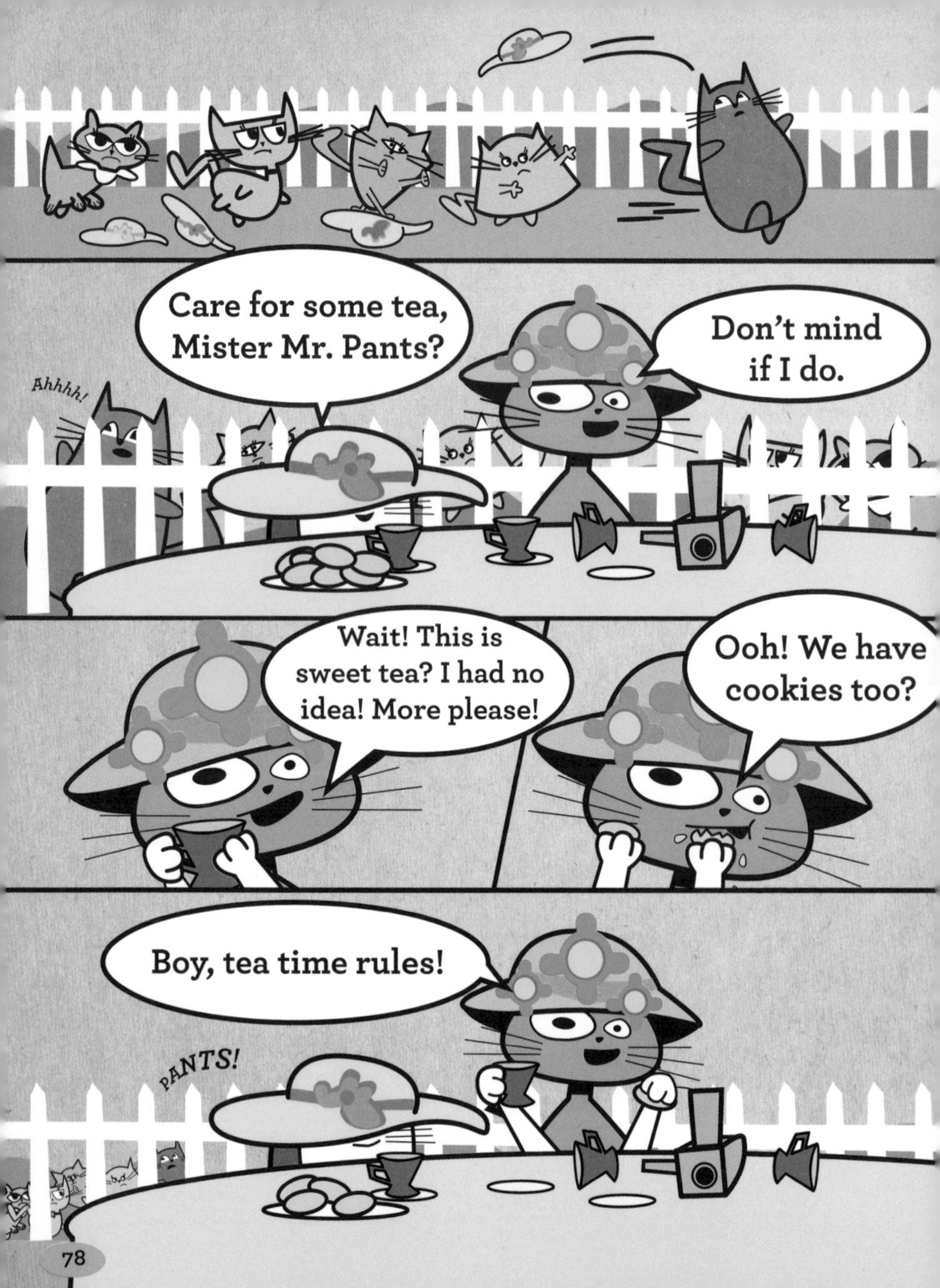
Care for some tea, Mister Mr. Pants?
Don't mind if I do.
Ahhhh!
Wait! This is sweet tea? I had no idea! More please!
Ooh! We have cookies too?
Boy, tea time rules!
PANTS!

Chapter Five:

THE SPY WHO PANTSED ME

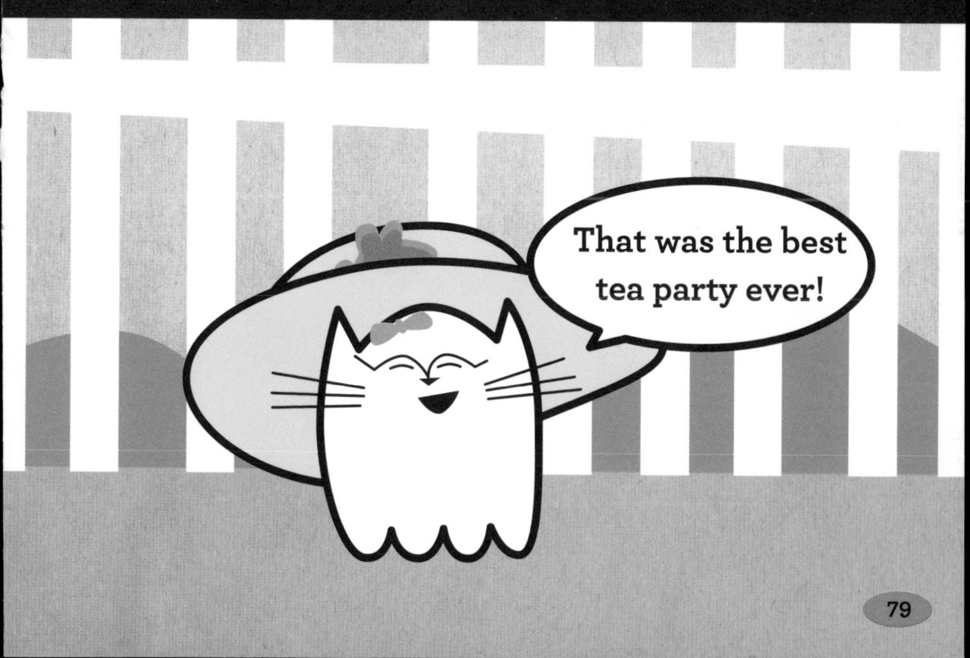
That was the best tea party ever!

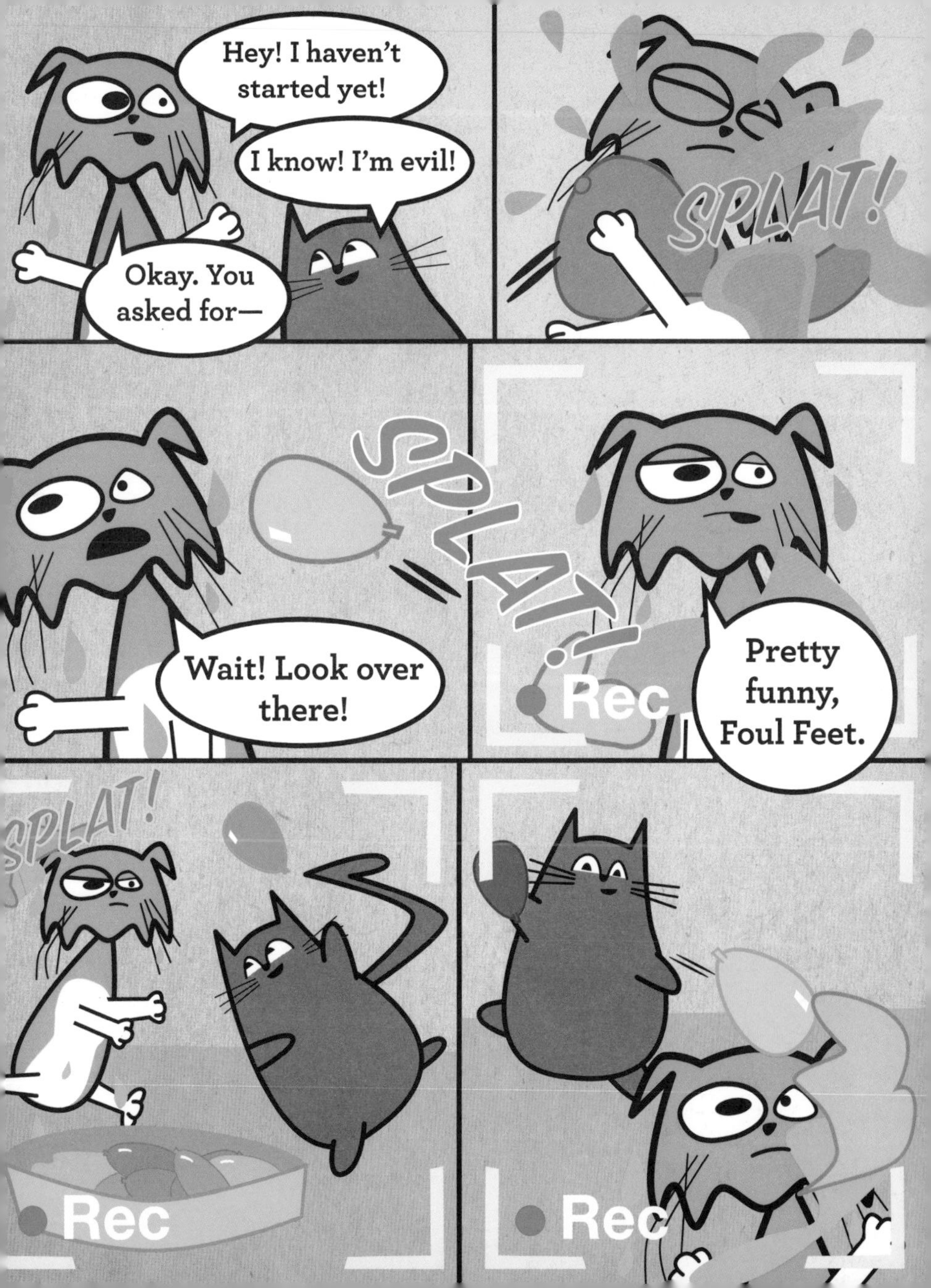

Hey! I haven't started yet!
Okay. You asked for—
I know! I'm evil!
SPLAT!
SPLAT!
Wait! Look over there!
Rec
Pretty funny, Foul Feet.
SPLAT!
Rec
Rec

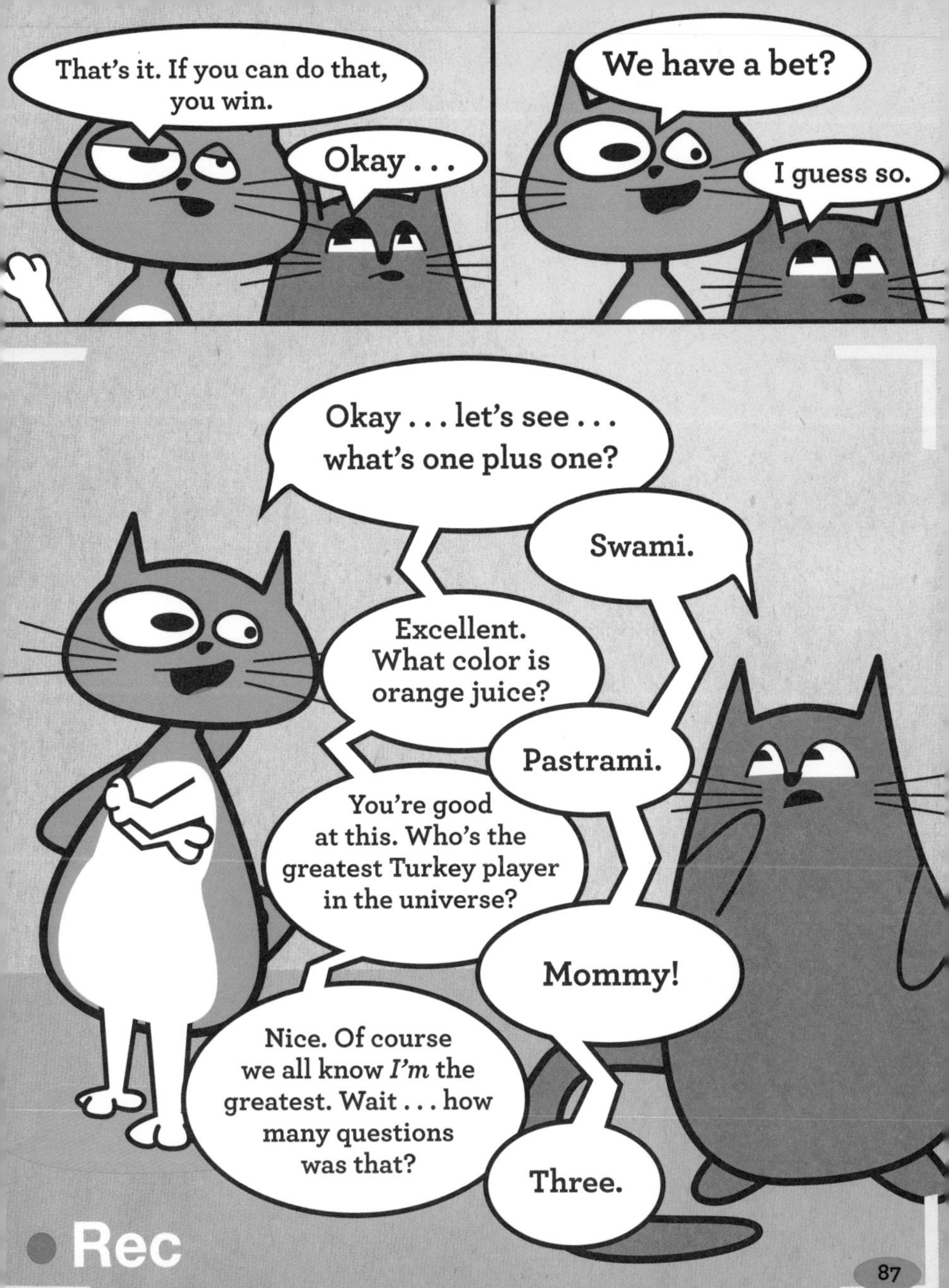
That's it. If you can do that, you win.
Okay . . .
We have a bet?
I guess so.
Okay . . . let's see . . . what's one plus one?
Swami.
Excellent. What color is orange juice?
Pastrami.
You're good at this. Who's the greatest Turkey player in the universe?
Mommy!
Nice. Of course we all know *I'm* the greatest. Wait . . . how many questions was that?
Three.
Rec

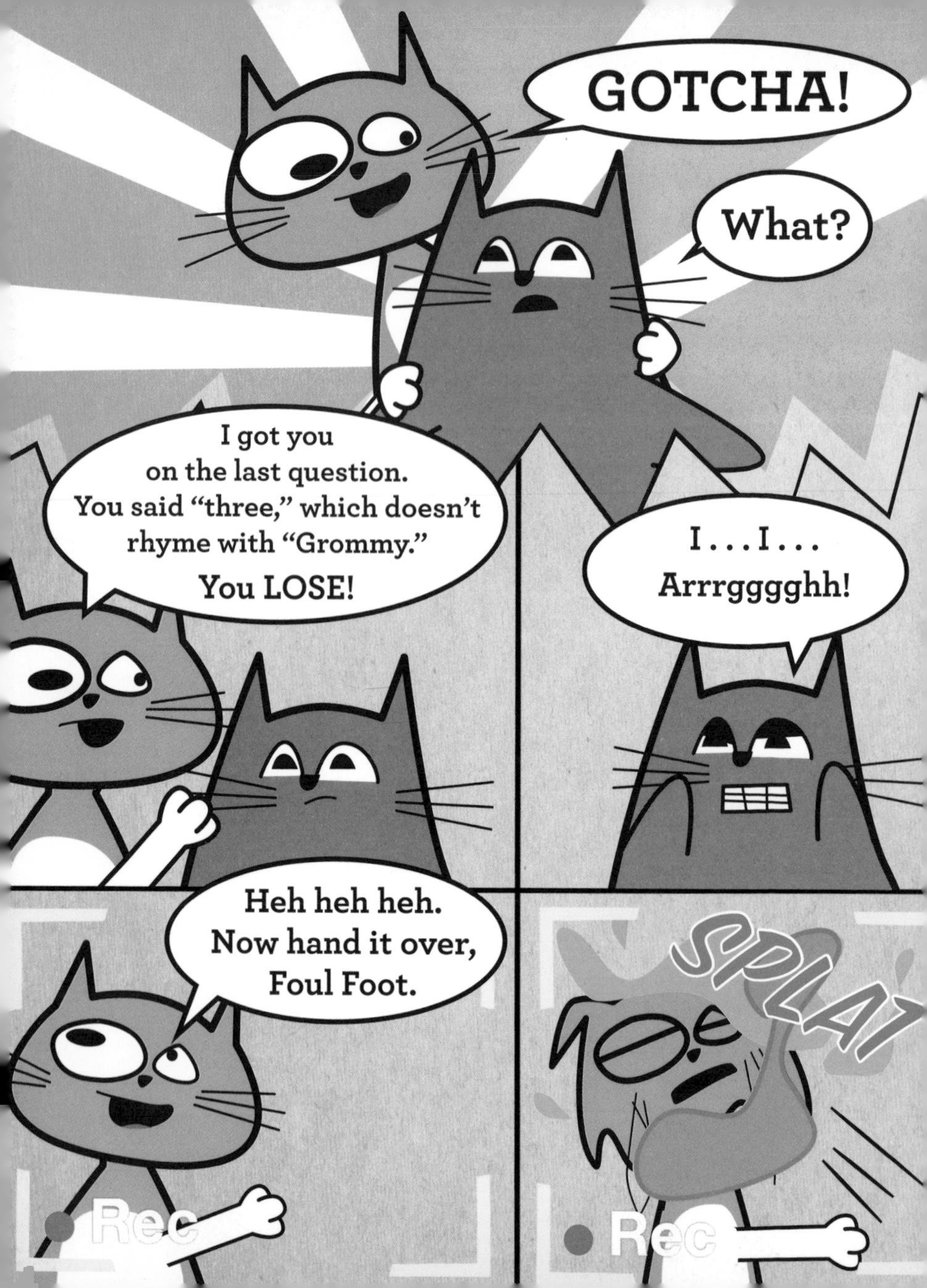
GOTCHA!
What?
I got you on the last question. You said "three," which doesn't rhyme with "Grommy." You LOSE!
I...I... Arrrggghh!
Heh heh heh. Now hand it over, Foul Foot.
Rec
SPLAT
Rec

Chapter Six:
BUM-BUM OVERDUB

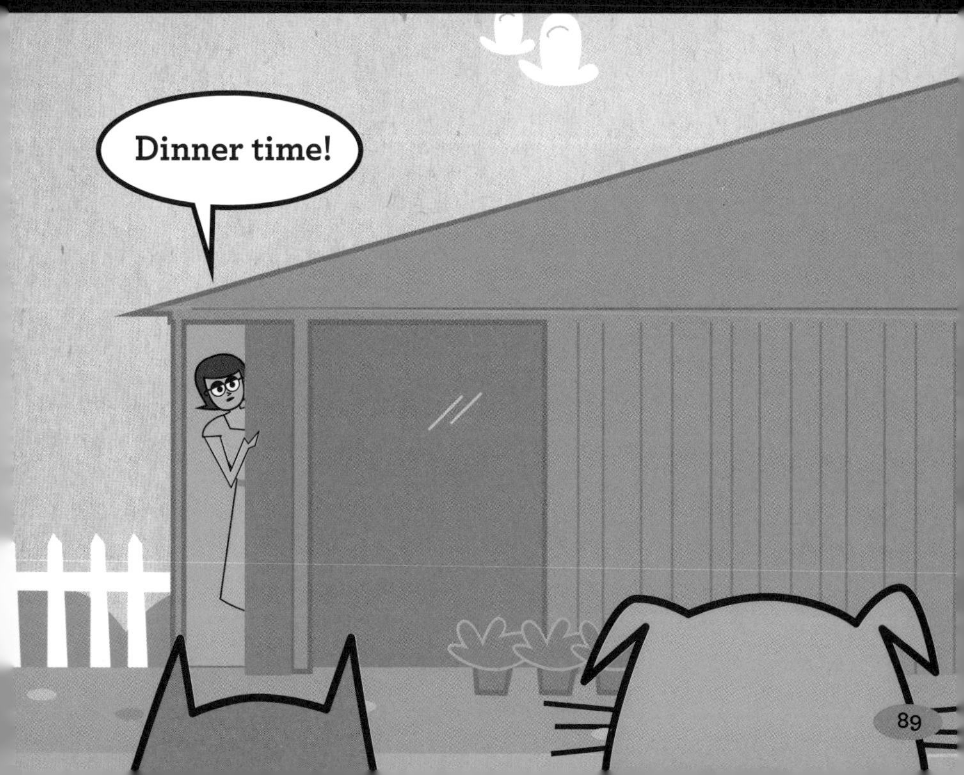
Dinner time!

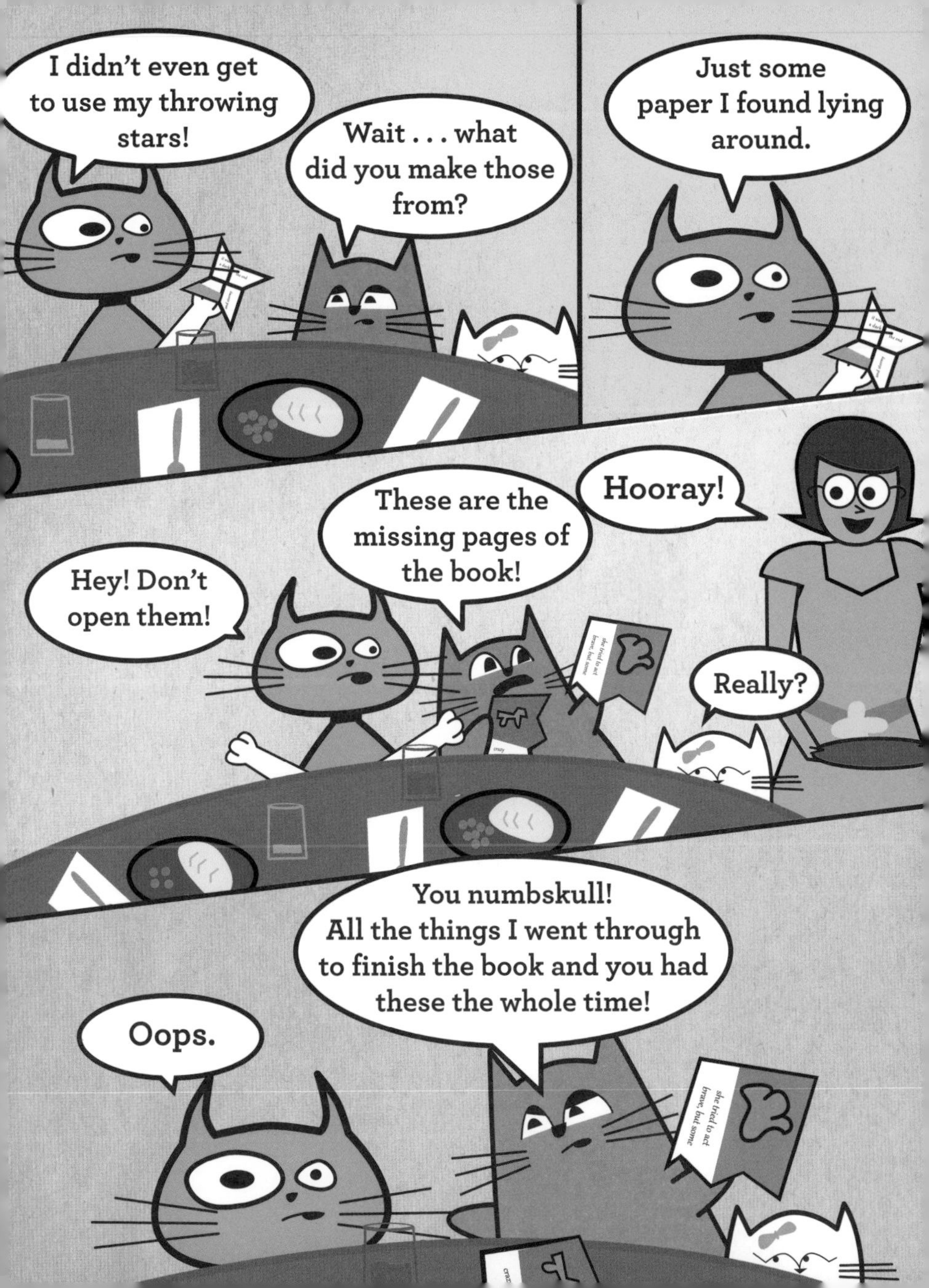
I didn't even get to use my throwing stars!
Wait . . . what did you make those from?
Just some paper I found lying around.
These are the missing pages of the book!
Hooray!
Hey! Don't open them!
she tried to act brave, but some
Really?
You numbskull! All the things I went through to finish the book and you had these the whole time!
Oops.

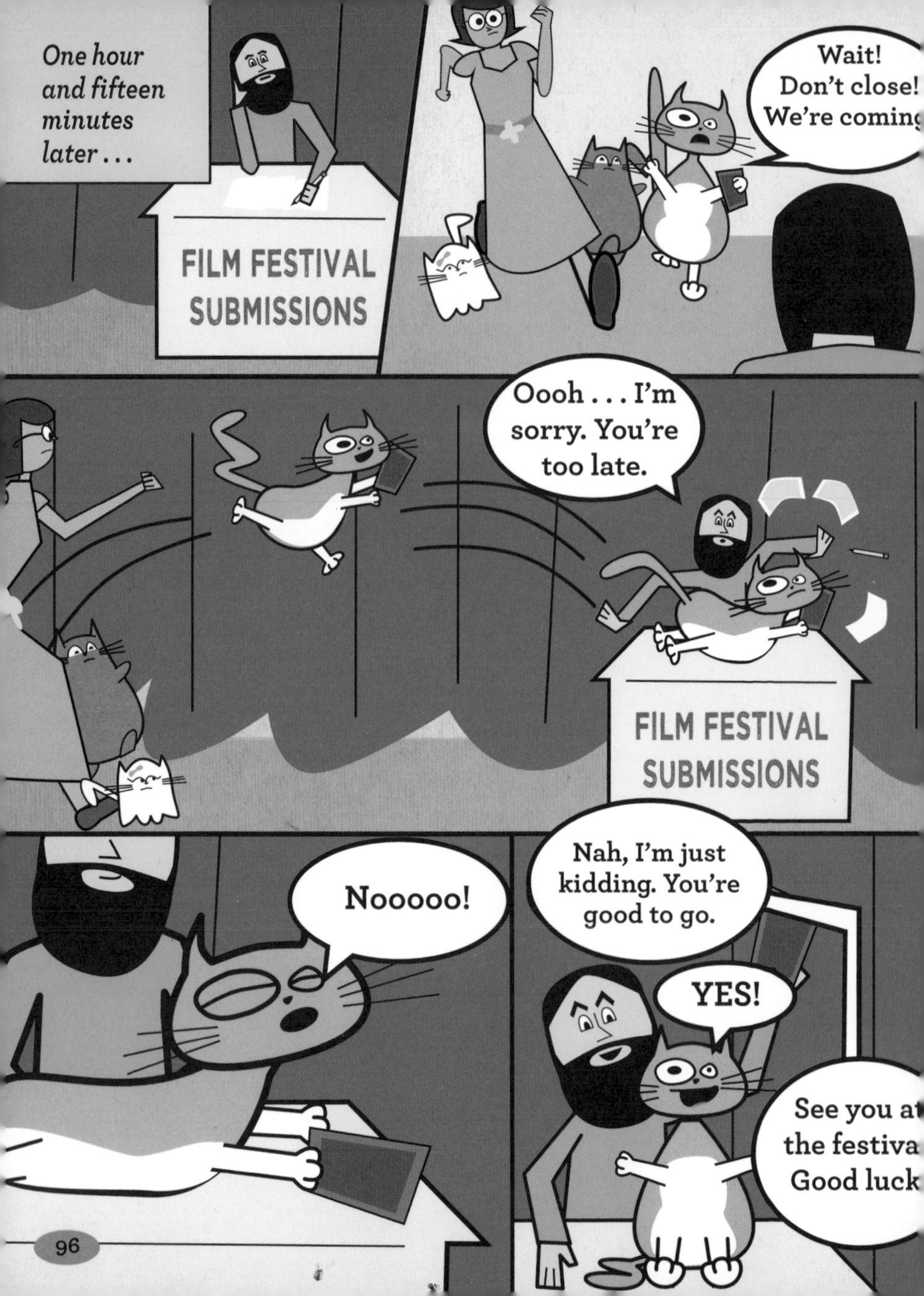
One hour and fifteen minutes later . . .
FILM FESTIVAL SUBMISSIONS
Wait! Don't close! We're coming
Oooh . . . I'm sorry. You're too late.
FILM FESTIVAL SUBMISSIONS
Nooooo!
Nah, I'm just kidding. You're good to go.
YES!
See you at the festiva Good luck

Chapter Seven: DOUBLE-O-AWESOME

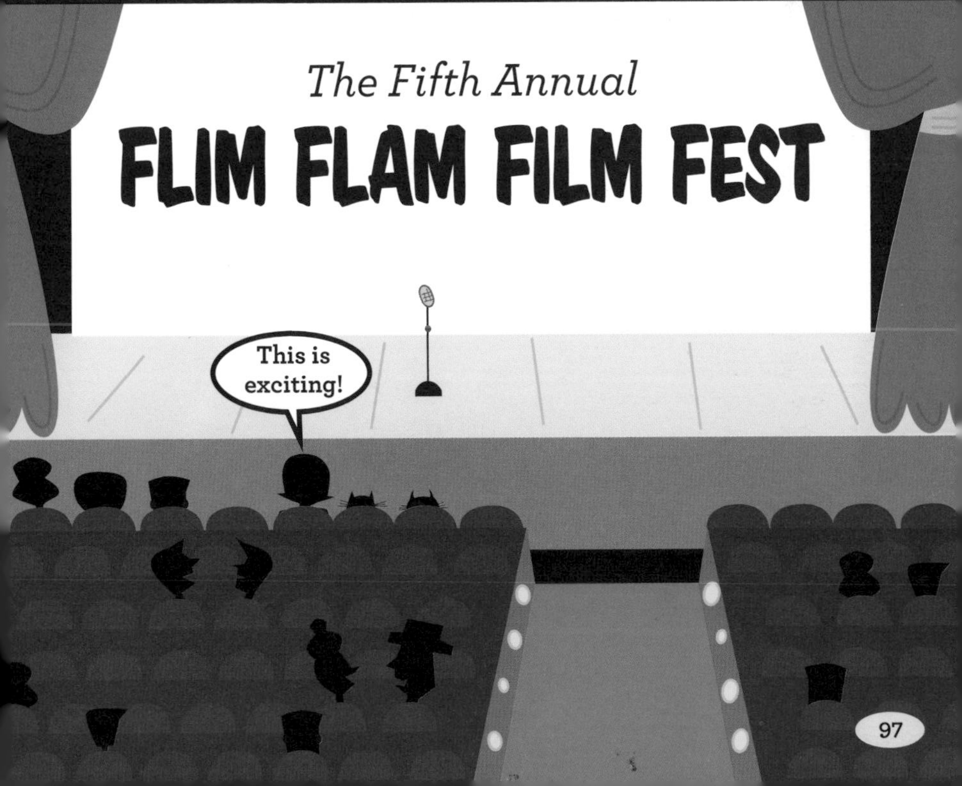
The Fifth Annual
FLIM FLAM FILM FEST
This is exciting!

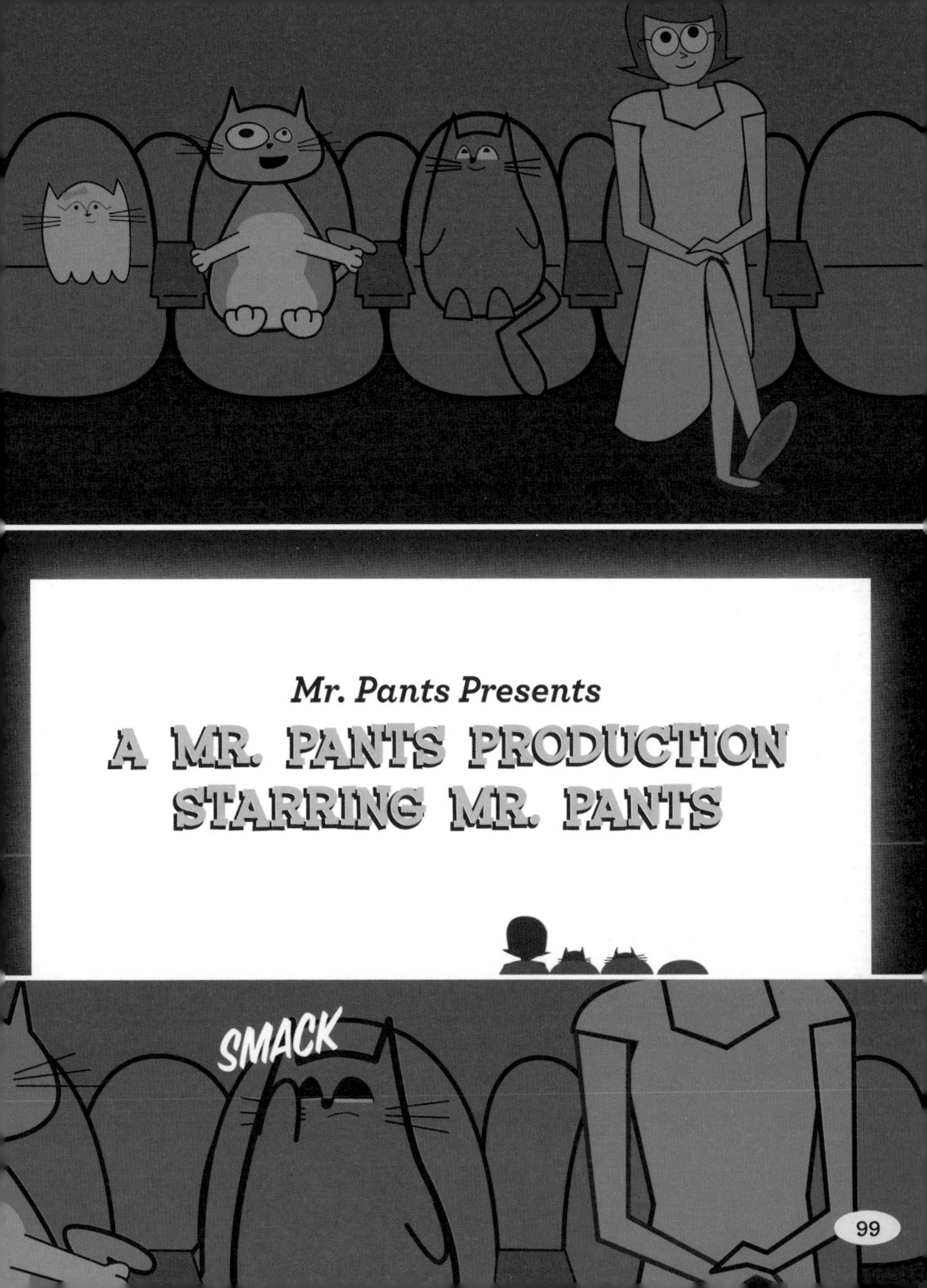
Mr. Pants Presents
A MR. PANTS PRODUCTION
STARRING MR. PANTS
SMACK

Agent Slacks Pantaloñez in:

BUM-BUM OR BUST

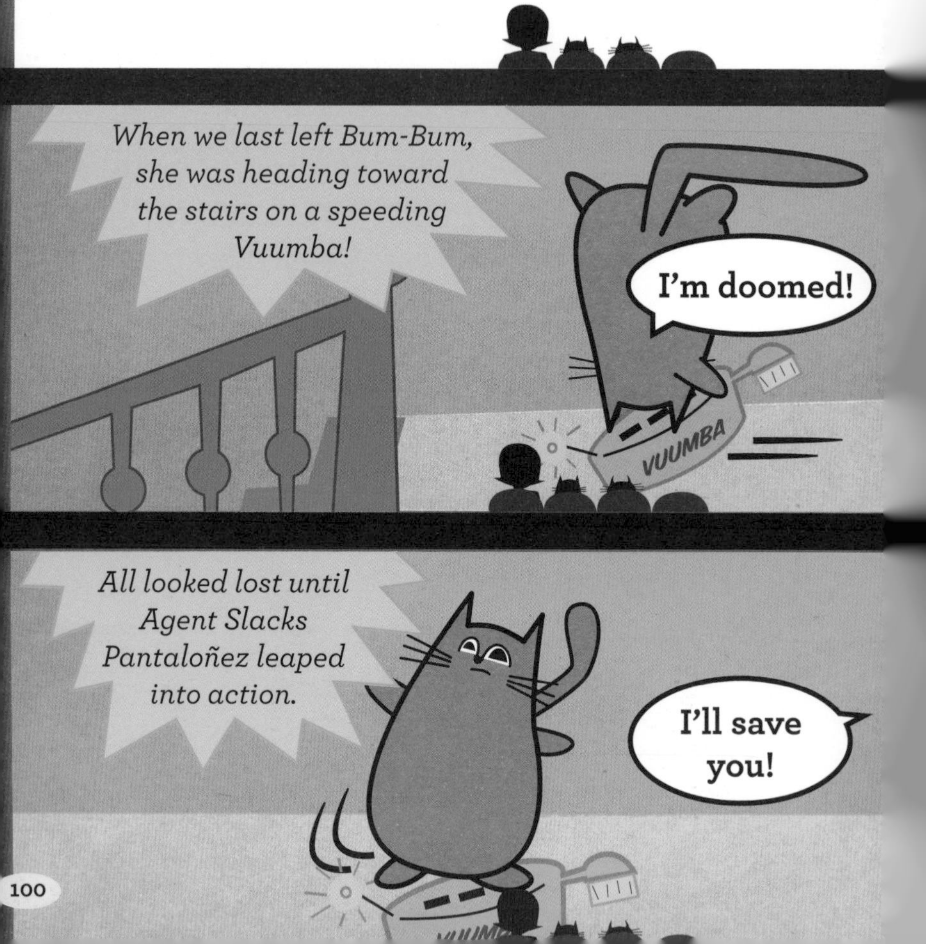
When we last left Bum-Bum, she was heading toward the stairs on a speeding Vuumba!
I'm doomed!
VUUMBA
All looked lost until Agent Slacks Pantaloñez leaped into action.
I'll save you!

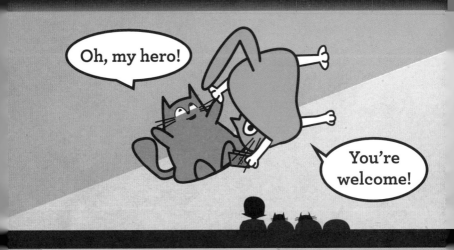

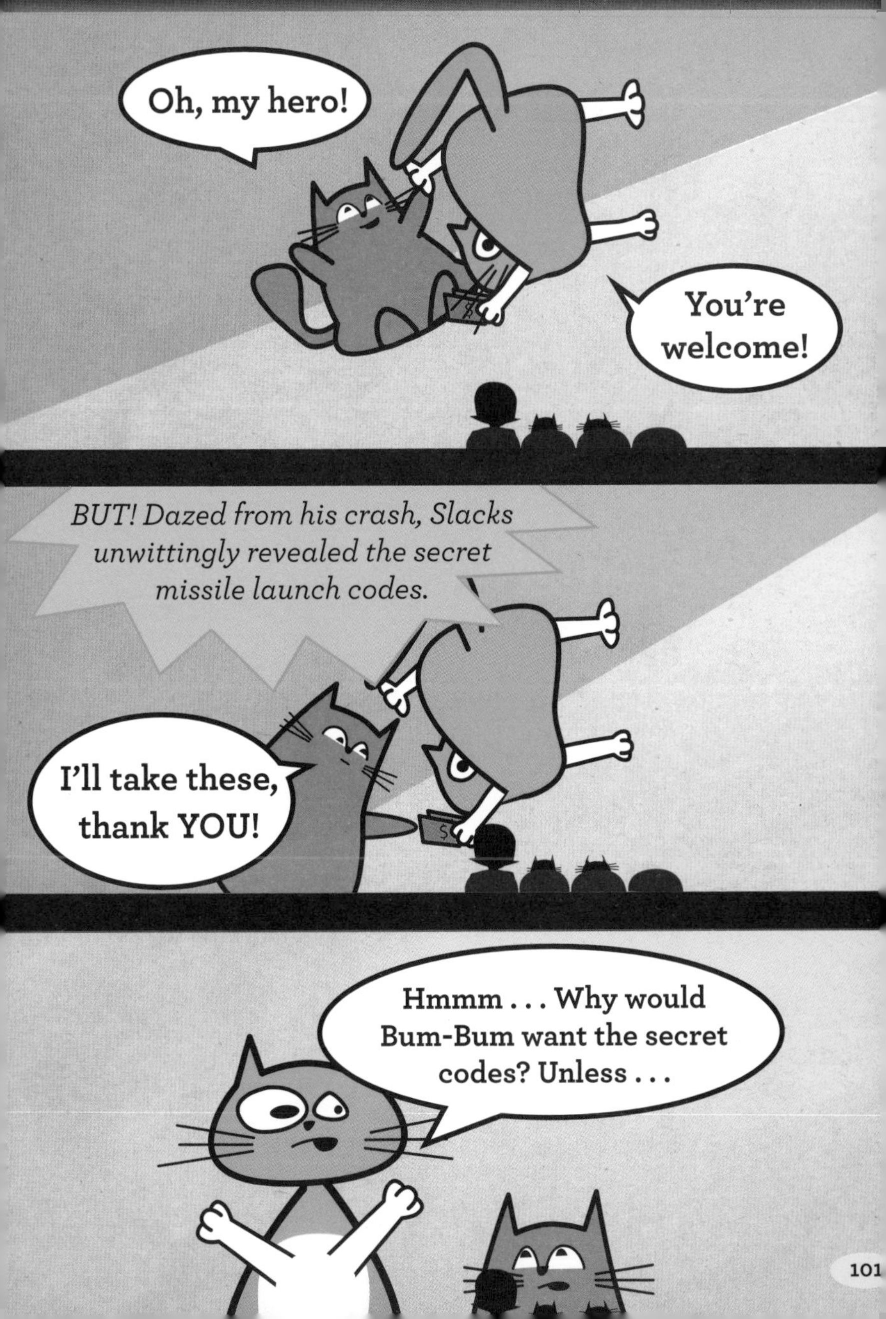
Oh, my hero!
You're welcome!
BUT! Dazed from his crash, Slacks unwittingly revealed the secret missile launch codes.
I'll take these, thank YOU!
Hmmm . . . Why would Bum-Bum want the secret codes? Unless . . .

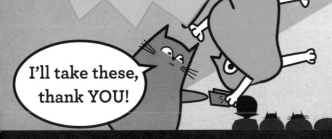

Suddenly Slacks realized that sweet, innocent Bum-Bum was really his arch-nemesis, the evil Dr. Foul Foot.

I KNEW she looked familiar. And evil. With those secret codes, she could blow up the whole world.

That would be bad!

Raise your hand if you want me to save the world.

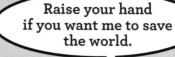

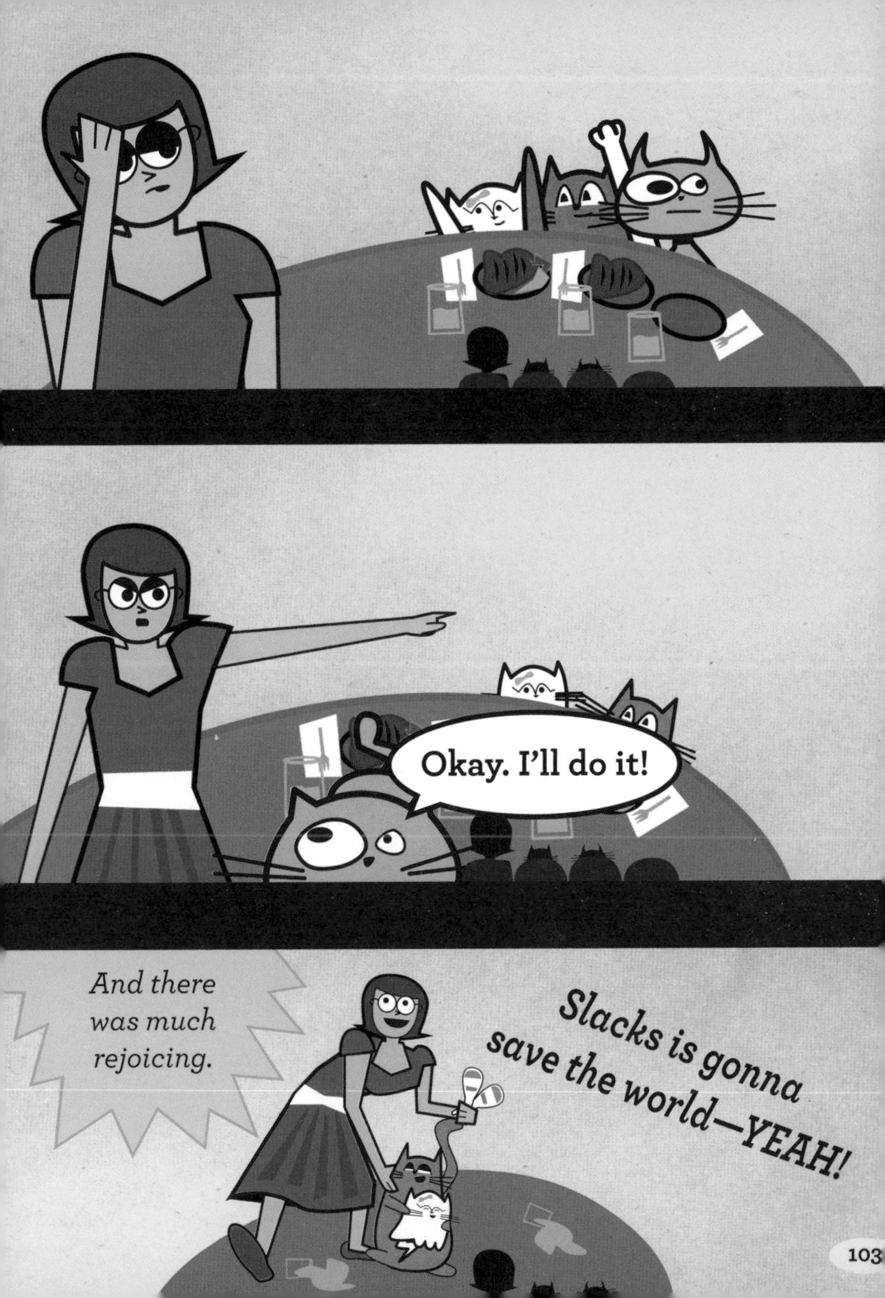
Okay. I'll do it!
And there was much rejoicing.
Slacks is gonna save the world—YEAH!

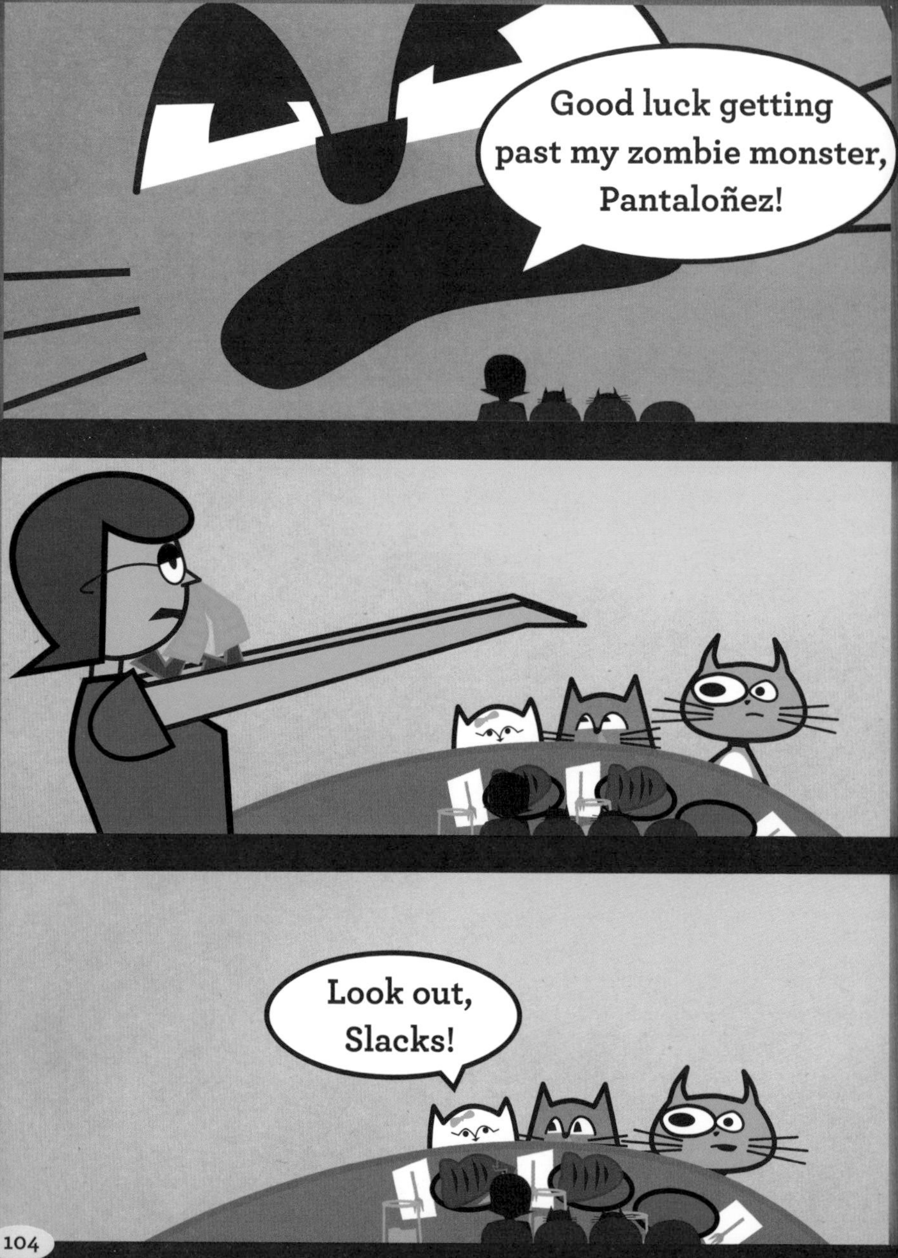
Good luck getting past my zombie monster, Pantaloñez!
Look out, Slacks!

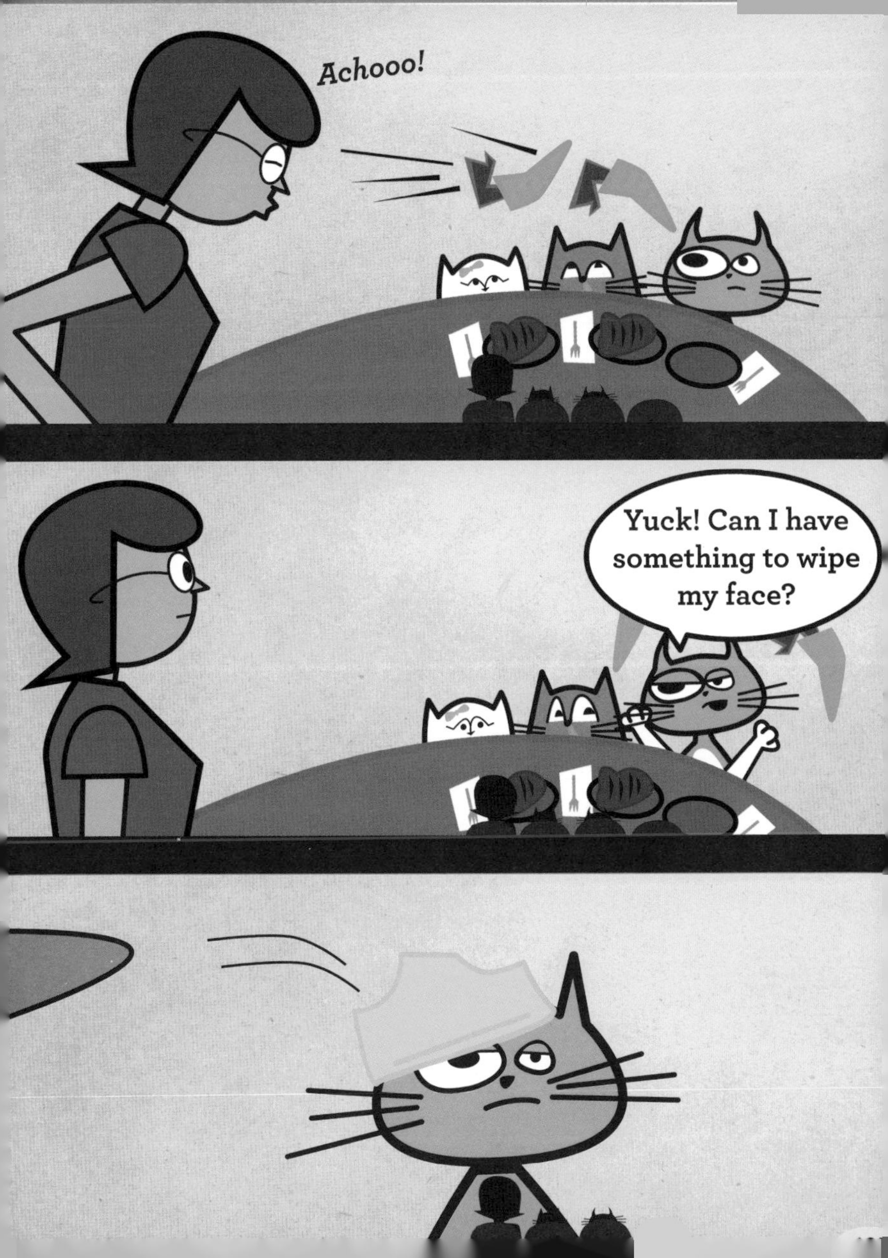
Achooo!
Yuck! Can I have something to wipe my face?

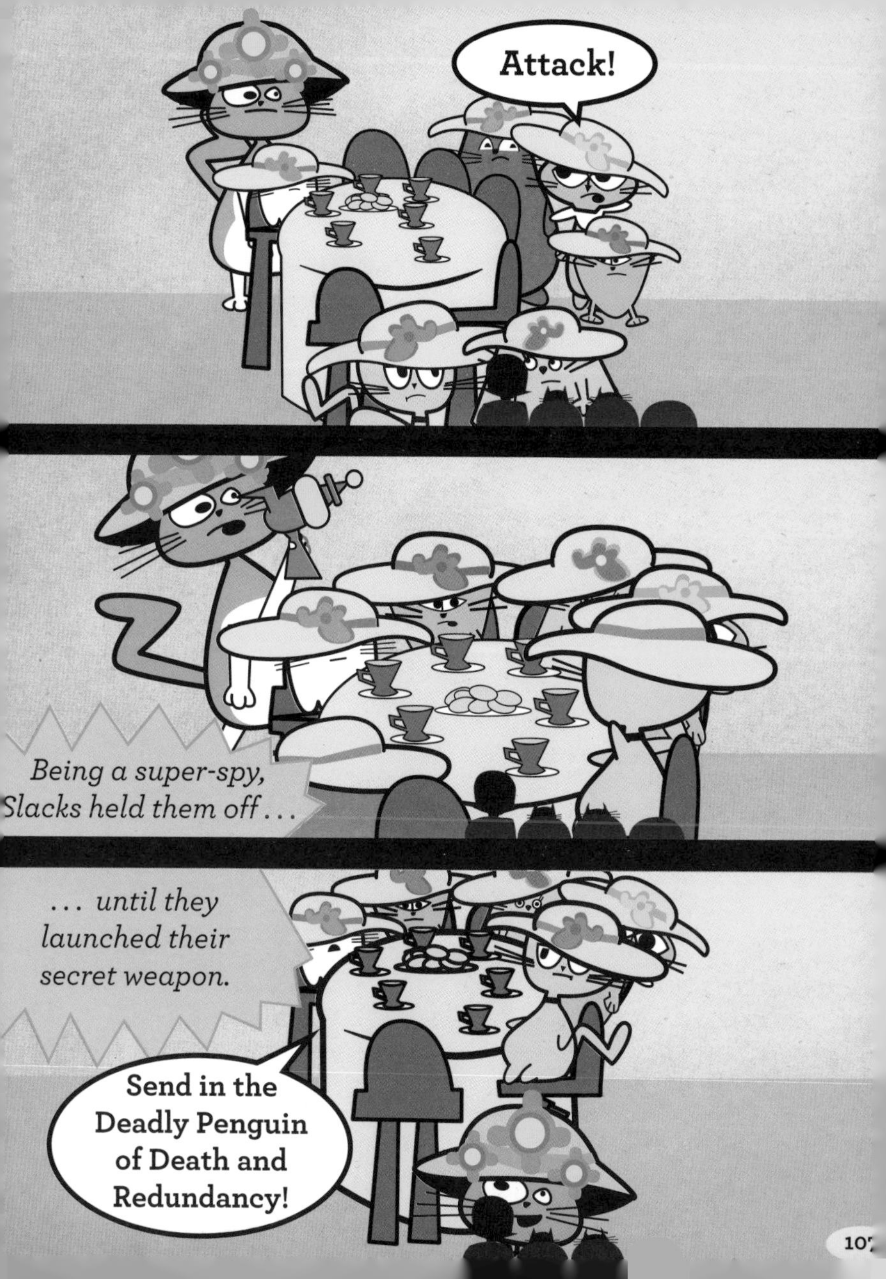
Attack!
Being a super-spy, Slacks held them off . . .
. . . until they launched their secret weapon.
Send in the Deadly Penguin of Death and Redundancy!

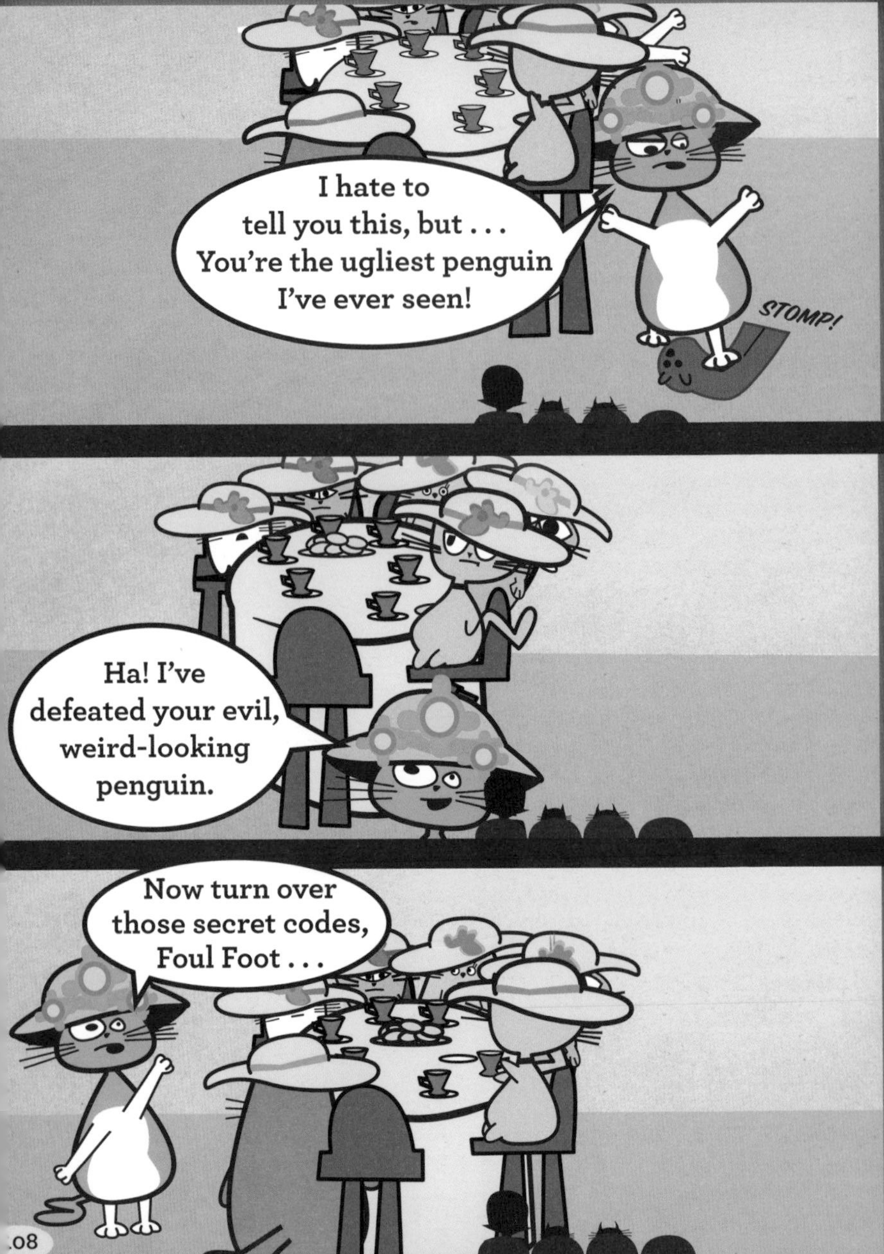
I hate to tell you this, but . . . You're the ugliest penguin I've ever seen!
STOMP!
Ha! I've defeated your evil, weird-looking penguin.
Now turn over those secret codes, Foul Foot . . .

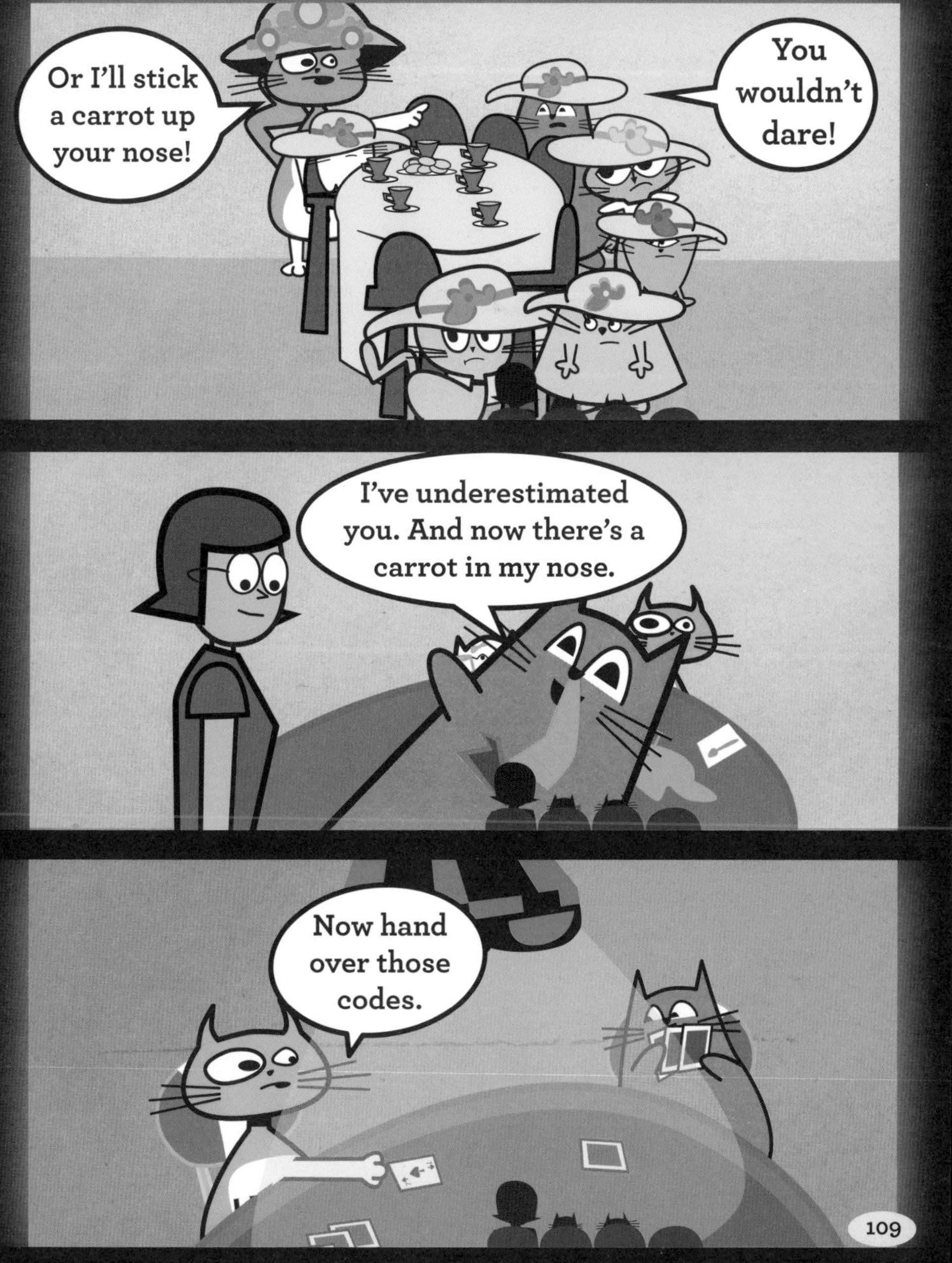
Or I'll stick a carrot up your nose!
You wouldn't dare!
I've underestimated you. And now there's a carrot in my nose.
Now hand over those codes.

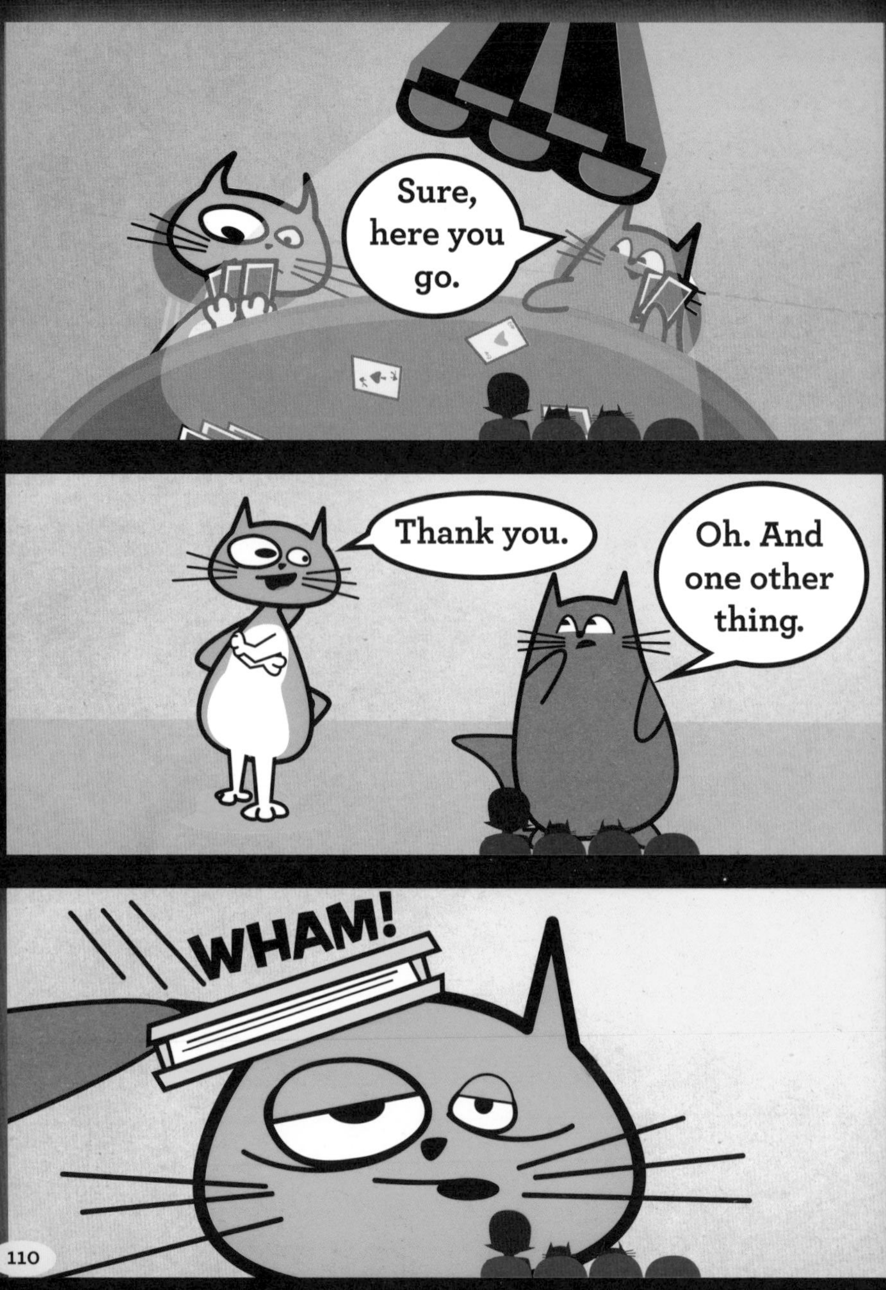
Sure, here you go.
Thank you.
Oh. And one other thing.
WHAM!

Oh no! Dr. Foul Foot's vicious volley to the head jostled something loose in Special Agent Slacks Pantaloñez's brain, causing him to act like a turkey!

Will Slacks ever recover? Will he catch Dr. Foul Foot? Will he find the secret codes in time to save the world?

Will he please stop gobbling like a turkey?

Tune in next time for another exciting episode of . . .

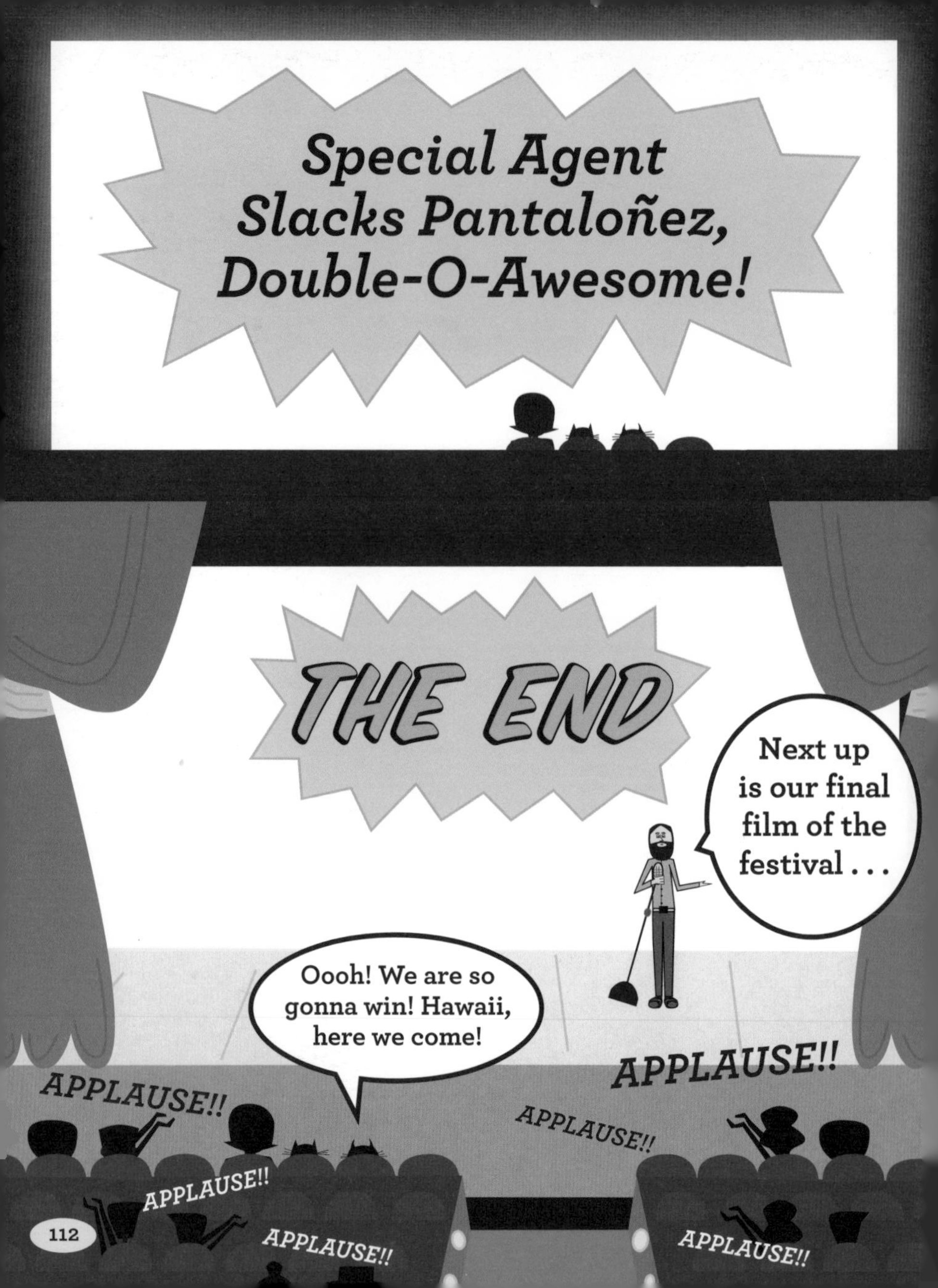
Special Agent Slacks Pantaloñez, Double-O-Awesome!
THE END
Next up is our final film of the festival . . .
Oooh! We are so gonna win! Hawaii, here we come!
APPLAUSE!!
APPLAUSE!!
APPLAUSE!!
APPLAUSE!!
APPLAUSE!!
APPLAUSE!!

Chapter Eight:
AND THE SORE WINNER IS...

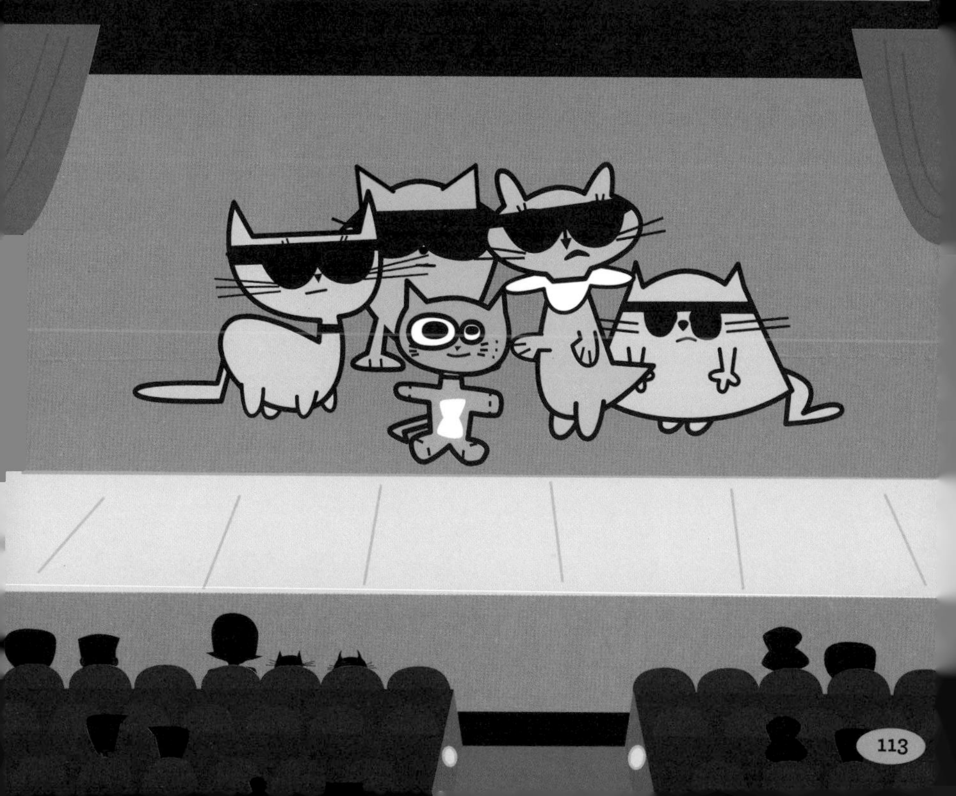

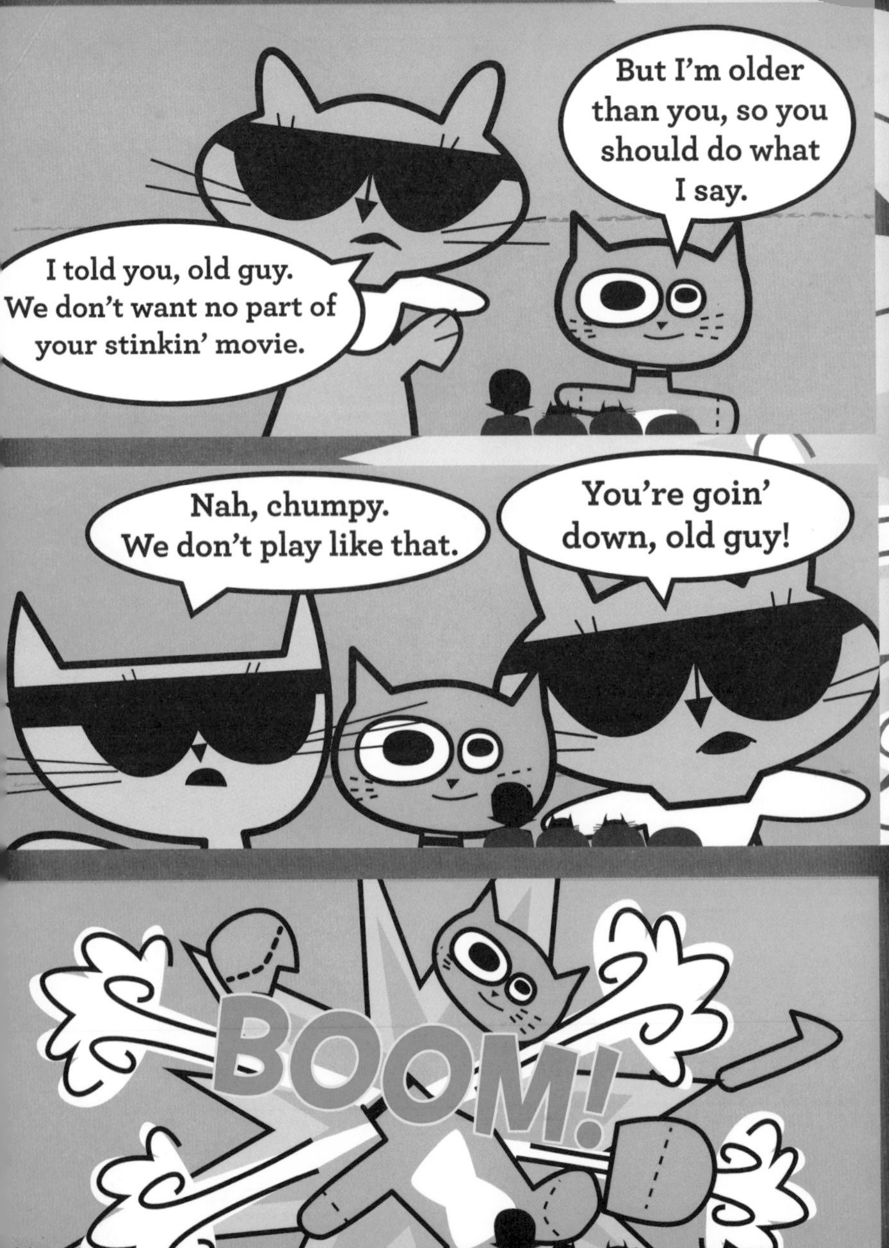
I told you, old guy. We don't want no part of your stinkin' movie.
But I'm older than you, so you should do what I say.
Nah, chumpy. We don't play like that.
You're goin' down, old guy!
BOOM!

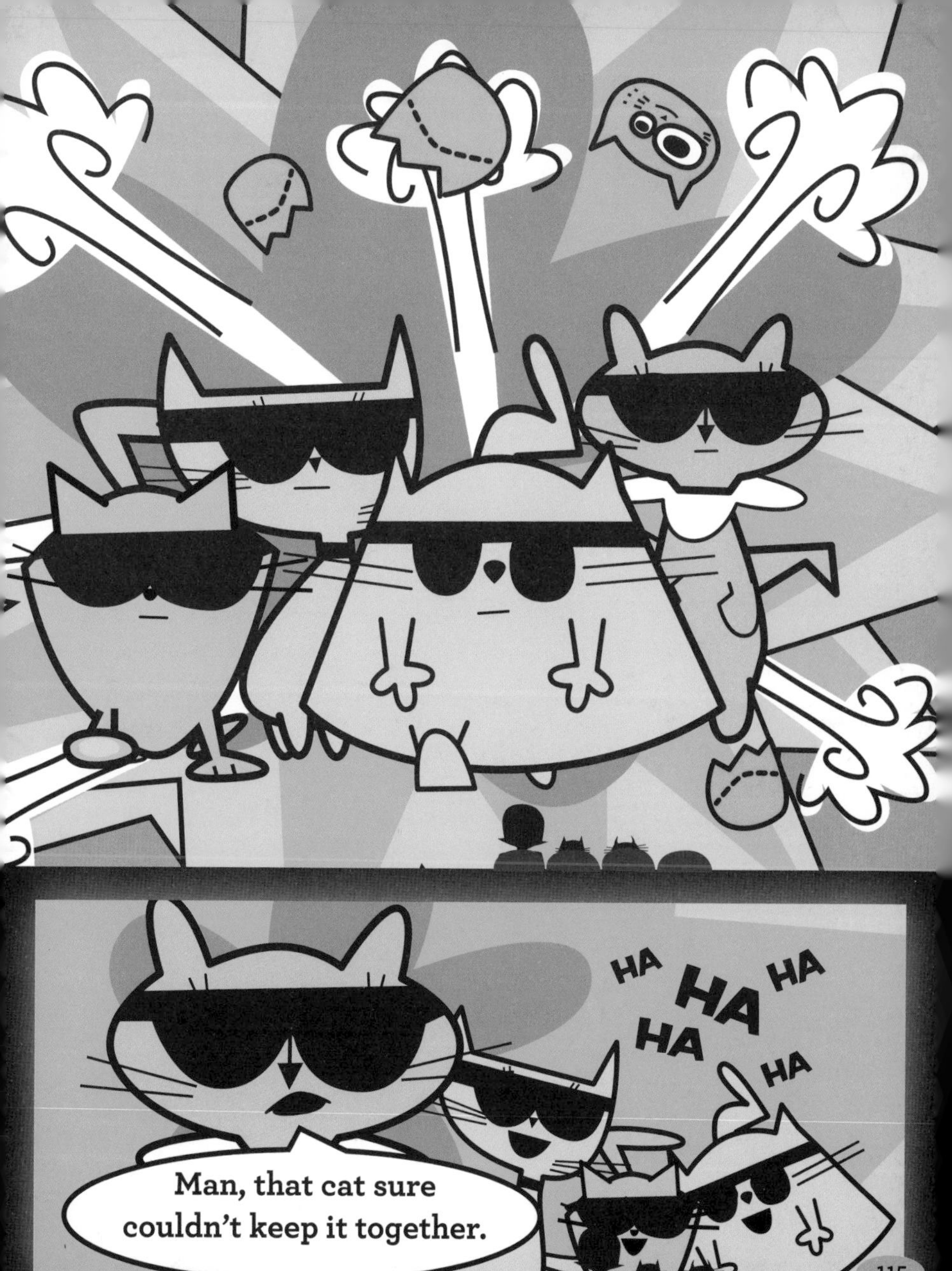
HA HA HA HA HA HA
Man, that cat sure couldn't keep it together.

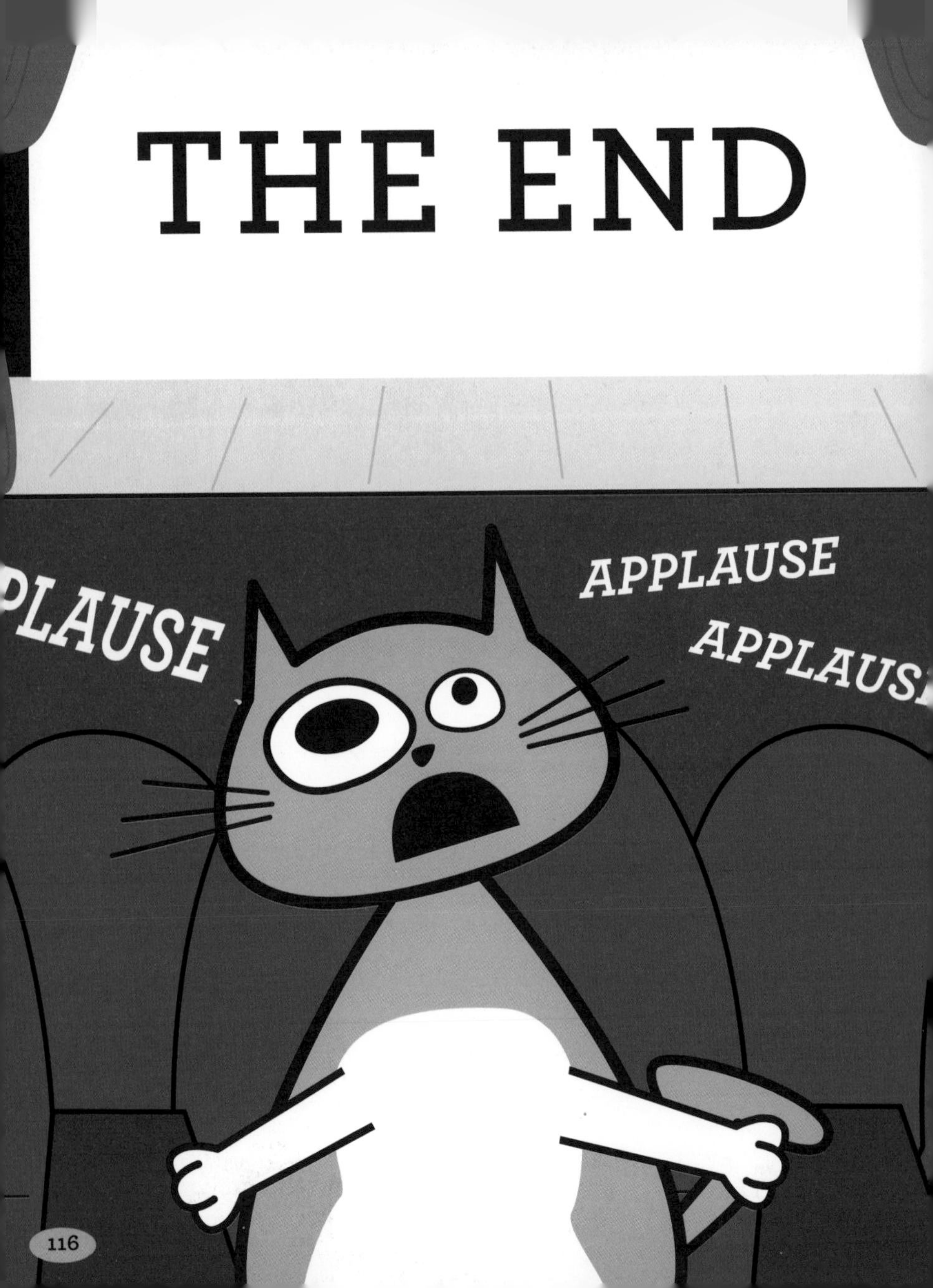
THE END
PLAUSE
APPLAUSE
APPLAUS

117

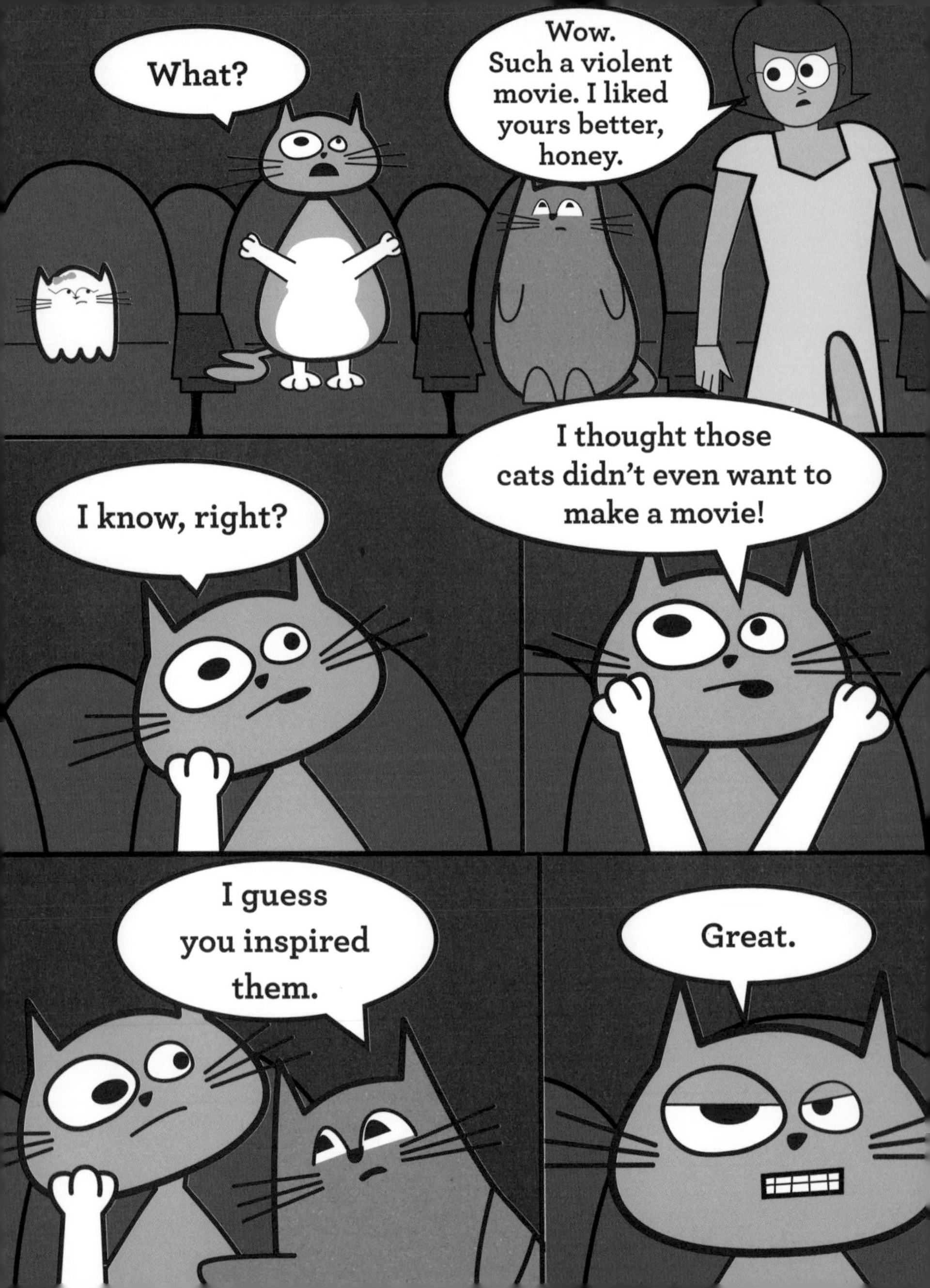
What?
Wow. Such a violent movie. I liked yours better, honey.
I know, right?
I thought those cats didn't even want to make a movie!
I guess you inspired them.
Great.

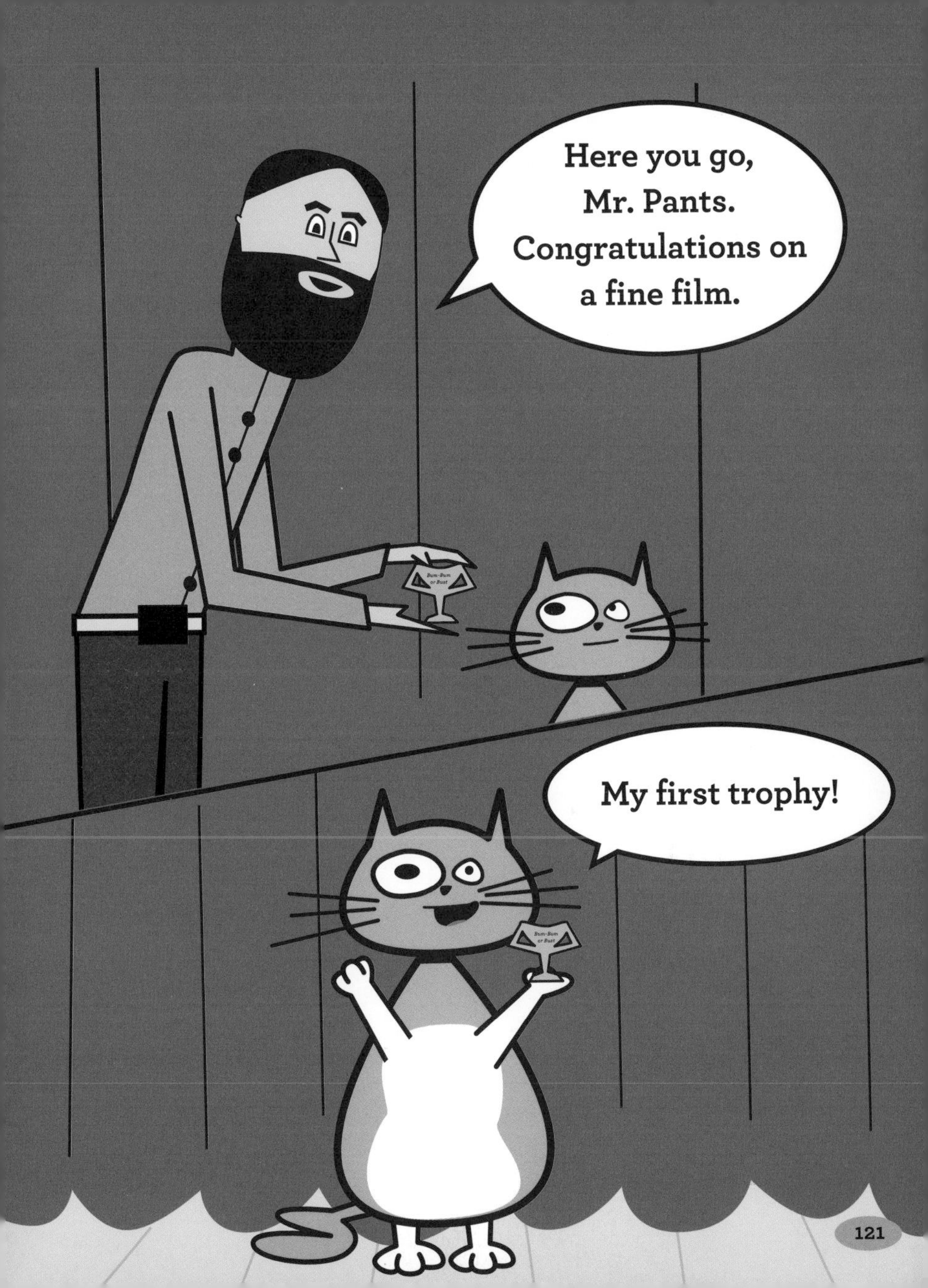
Here you go, Mr. Pants. Congratulations on a fine film.
Bum-Bum or Bust
My first trophy!
Bum-Bum or Bust

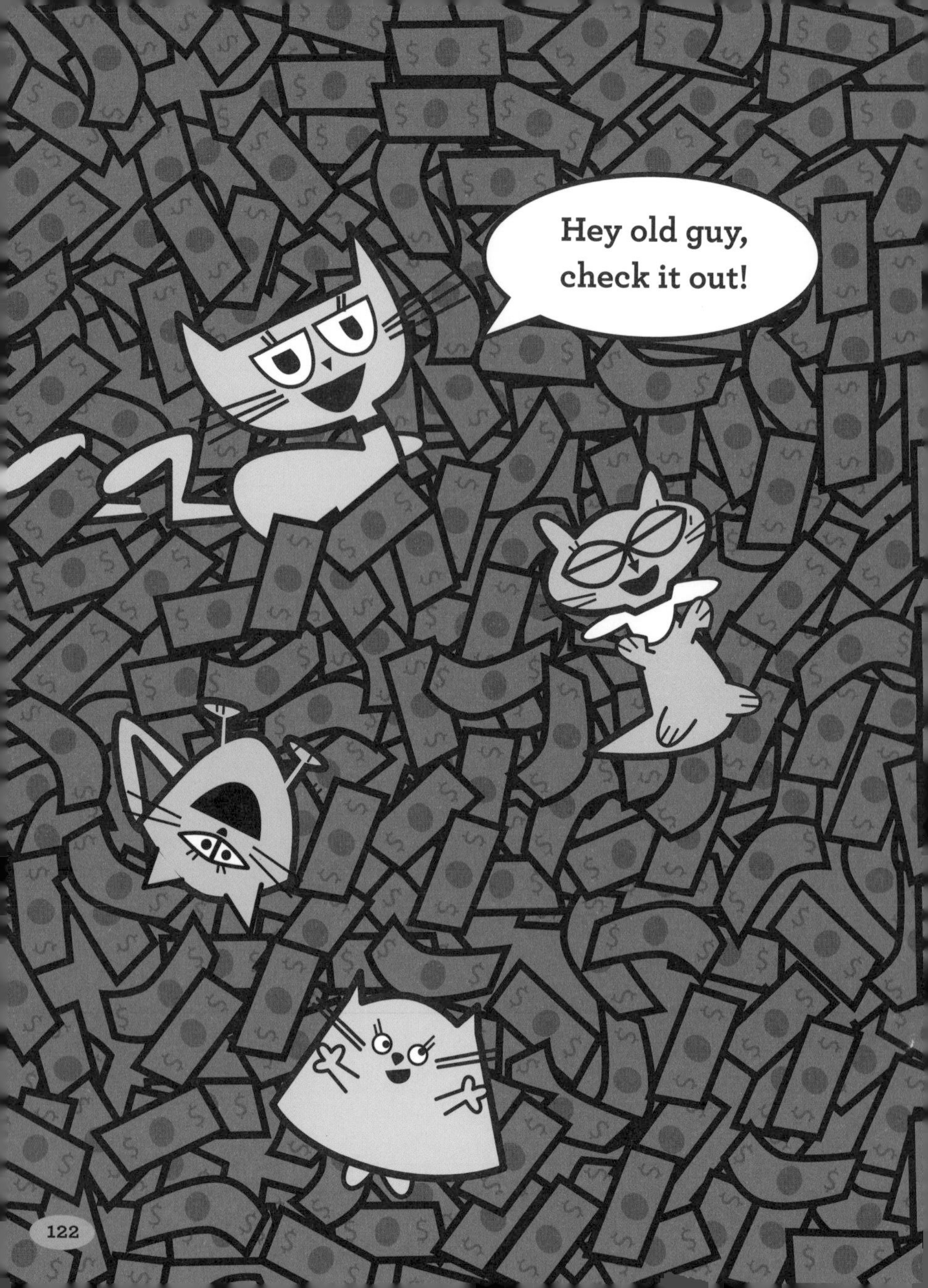
Hey old guy, check it out!

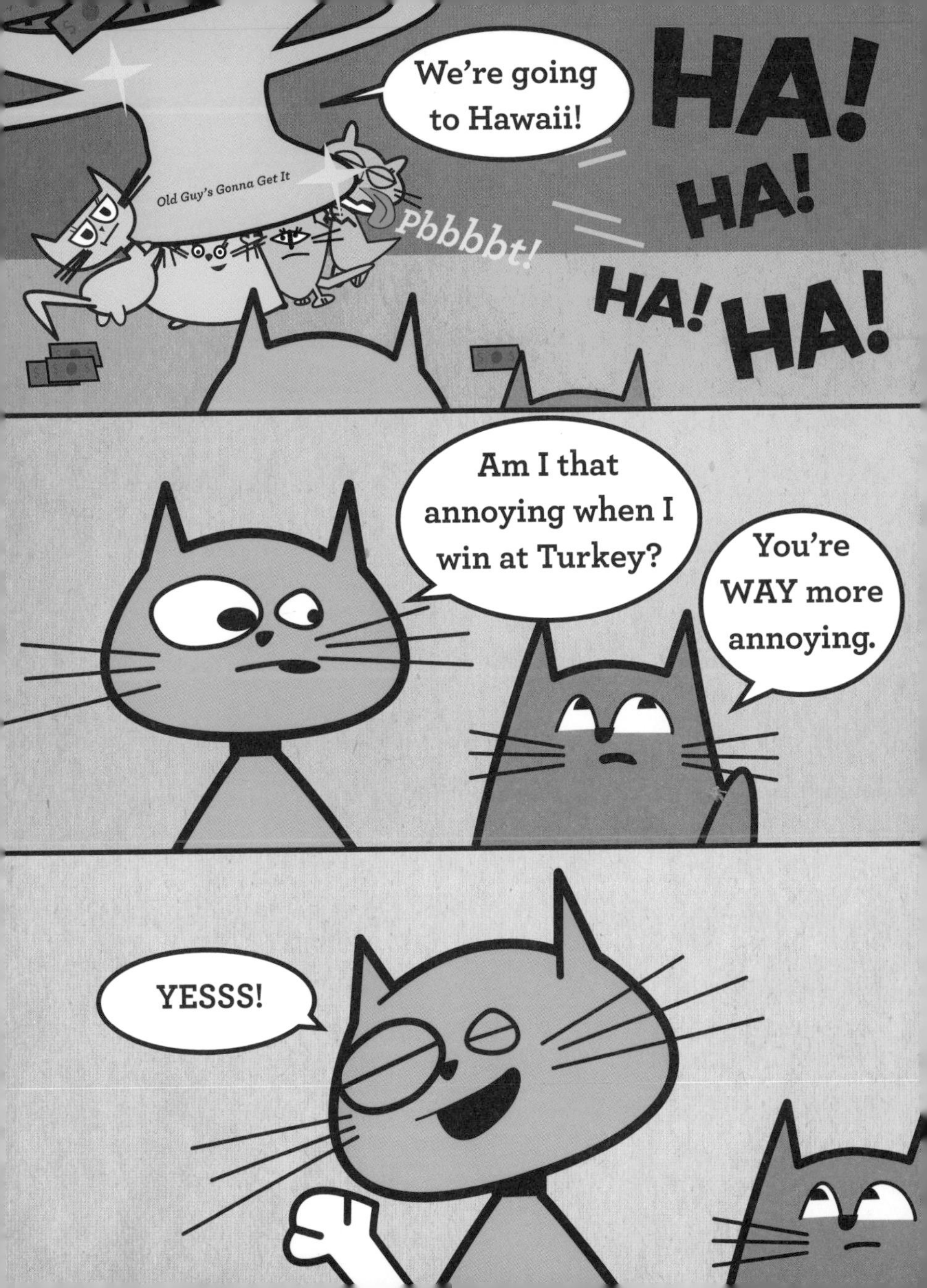
We're going to Hawaii!
Old Guy's Gonna Get It
Pbbbbt!
HA! HA! HA! HA!
Am I that annoying when I win at Turkey?
You're WAY more annoying.
YESSS!

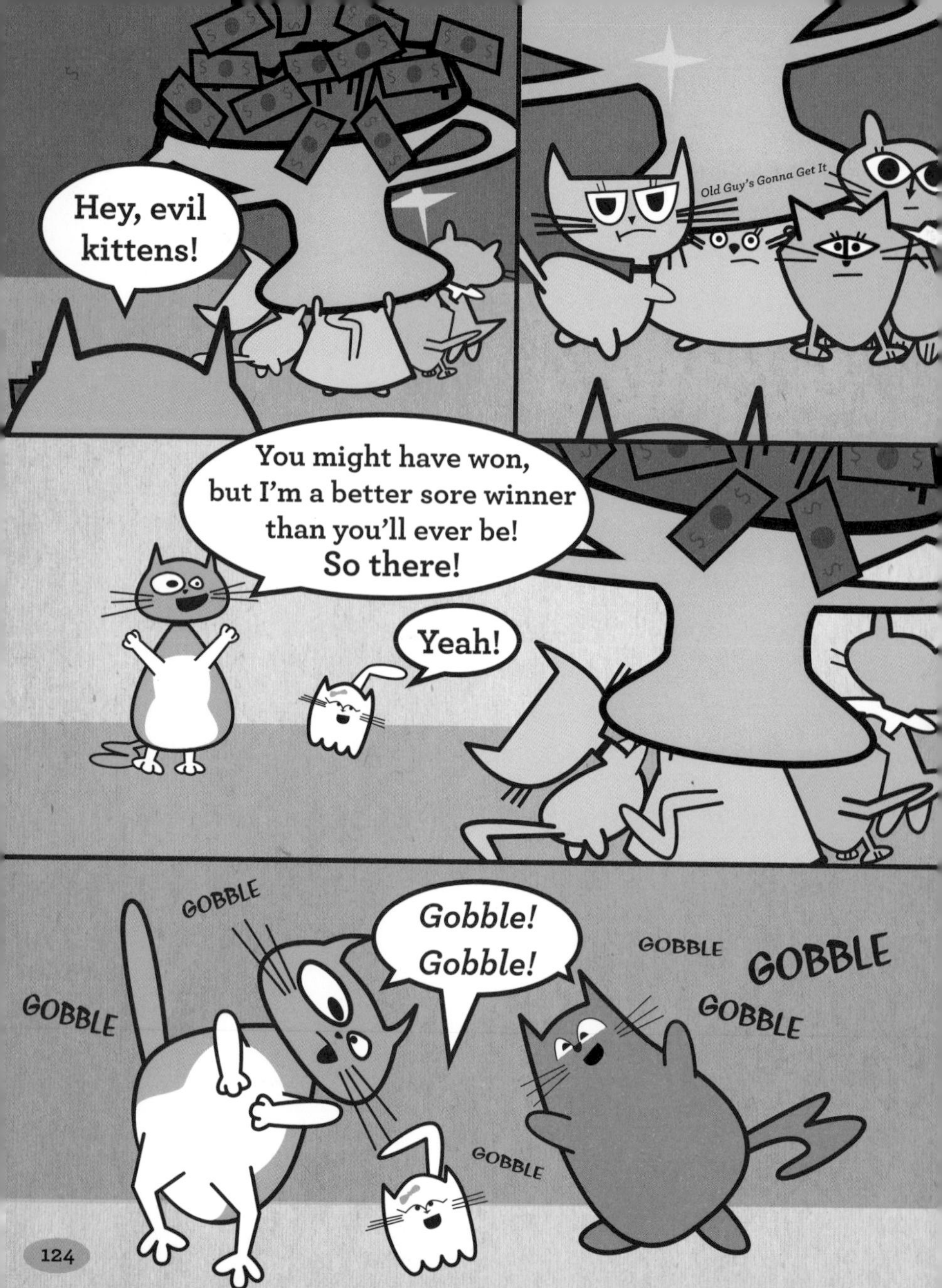
Hey, evil kittens!
Old Guy's Gonna Get It
You might have won, but I'm a better sore winner than you'll ever be! So there!
Yeah!
GOBBLE
Gobble! Gobble!
GOBBLE
GOBBLE
GOBBLE
GOBBLE
GOBBLE

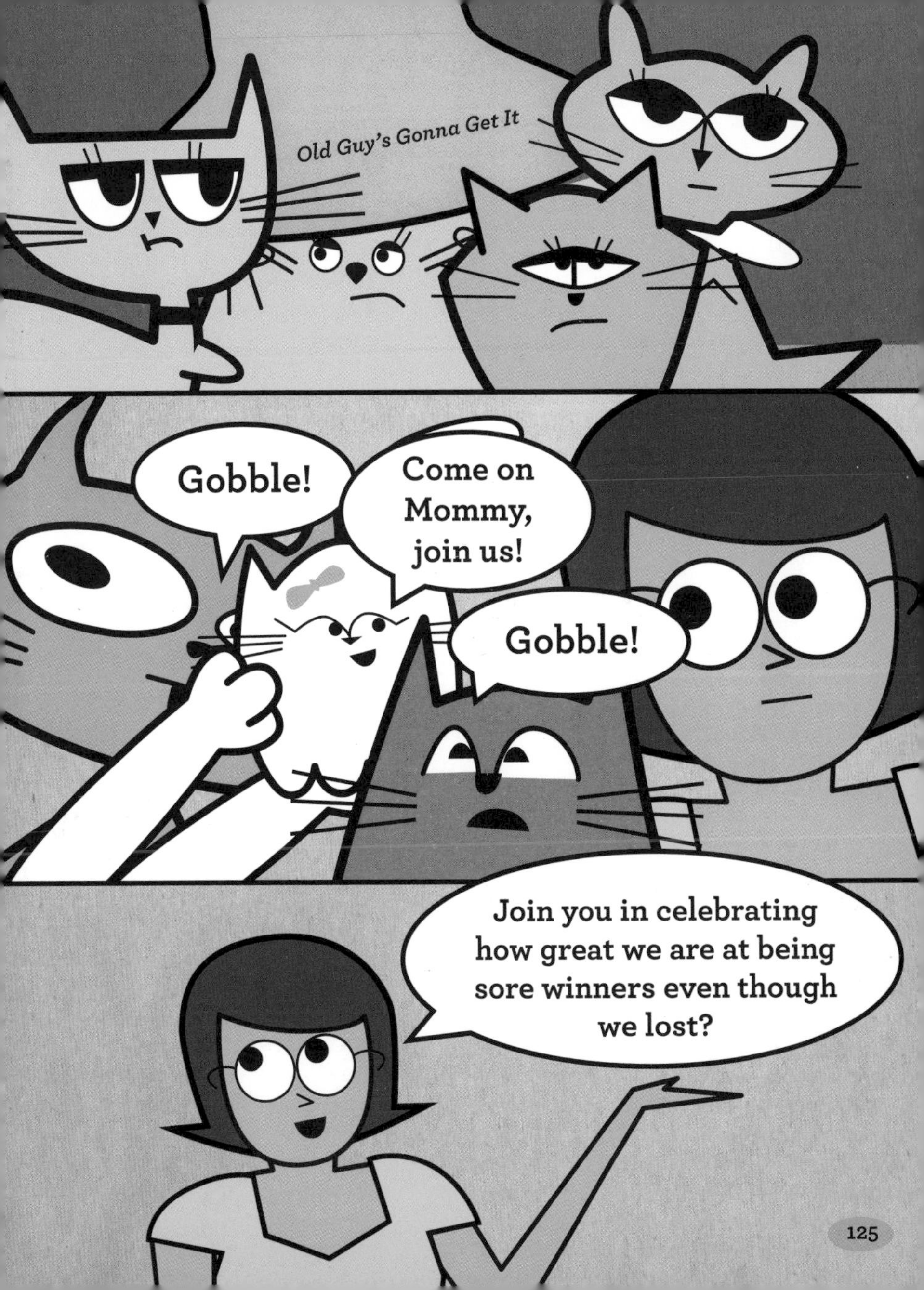
Old Guy's Gonna Get It
Gobble!
Come on Mommy, join us!
Gobble!
Join you in celebrating how great we are at being sore winners even though we lost?

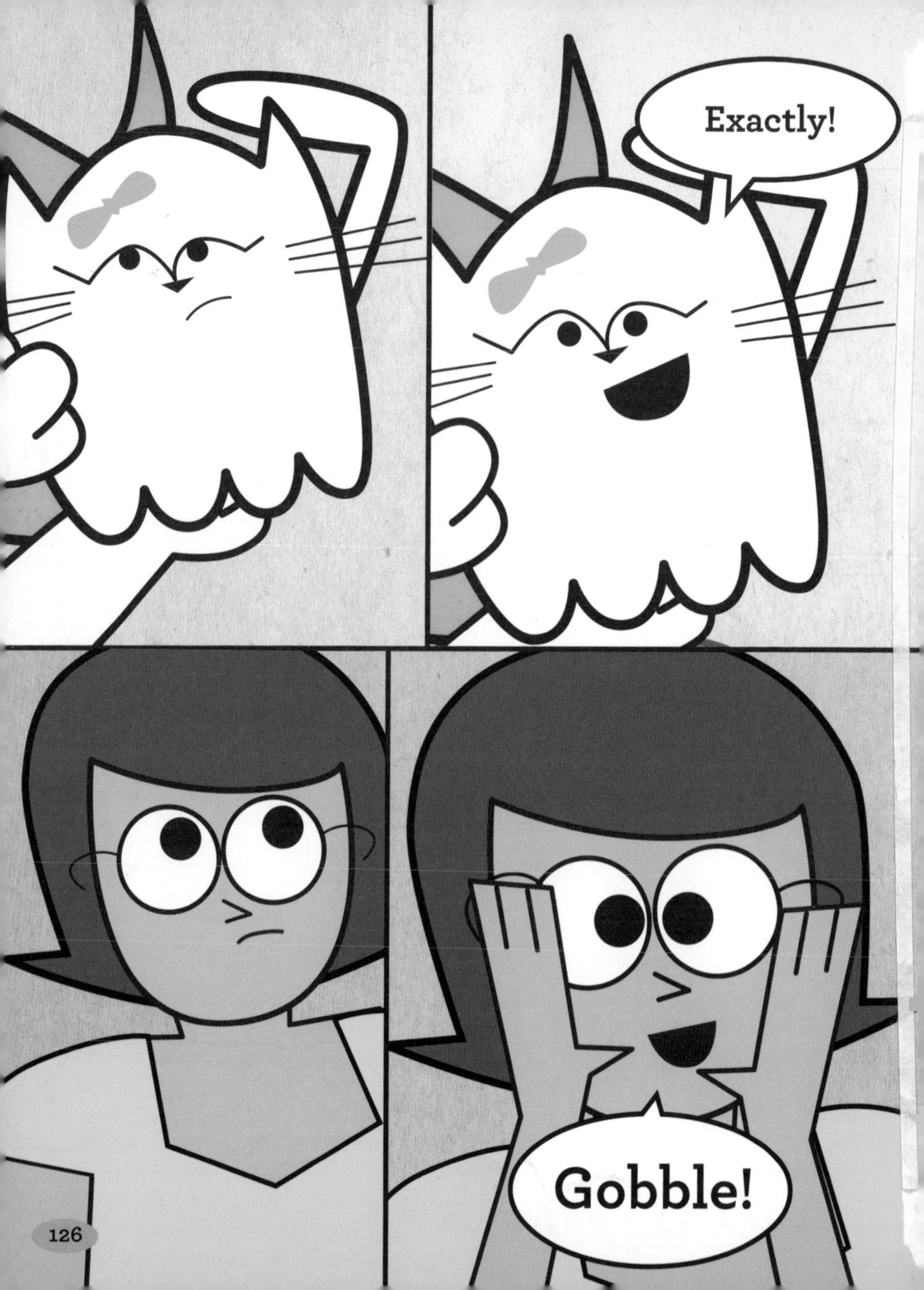
Exactly!
Gobble!

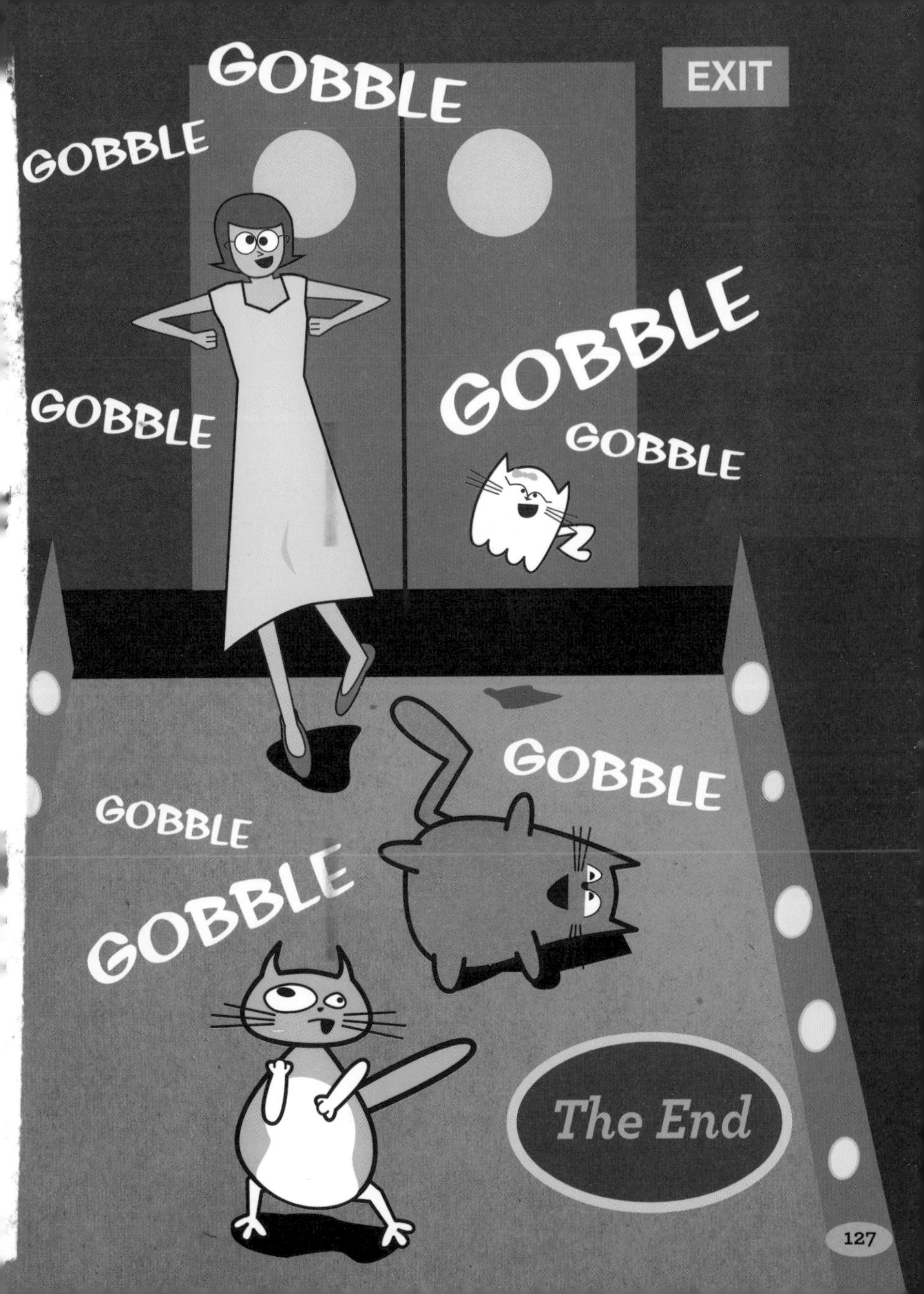
EXIT
GOBBLE
GOBBLE
GOBBLE
GOBBLE
GOBBLE
GOBBLE
GOBBLE
GOBBLE
The End

About the Authors:

SCOTT MCCORMICK is the greatest Turkey player in the universe. (Don't tell his kids.) His favorite part of being an adult is that he can have ice cream whenever he wants. He lives in North Carolina with his family and the real Grommy LuluBelle.

R. H. LAZZELL is a freelance illustrator who enjoys entering film contests so he can win trips to Hawaii. He lives just outside of Philadelphia, Pennsylvania, and has no cats. (Mr. Pants is enough.)

Visit **PANTSANDFOOTFOOT.COM**
to find out more!

And don't miss these cats' first escapade!

"Fans will wait excitedly for the next book in this fun, rollicking series."
—*School Library Journal*

"Readers . . . will find plenty to recognize in this family's harried day of activities and errands, while enjoying Mr. Pants's lighthearted comeuppances."
—*Publishers Weekly*

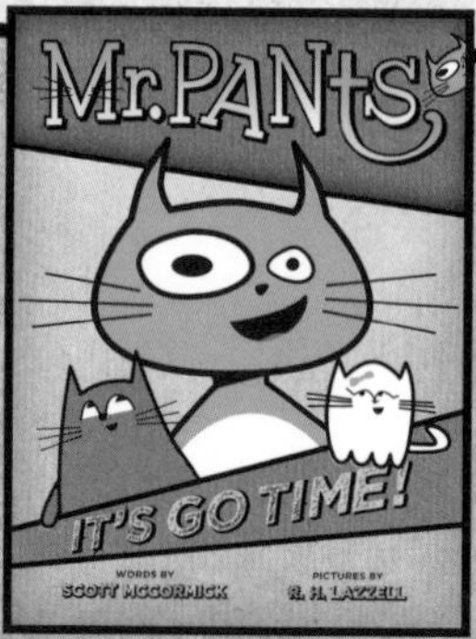
Mr. PANTS
IT'S GO TIME!
WORDS BY
SCOTT MCCORMICK
PICTURES BY
R. H. LAZZELL